KELLY BLUE

Also by Peter Bowen

YELLOWSTONE KELLY

KELLY BLUE

Peter Bowen

Crown Publishers, Inc.
New York

Fer Greg and Jamie, Swamp Knights of the
Frightful Hawg, and McFudge
The Sweetest Thang in All the World,
and I Respect Her, Too

Published by Crown Publishers, Inc., 201 East 50th Street, New York, New York 10022. Member of the Crown Publishing Group.

CROWN is a trademark of Crown Publishers, Inc.

Manufactured in the United States of America

Library of Congress Cataloging-in-Publication Data

Bowen, Peter, 1945–
Kelly Blue / Peter Bowen. — 1st ed.
p.   cm.
I. Title.
PS3552.0866K45   1991
813'.54—dc20   90-47137
                                                                CIP

ISBN 0-517-58286-4

10 9 8 7 6 5 4 3 2 1

First Edition

1

You know, damn near all the real trouble I ever got into was caused by my friends. I ain't hardly ever had an enemy do anything bad to me at all.

Take Cody, Buffalo Bill to you—I got into more genuine mortal embarrassments due to him than I care to recall, some of which was spiced up with me being shot at, and even Cody dying warn't no different. On account of that damnable Ned Buntline, Cody spent about three years total killing buffalo and Indians and taking hunting parties here and there and over forty in a circus tent somewheres telling lies about it.

My luck, which has never been worth a damn anyway, especially if my friends is around and helping out, caused me to be in Denver on the eighth of January 1917. I had been back East seeing those members of my family still surviving—the good die young like the saying has it, the vile go on forever—and I had come into Denver on the train. I thought I'd stay a few days at the Brown Palace before heading back to my little cattle ranch in California. So I gets off the train and I'm waiting on my bags and I hear this voice behind me.

"Luther," says this voice. I think it's probably a newspaperman and I'm looking around for a handy club when the voice bellers again.

"Luther, goddamn it, it's Lew."

Cautiouslike, I turn around, and by God if it ain't Lew. Lew Decker, that is, brother-in-law to Buffalo Bill and a right good man save for what his wife had in the way of brothers.

Lew looked sad as hell. "Bill's dyin'," he said. "I know he'd admire to see you."

Well, that hit me hard. I wasn't sure what other feller in all the world I could possibly hate as much as Bill, unless it was good old Teethadore Roosevelt, God rot him, and without them the world would be a more quiet and restful place and I wouldn't have to worry so much about what's coming *next*. (I'll tell you about the year touring Europe with Bill's Wild West Show sometime. It'll curl yer hair.)

"He really gonna *die* this time?" says I, trying to sound sympathetic.

"He got told at the sanitarium over to Glenwood Springs yesterday, and now he's at a nursing home here over by the Brown Palace, with a couple of quacks pokin' at him. He feels like hell, Luther, I know he'd admire to see you."

"Yah, yah, I'll come," I says. "Right now." (I wanted to make *sure*.)

I got my bags trundled off the train and we took a horsecab to the hotel and sent 'em on up to my room and I followed Lew down the street a ways. This nursing home was a big old mansion sort of place squatting like a dirty gray setting hen on filthy black snow. Denver is plumb up to the front range of the Rockies, and all the smoke and soot from the coalfires just stays there.

Well, we went in through the front doors and of course the stink of medicines and dying folks hit us like a blast of sour wind, and then I could hear something else. It was a fat voice runnin' whey; I'd never heard one before.

"He's up here," says Lew, looking back like he thought I might have made a dash for the door—he knew me pretty good, you see—and he leads me down about five doors and goes into a room.

Well, I wish to hell that I had a magic lantern slide of what was in that room. That fat voice belonged to this fat doctor—he musta weighed five hundred pounds, all poured into an ice-cream suit looked ready to bust and a white doctor coat looked like what you see on an organ-grinder's monkey. The fat doc is looking at the ceiling, and there on the bed, just setting, is Buffalo Bill. Bill's dressed like Buffalo Bill—buckskins, lacy shirt, skin-tight tan trousers, high dragoon's boots, and a hat big enough to cover Nebraska.

"Mr. Cody," says the fat doc, "it becomes necessary for the physician at times to turn the case over to a Higher Physician, one who . . . . . . uh . . . . . . ah . . . . . ."

This musta been going on for some time, as Bill was reddening up like a cock turkey. He stood up and grabbed this doctor by the throat.

"HOW THE HELL GODDAMN LONG DO I GOT, YA FLANNELMOUTHIN' SON OF A BITCH?!" Bill roars. The doc began turning purple—his face looked like a blood pudding.

"If ya would take yer thumb outa his windpipe he'd likely tell ya," I says.

Bill relaxes his grip a bit and the doctor gasps like a beached whale for ten minutes 'fore he can speak, and then he wheezes out, "About . . . . . . thirty . . . . . . hours," and the bloated Hippocratic makes for the door and manages with some puffing and blowing to squeeze through.

The red color in Bill's face drained off. He looked at me and his eyes was twinkling.

"Well, goddamn it, you two," he roars. "Go and get some whiskey and some cards and all the dancin' girls you can find and get back here pronto. I may have to die, but I sure as shit don't got to be bored."

Well, Lew and I drew straws and I got to go for the cards and whiskey and Lew went for the dancing girls. I come back long before Lew with a couple cases of Panther Sweat and some cards and chips.

There was this circular table out in the lobby didn't have nobody watching it, so I tipped it on edge and rolled it down to the room. We spread the blanket from Bill's bed on it, pulled up some chairs, lit seegars, and commenced into playing five-card stud.

The smoke went out into the hall and flushed this big mean nurse out of her catpit. She come sailing in like the good ship Wrath and informs Bill that smoking ain't allowed.

Bill pulls out a little six-shooter and commences shooting it into the wall some. The nurse swaps bow for stern and sails back out, and that's the last we hear about *that*.

"What the hell are we doin' with these things?" says Bill, looking at the chips and curling his lip. He took a long pull at his bottle and belched happylike.

So we toss the chips in the trash and dig around for our gold and silver.

"See?" says Bill, holding up a double eagle. "This is the real pure quill."

We'd played ten hands and I had maybe a hundred of Bill's gold when Lew come back with some lovely ladies, all bundled up against the cold. When they took off their wraps they didn't have enough on to wad a shotgun with, lessen you counted the feathers, and they commenced into cooing at Bill and cuddling up to him. Thus distracted, he lost two more hands. A couple sat down by me, one on each side—I'd swiped a piano bench from the chapel—and I tried to keep my mind on the cards and not on all this pretty white flesh about to bust out of the tiny silk rags they wore. Waves of sweet perfume mingled with my seegar smoke. It was most enjoyable in the nostrils.

One of 'em was rubbing up against Lew, who wasn't drinking or smoking neither.

"You get bit by Jesus or something?" I says. Lew was a man knew how to enjoy himself once. Well, friends fail you.

"He did that," says Bill. "Ain't been worth a pinch of dried coon shit since."

The girl took on Lew as a challenge, rubbing him with various of her parts.

"Goddamn it, Lew," Cody roars. "If ya can't be nice to the lady then go find a church to flog yer knees in. Luther'll take good care of me. We don't want yer lily-livered soul smirched, now do we?" Lew scuttled out the door and one of the chippies closed it, and then she started removing her feathers while doing a slow dance.

"This is right fun," I says. "You ought to die more often."

"Give me two," says Bill, glaring at his hole cards.

We was intent on this couple of hands, and then one of the girls' screams about knocked the paint off the walls. She was pointing to a window that had faces in it like figs packed in a box.

"That will be the gentlemen of the press," Bill says, pulling out his revolver. He made a couple offhand shots in that direction. A couple panes of glass busted and the faces disappeared.

"I think yer breakin' the law doin' that," I says. Bill was looking at the smoke twirl up toward the ceiling.

"Might even hang me for it, this being Denver," says Bill. "I'm full of the trembles about what all they might do to me."

There was a draught coming in the broken window.

"Pull them curtains, will you, honey?" says Bill to the girl who had been taking off the feathers. She drew the heavy velvet drapes.

A few minutes later there was a heavy pounding on the door.

"That will be the gentlemen of the police," says Bill. "Go talk to 'em, will ya, Luther? Don't hurry back." The girls was undoing his buttons.

I slipped out into the hall and there was four cops there—two in uniforms and two in overcoats.

"We have a complaint . . ." one of the overcoats says.

"That's Buffalo Bill Cody in there and he's dyin'," I says. "You keep the damn reporters away, he won't shoot at them."

Well, when I said Bill's name and that he was dying these four fellers got horrified looks on their faces, said, "Buffalo Bill? Dying?" in chorus and they hotfooted it toward the front door. Ten minutes later there must have been forty of Denver's finest scattered around in the hallway, hiding in the shrubs, and guarding all the doors.

Time to time we'd hear voices raised in argument, and time to time we'd hear a sound like a watermelon makes when you drop it on the sidewalk. The watermelon sound usually come right after the journalist started bellering about the Constitution.

"Such a privilege to be sittin' here skinnin' a legend," I says, raking in another pot. Bill had lost his pants and shirt in some sort of accident, I guessed.

"Why don't you go screw a lame coyote?" says Bill. More fists pounded on the door.

"Luther?" says Bill, checking his revolver.

I stepped out into the hallway to find several inflated-looking gents in dark-rich-looking overcoats and self-satisfied smiles standing there.

"We need to see Mr. Cody," says one.

"Mr. Cody don't want to see nothing but friends," I says. "And I know he ain't got any friends look like you."

"Do you know who this is?" one of the fellers says, pointing to a smug-looking, portly feller with lawyer's eyes.

"No," I says.

"It's the Governor!"

So I opens the door and says, "Bill, the Governor is here to see you."

"Shut the door and get out of the way," says Bill, tearing himself away from a long kiss.

So I shuts the door and does a fast sidle behind some cast-iron drainpipes. The four gents look at me like I'm touched. Then Bill puts four shots through the door, one going through the Governor's homburg. All four move right smart for such fat crooks.

"He don't want to see you!" I hollers at their fast waddling backs.

Well, we had a right good little card game there all night, interrupted from time to time by senators, newspaper editors, silver magnates, and riffraff like that, all of whom went quiet or got shot at.

Long about sunup I paid off the girls handsomely and sent them off in a horsecab. I'd won sixteen hundred dollars off Bill.

6

I was tired and commencing to yawn a lot when I heard a fearful bellering in the hallway and sounds of a scuffle. I opens the door to see Mulligan, barefoot as he always was, standing on a couple of unconscious coppers. Mulligan had a nightstick in each hand.

"Guudun un," he says through his adenoids, which must have been the size of plums, "Wiz Bilph?"

Mulligan ain't well known on account of he weighed about eighty pounds, never bathed, and couldn't talk, but he was a fine scout and a brave man.

"Bill," I says, sticking my head in the door, "Mulligan is here and I'm needin' some sleep. You're dragging out this dying business, hard on an old man like me."

"Mulligan?" says Bill, delighted. "Send him in and go rest your pore old worn ass a while. Never could stick it, anyway."

"Thunka," says Mulligan, passing by me.

Well, I went to the hotel and got some sleep. I woke up about four in the afternoon. I thought that I'd take some food back with me. I had the hotel make up sandwiches and filled a hamper with cheese and sausage and took a horsecab back, just a little apprehensive. Maybe, I says to myself, he's dead and this is all over.

There was a big crowd in front of the nursing home, so I guessed he wasn't dead yet. There was a big black column of smoke coming up from a hole in the crowd on the lawn. I managed to elbow and cuss my way up to it, and there was several full-dress Injuns feeding a fire with the shrubbery and such trees as was within easy reach. There was a whole buffalo carcase on a spit sizzling away, and Dirty Dack Tom, best camp cookie ever, slathering on his tonsil-melting barbecue sauce.

It smelled wonderful and sure took me back. The smoke got to me and my eyes teared some.

"Just a holdspell," I says to Dirty Dack Tom. "Where in the hell did you get a buffalo?"

"Think, Kelly," says one of the Indians, Black Lynx, a Brulé Sioux I'd known for years, "where would you go to get a buffalo in these sorry times?"

7

"The City Zoo," I says.

Black Lynx patted me on the head like I was an especially promising idiot. When he wasn't riding in Cody's show he was a lawyer.

"You goin' in to see Bill?" says Black Lynx.

I nodded, hoping he wouldn't ask to come along. There were hundreds of folks who'd like to, and they would in a moment if they was asked, but Bill was dying and he didn't want to see everyone.

Black Lynx had taken out a skinning knife—I recognized it, it was his father's, Spotted Tail—and he cut off a heaping plateful of hump meat.

"Not so bad dyin' with that taste in yore mouth," says Black Lynx. He turned away sudden.

I didn't have to fight my way in—just hollering that I had a plateful of Bill's favorite meat and the favored cut of that parted the crowd right smart. I walked down the hallway and rapped on the door with my cane.

A tall blonde whore opened the door. I could see Mulligan's bare, dirty old feet sticking out from under the bed, they was pointed down between two clean lady feet pointing up—a scene of terrible debauchery, which I have always found pleasant in comparison to wars and disasters. So I clapped my hands and whistled.

Bill was sipping his whiskey out of a beer stein, genteel-like, and playing cards with four pretty ladies wearing nothing but smiles.

"Luther's pecker is this long," says Bill, holding up his hands like a lying fisherman.

"Christ," I said.

Well, we played cards and the sun went down, and I would have been further ahead but for various distracting attacks upon my person by the dancin' girls. Long about midnight the door opened and one of the Paddy cops says "The Bishop to see . . ." but he didn't finish because there was this despairing "Jaysus, Mary, and Joseph" behind him, which I guessed belonged to the Bishop, who saw right off his comfort for the dying was like to being underappreciated. Fast mind like that, no wonder he was a bishop.

"Four sevens," I says, turning up my hole cards, "and I think your soul just went to Texas."

"A pair of twos," says Bill. "Gawd I hate to lose like this even if it *is* the last time. Glad that whatever he was went away. I'm sort of enjoyin' myself and them godwallopers take the enjoy out of everything."

I cut and shuffled a bunch while Bill pulled on his half-quart of Panther Sweat. "Where's Mulligan?" says Bill, coming up for a little air.

"Fuckin' like a mink under the bed there," I says.

"Good," says Bill, "I thought we was having an earthquake."

We played a lot of cards, and about the time the light was coming up Bill started sweating a lot and scratching his wrists.

I stuck my head out the door and saw Lew Decker and asked him to take the whores home. He nodded and in a few minutes they had flounced out, jingling a lot of gold in their pretty hands.

Mulligan was snoring—a strange sound, like unbuckled galoshes make—and I hauled him from under the bed and carried him down to a couch in the lobby. The cops sort of rolled their eyes, remembering what he'd done to a couple of them the night before.

Bill crawled painfully up to the bed. He was white and cold and shivering now and the sweat was running off him.

"Give me another piece of buffalo," says Bill, and I stuck a cold, greasy hunk of it in his mouth. He chewed it and it seemed to take his mind off the pain a bit. Took him a long time to swallow it, but he finally did.

"Luther," says Bill, "there's a bag of gold in my bag over there. Could you get it?" His eyes seemed troublesome to him, he rubbed them hard for a few minutes.

I found a blue leather bag that was full of something so heavy it could only be gold. I figured about ten thousand dollars' worth.

"I want you to take that down to Susie's and give it to the girls," he says. "They was always square with me. Buy 'em a few new feathers, anyway."

"Sure, Bill," I says. They was as good as any and better than most I could think of. Time you get the gold they're all dead anyway, the ones you got it for.

Bill fell asleep, snoring deeply, and then sometimes he'd just stop breathing for long enough to where I'd think he'd gone under but then he'd fire up and go on.

I had a couple of drinks and nibbled some cheese and polished off the last dozen oysters some kind soul had sent. I lit a seegar and looked at my fingernails. It's uncomfortable waiting for someone to die. You wish they'd just do it and be gone.

There ain't nothing useful you can do, and I've shot my share of partners who were suffering off to Hell. Smile nice at 'em and when they look away you shot and it's better all round. But I couldn't do that here, and anyway, Bill wasn't seeming to be in fierce pain.

A nurse stuck her head in the door and I went over to her—nice woman, just wanted to know if we needed anything.

"That really Dirty Dack Tom out there?" said Bill. "Awful nice of them to roast a buffalo on my account."

"It was that," I said. And for all us poor bastards came out here before them as herds turnips come in their thousands.

He lay quiet for a long spell, then he looked at me and he grinned, and just for a second I could see the young feller I had first met over fifty years ago.

"We had some good times," says Bill, "and it was some good country then. Mighty good. I'm proud to have known it."

And Bill closed his eyes and died, just like that, grinning and remembering how it was. I touched the artery in his throat. Nothing.

"Goodbye, my friend," I said. I was almost tearing, but I commenced counting the scars that son of a bitch had got for me and regained some of my sand.

I put the sack of gold in the hamper I'd brought the food in and I walked out, leaving the door open, and nodding at the nurse.

I didn't want nothing to do with what was going to come next—every booster club of every town he'd ever been in would want him buried there (they did; they had to guard Bill's corpse like it was gold)—and so I walked out the front door of the nursing home and looked out on a silent crowd of cowboys and Indians and cops and reporters and just plain folks.

I shook my head and shrugged and walked down the steps and all the way back to the hotel in the sleet. I washed up there and put on a clean shirt and took the sack of gold over to Susie's. The place was all shuttered—noon is the dead of night to fine establishments such as that.

My gold-headed cane about beat the damn door through before a bouncer come. He greeted me civilly and let me in and went off to fetch Susie. When she come I told her about the gold and Bill's last request. Susie let out a beller of pure mirth.

"Damn," she said, "he was the pure quill, wasn't he? Him and you and Pardee and McKinnick come here drunk as lords and sing hymns till you passed out."

Susie went on remembering for a while. I didn't mind.

"Pure quill, sure enough," she said, and she went off dabbing at her eyes and rousted the girls out. They took quite some time getting as dressed as they ever do and come downstairs in twos and threes, yawning and making tabbycat sounds.

Susie tried to explain it, but the whores just crowded around the little table I'd put the gold on, and some grabbed and then they got to shoving and in about three seconds there was the biggest damn catfight I ever saw in my life. I left when the crockery started flying and other weapons such as fireplace pokers and curling irons was picked up and used. They was fighting over Bill's gold like the buzzards in the watered-silk vests was fighting over his body. I have never much liked critters that bunch up unless they eat only grass.

I caught the next train from Denver to California. I looked out the windows of the club car at the country, passed places where I'd killed good men and bad, saw farms where there was once nothing but grass, went through little cities got electric lights and trolley cars, fer Chrissakes.

It was a fine country back then, and I don't like it so good now. The train wheels clacked over the joints in the track and I began to think of how I came to be here at all. Like all of life, it wasn't much of a thing got me headed this direction. I had wanted to go to sea, and I'd ended up in a sea of grass, back when the Indians ruled all the Great Plains and most of the mountains.

My little ranch is a tiny part of old General Bidwell's spread. He used to own everything from Sacramento north to Oregon. He'd given me a little piece a long time ago, and I raised horses and a few cows, didn't need the money but it kept my hand in.

I knowed when I got back there would be a lot of hell to pay, and there was. I had bags of mail and telegrams and five reporters in the shrubbery who had found out I was with Bill when he died.

The reporters let me into the house civil enough, and when I come out I had a shotgun and shells full of rock salt and I run them off civil enough. (When their editors complained I said it could have been buckshot.)

There was a telegram from Teethadore Roosevelt. He'd been on a trip down the Amazon and survived the piranhas and bushmasters and crocodiles, damn it. Our ex-President wanted a full and found report on Bill's dying breaths. Likewise Miles wanted a report, likewise about three hundred newspapers.

I took all of this garbage down to the big irrigation ditch and tossed it in.

The hell with you all, I thought, watching the paper flow away on the water, he was my friend, and I don't owe none of you bastards nothing at all.

2

I was born in Oneida, New York, in 1851, and I run off in January of 1865, almost fourteen, and joined the Union Army. Now there's a lot went on between those two dates, but I ain't going to tell you that now. Other than I found it a fine idea to leave Oneida in the dead of night, over a woman.

Me being a young pup of thirteen, it was an older woman of sixteen that caused all of the trouble, her and a mule name of Oxnose. If this here woman hadn't been the daughter of the Episcopal Bishop I'd maybe have got off with a stern lecture and I would have been spared much.

I was out late that afternoon helping old man Hoeft haul ice up from the pond to the icehouse. We'd slide a block up on a stoneboat and brace it down on the pond, and mule-haul it up the hill to the icehouse, slide it inside, and shovel sawdust all over and around it. I got to scamper up to the loft where the sawdust was stored and fork bushels of it over, and the fine wood dust made me sneeze.

It was about ten degrees above, with a bitter wind off the lake, and that summer lemonade was sure a damn long ways off. I never did get any, come to think of it.

The haul road from the ice pond was a snakey, churned-up thing, and unusable unless it was frozen. There was a spring seeped out of the hillside and leaked down to the pond, and it filled the tracks the runners on the stoneboat cut with water that froze right off. The stoneboat slid better on that ice, but Oxnose had trouble with it, never knowing what he'd step into next.

The Bishop's house was just uphill from the icehouse, a huge building with gables and turrets and bay windows and a lot of ugly ornamental trim. The architect tried to hide his mistakes under a lot of foolery.

Old Oxnose was a placid sort of mule, the kind that will wait for years for one good shot at kicking you into eternity. One of the hames got foul on his harness and I jumped down to release it, leaving old man Hoeft with the reins, and dashed across behind old Oxnose. Oxnose decided to kick then, but he was some out of practice, and he missed me by an inch or two and both hooves hit the crosstree and busted it all to match-wood. One of the strap-iron caps on the end swung off on a bust leather and caught me right where my spine joined my skull. It probably would have killed me but for the heavy rolled stocking cap I had on. As it was I fell facedown in the snow, out like a poleaxed shoat.

I come to in a bed in a strange room, with a cool wet cloth on my forehead. I blinked my eyes. Someone had took off my clothes. There was a rustle of cloth off to my left. I moved my head slowly that way, and where the iron had thumped me I got a quick stab of pain.

There was this beautiful young woman sitting on a chair next to the bed. Deep blue eyes, black hair, pale skin—after all these years that face comes back to me unbidden.

There was an oil lamp off somewheres turned down low and a candle, which she picked up and held over me. She bent down and looked at my eyes, and I could smell her, lavender and thyme.

"You're awake," she said. She looked at my eyes for a long time and then she turned the cloth on my forehead.

"Thank you," I said. I must have been breathing through my mouth when I was knocked out, my throat was dry and I croaked.

"Pretty," she said, stroking my cheek. Her eyes was

glittering a little. I was still sort of groggy, and it took me a few minutes to grasp that she had set the candle down and was removing her clothes.

You know, the first time I saw a beautiful woman taking off her clothes I thought that this was what I wanted to do in life, and I sure have and don't you know, I love them all still, even after all the damn trouble they have caused me.

I laid there paralyzed while she took off the last of her things, and she stood there for a moment, curve of hip, dark thatch between her thighs, lovely breasts, slender and poised. The roof could have fallen in at that moment and I wouldn't have knowed or cared. She slipped into bed with me and she began to kiss me and run her hot hands over me and it occurred to me that I didn't have the foggiest notion about where exactly I'd fit into her. I don't think she did neither, and we thrashed around for a while, tossing the bedclothes off on the floor. Finally I slid in and we both gasped and I went off right then.

Well, bless youth. I hadn't given off but about four gasps and the odd moan of pleasure when my dick rose up and we went at it again. She was drawing long red weals over my back and moaning and she give off a little shriek and that was what did us in.

The door slid open, and I looked over my shoulder to see the Bishop, his own self standing there in a long red flannel nightgown and a tasseled cap. He was holding a candle and seemed stunned.

The poor son of a bitch was so shocked he just stood there for several moments while his daughter thrashed and panted under me.

Finally he give off this strangled croak. "Charmian?" he said. Her head shot up like a spooked horse's.

"Papa?" she said. I wondered who else she might have been expecting.

Then she looked back at me, her eyes white and wide all around.

Now, as bad as my luck has been sometimes, it always

manages to hold just enough for me to miss judgment. I ain't making a case for the justice of it, but there it is.

The Bishop fainted dead away, and he fell into the room, taking a good chunk of the doorjamb along with him. He weighed a good two-fifty and all small objects in the room rose up and settled back down. And there was me and Charmian, all hot and distracted.

She slithered out from under me and made a dive for her clothes and I made one for mine. I noticed she was tearing her underclothes up some, and having a quick if not exactly decent mind the conniving little piece had sure showed me which way the wind blowed.

While she was bent over tearing a few holes in her stockings I crowned her medium hard with the Meissen pitcher from the washstand. It was full of water so it put her to sleep pretty good.

I shucked on my boots and looked one more time at this father and daughter and left them to sort out their differences as best they could. I took off like a stripe-ass ape.

I skedaddled to home, leaped up on the woodshed, prised up the window to the room I shared with my far too many brothers, pulled my few possibles out from under my bed, stuffed them in the sack I used for schoolbooks, and then slid back down the roof and made a beeline for the rail yard.

My luck was running good. There was a freight made up and moving south, and I wiggled in between a couple of crates. It was an open car and the wind was cold, so I hunkered down and tried just to stay warm.

My crazy uncle Arthur, when we'd go camping and fall out of the canoe or the storm would tear our tent away, used to holler happily, "Jaysus Kay-rist, Kelly, I can't remember when I been so happy!" I hated him for it some, but that was what I chanted down there between the crates, which weren't braced and tied good and sort of kneaded me whenever we went around curves.

I rode till almost dark and then the train got to pulling into Albany and I wriggled out of my hidey-hole and jumped off. I had about a dollar on me, in coins, a pocketknife, and no idea in all the world what to do except stay the hell away from Oneida. Jails never appealed to me much.

The police, I figured, would likely be looking for me, so I steered clear of the railroad station and hotel lobbies and spent a cold night stamping my feet and walking. Early in the morning I come across a pieman who sold hot fried cakes to the men who worked in the mills. The cakes was three for a penny. Little ways along I found another vendor who sold a big mug of sugared tea for a penny. The mug warn't too clean but I didn't complain.

It was a bright day, and the wind was brisking up. I was dressed warm enough as long as I was moving, and I wandered the streets, looking at the shops and officemen hurrying to their tall buildings.

Then I heard a fife and drum heading my way. They warn't much good, but they was loud and pretty soon the scrawny soldiers come round a corner, strung out behind a big flag. Some of the men had a banner saying that Old Glory and the Union needed me. I followed them down the street. They made a smart right turn into a barracks was part of the Armory.

Having left home so hurriedlike I of course had no plans other than not getting hung. I had a good idea right then. My parents had instilled in me all sorts of good virtues, like not telling lies, so I dug around in my sack for a stub of pencil and a scrap of paper—had to tear the flyleaf out of a schoolbook. I chucked the schoolbook into the gutter, thinking I likely would not need it. I scribbled eighteen on the paper, unlaced my shoe and put the scrap inside, put the shoe back on, and stalked across the street to save the Union.

A gross, potbellied Kraut recruiting sergeant was setting in front of a plank desk in the first building, the mess hall. He had a stack of forms under his elbow. (You may wonder how I knew he was a Kraut. Well, there was this sort of mudslide down the front of his misbuttoned tunic made up of sausage scraps, pretzel dust, and beer.)

"Yaaassss?" says he, blowing a breath would've singed pinfeathers off a turtle. "Wass veyou?"

"Aim wantin' ta jine up," I said, imitating the nasal whine of the laborers who came to Oneida for the harvest, men mostly from Maine.

"Vhow olt?" he said. I thought maybe he'd speak better if he'd had a few beers.

"Eitch-cheen," I says, "free, white, and over eitch-cheen."

And that was all it took. He shoved a form at me, which I signed, thinking up a new name on the spot. He then tossed me to a dentist and a doctor who looked at me for maybe three minutes total and pronounced me fit. The recruiting sergeant took me to the quartermaster, who issued me boots and kit, and then a miracle happened. He took me to the paymaster who paid me one thousand dollars in greenbacks. I'd have preferred gold, but I took it.

The Union Army was real close to whipping the Rebs. And so many men were sneaking away to be home for spring planting that it was a real worry to Lincoln and Grant that Grant have enough soldiers to whip Lee when they met. So worried that they were paying good money—damn good money, a doctor made maybe five hundred a year—to keep and to get soldiers.

As an almost-fourteen-year-old accused rapist, I thought it damn handsome of my government and I have never wavered in my regard for my country or them as runs it.

Of all things I even had a money belt, belonged to my crazy uncle, and I put the money in it and put the belt on and wondered when I'd get a musket.

Luke Pabst I was, private, 33rd New York, and for three days I did nothing but guard my money from my fellow soldiers and try to march in step with the rest when we marched out to snare some more recruits.

"If you run with that Union bounty we'll catch you and hang you," the paymaster kept reminding me. It was the first time that the army throwed in with the civilian government but not the last, by a long goddamn.

One morning a sergeant bellered us out of bed at four in the morning and we was given twenty minutes to pack and then we moved out, slipping on the frosty cobblestones. We was marched down to the rail yard and put on a troop train with some regulars.

These was tough men, these regulars, and they had been fighting for a long time on seven dollars a month and eating what they could find. They was tanned and hard-bitten and their uniforms were faded and patched and they didn't wear socks and they were lean and scarred and good at their business.

The rumor that there was bounty men on the train had come to them, and they was not a bit happy at sharing the train with green boys who each had been given the price of a farm and this late in the war would not see any fighting at all. For a lot of the men, the hardest of all was the knowledge that their families had done without or starved, and here with victory in sight the damned government was insulting them with these useless, rich, fat boys.

One of my fellows who warn't too bright wandered off up into the next car to jawjack, and a few men stood up and I heard one startled yelp and after a while the men sat down again and divvied up wads of greenbacks taken from the feller they'd killed and tossed out the window.

We rode all day and the next night and then come down to the big yards in Washington. The regulars formed up and swung off and was gone.

All but the one of us didn't survive the trip down stood around in the cold for a few hours. We had no officer with us and other than a rumor that we would be guarding prisoners we knew nothing at all, not even how to get fed. I was feeling good and sorry for myself now, and I didn't have anyone to blubber at. I wanted to write my mother and tell her I was all right, but I couldn't. (Later on my mother told me she never worried once. She understands me, you see.)

Then an officer and two sergeants and a paymaster carrying a paybox come striding around the end of a freight line and up to us.

The officer greeted us and the paymaster said that any soldier who wanted his bounty safe should deposit it with him. So all of them did but me. They never saw their money again, and I think maybe the army was smart enough to know that any fool who'd trust them didn't *deserve* a thousand dollars.

We was marched off across the city, headed west, and finally to a tent camp—not so bad as it sounds, all the tents had wood floors—and we was assigned tents and given some salt pork and hardtack. First time you ever encounter salt pork and hardtack you know right off the enemy is nothing compared to the food.

The paymaster's clerk tracked me down and hauled me off and the paymaster and then a one-eyed, one-armed, one-legged captain come in and said something in a low voice and the paymaster turned his hands up and looked heavenward. The captain laughed and he clapped him on the shoulder and I was told to go get some sleep.

The camp was all wired and fenced except where we come in, and by the time I got back to where I lived now there was three sutler's wagons pulled up and the troops was buying food and notions from them at outrageous prices.

I bought some coffee and a big tin coffee cup and a couple of ginger cakes, but they was glycerine and sawdust and cinnamon mostly so I spat it out and attacked the hardtack and salt pork, which was filling and made me thirsty as hell.

We still hadn't been issued guns and so I went back to the sutler and showed him some greenbacks and he sold me a two-shot derringer and ten rounds of bullets for it for forty dollars. It was an English gun and I still have it. I said I wasn't buying until I knew the gun worked, so he prised the top off a flour barrel and fired the gun twice, and the noise was lost in the racket of camp.

Next morning a couple sergeants from the 33rd New York come by and chose five of us. We tossed our gear in a wagon and went off walking behind. We did that for three days and ended at a miserable camp of wet tents along the Rappahannock. We was to watch—and shoot if they tried to escape—a huge batch of Confederate prisoners all jammed into a barbed wire depot, mostly without blankets or shoes. Dozens was dying of pneumonia every day. All they had for shelter was old Union Army bell tents too rotten and torn to use much. The word had got round that the South was starving Union prisoners and so this is what we done. The whole South was starving and had been since Sherman went through Georgia, which was the pantry, so to speak.

They give me a muzzle-loading musket with a long bayonet on it, called a "lunger," and put me to marching twelve hours a day up and down the fence. Since I hadn't got my real growth yet the gun was taller than I was, and them Confederates found me very amusing and commented all the time on whether or not I had a stool to use when I cleaned the thing and if they'd mowed down every Yankee all the way to the sprouts and pips maybe it was time to quit since they'd won anyway.

The Rebs wasn't much interested in escaping—the war was over as soon as Grant caught up with Lee. Ulysses chasing, Robert E. running, and half a million dead scattered round— mostly killed by the doctors, to be sure, but they wouldn't be coming home.

I spent the first half of March walking up and down on frozen earth and the last half staggering through mud damn near up to my money belt. The winds got raw and blustery and sleety rain come down by the lakeful. It turned the whole camp into a bog festering with shit and even some Reb corpses come up, buried hastily so the survivors would go on getting their rations.

The great cheer when the war ended was given up by the Rebs, who could now go home. I marched along in the mud wondering what the hoorah was and when it hit home I wondered what I'd do now. My manner of leaving Oneida wasn't so stuffed with thinkin' time that I had made any plans, long or short.

Though a lot of the healthier Rebs just run off, the others was waiting on news of someway they could get home. Many died in that week right after the war, almost as though they'd stayed alive just for that.

Then the news come that President Lincoln had been shot at Ford's Theater by John Wilkes Booth.

The soldiers of the 33rd went clean crazy—they weren't

soldiers at all, just boys like me who they'd give a gun to. One company loaded up their muskets and marched over to the Reb pen, they was just going to pour fire into the prisoners. John Wilkes Booth wasn't in there, I was sure of that.

Then the one-eyed, one-armed, one-legged captain came riding a big sorrel horse, holding his saber with his left hand, and he bellered that he'd kill the damned cowardly lot of them if they didn't form up and march back and leave their damned guns where they stood. Some of the mulier fellers thought they'd see if he meant it and he charged them, cracking a couple on the head with the flat of his sword—saber, I guess, I thought it was a sword then—and he run all of them off like so many clipped sheep.

Then the captain rode over to the wire pen and he looked at the Rebs until they was quiet. Then he said they was his countrymen and that he would not see them humiliated. Any of them that wanted to could go; the sick would have to wait until transportation could be arranged. So while he stood there beside that sorrel horse maybe two or three hundred men come by to shake his hand and thank him, and he said God Bless You to every one who did. I thought it pretty good for a feller about half-trimmed up by Reb guns.

The captain struggled up on his horse and rode away, and the men left in the camp gave him a cheer, and I joined it.

I was awful young but I'd read enough books to know wars aren't all that glorious to those who fight them. They was a dirty, bad business stupidly thought out and done by fools and ignorant amateurs, blood and stink and nothing for the soldiers at the end, lessen you're someone like a general and you want to go on to Congress or the White House. A wooden leg, an empty sleeve, a furrow cross your skull where your eyes was, and, like the Brits say, the thanks of a grateful nation.

Next day rumors flew around the camp like drunken bats. Booth was headin' south, headin' north, headin' west, on the moon, or in the basement of the White House eatin' shepherd's pie with Mary Todd Lincoln, who was crazy and supposed to be chained there.

A couple of companies of the 33rd was detailed to sweep the countryside for Booth. We went back and forth, not finding him and having to buy all our food from the sutlers who followed us like stink on a skunk until the word came that Booth had been shot down in a burning barn. Booth being an actor I thought that the barn was a nice theatrical touch. (I was righter than I knew, or was to know later.)

We marched back to the prison camp and found it empty except for a couple men dying of brain fever. A good half of the 33rd had deserted—no one was going after them and they knew it—there wasn't enough jails in all the country to hold the men streaming away. The real soldiers was so fed up with war and everything about it they was hurriedly let go before they shot their way out. After a feller has a few years of good, hot war and he eats the garbage they call food and lives with death every minute, what that feller wants most is a good meal and a soft bed and a big jar of good whiskey. A lot of the men took their muskets home with them and year by year they watched the rust eat them and they nodded and smiled.

As you may well imagine, I did not wish to return home right away, where I would be strung up for rape and many other crimes.

So I nosed around a bit, telling anything with stripes or gold on it that I liked soldiering. They mostly looked at me like I was simple and smelled bad to boot.

The country still had a lot of need of soldiers, so while the 33rd melted away the peacetime army was looking for recruits. Out where the Indians was the North had had to make do with paroled Confederate soldiers—galvanized Yankees—all of whom left about three minutes after the news of Appomattox got to them.

The army is a mysterious thing. A sergeant come for me, took me and my kit to a train, shoved me on it, and said I should report to Fort Semple, way out in Minnesota, wherever that was. There was trouble with the Sioux, whoever they were. I had long thought I'd go to sea, but fighting Indians didn't sound so bad. Christ, I was as green as spring grass.

I got a lot of gossip from the folks on the train—civilians, and many of them immigrants who didn't speak English. Seemed that there was this Sioux chief, Red Cloud, who had whipped the army so much and so often that they had to abandon the Bozeman Trail. (Red Cloud called it the Thieves' Road. He was to tell me so himself.) Red Cloud was now raising hell worse than Nathan Bedford Forrest ever did. The Sioux ate their captives after torturing them to death.

There had been hundreds of settlers killed, scalped, and eaten. (Actually three, and none of them were eaten.)

I changed trains in Chicago and on I went seeing new country and listening to the same gossip. The train got to Minnesota and then the cars began to fall away until there was just two flatcars with iron rails on them and we come to the end of the railroad—easy to spot, the crews was building it right there. I asked where Fort Semple was and the foreman pointed a finger off to the northwest and I took off. The fort wasn't more than five miles from the end of the track, a palisaded business with raw log walls and the same tents up on wooden puncheons. It was starting on real spring there, and flights of Canada geese were going overhead all day and all night.

I found a lieutenant with the red sash of Officer of the Day on, and I handed him the crumpled orders I had been given back in Washington. And that was the first time I laid eyes on Lt. Gustavus Cheney Doane, USA. If I'd have known what he was going to do to me over and over I'd have shot him there and banked on my age.

"Son," said Gus, "would you mind telling me how old you are?"

"Eighteen," I said, standing at what I thought was attention.

"Port arms," he barked. I blinked and looked at him, having no idea what he meant.

"Jesus," said Gus.

He called over a sergeant who took me to a barracks and gave me a bunk. The place was low-ceilinged and stank of sweat and tobacco. I dropped my kit on my bunk and my shoulders slumped.

The sergeant barked at me to hurry and get out for drill and since I hadn't ever had any I was curious. I was utterly hopeless. I caused anarchy in the movements of Company "C" and my stage fright wasn't helped by that goddamned Doane laughing like a madman every time I fell over or took somebody's head near off with my musket butt. The sergeant ran me back to the barracks steps just before he would have died of a stroke.

Gus sauntered over, a big smile on his face.

"Eighteen, huh?" says Gus. "What's your name?"

"Private Pabst, sir," I stammered. I was trying to stand at attention but I don't guess I was doing very well.

"Private . . . . . Pabst," said Gus. "How old are you really. Just tell me. I am trying to help you out."

"Fourteen, sir," I said.

"Jaysus Kayrist," said Gus. "Infants and idiots. The perfect soldiers."

"My uncle always said so," I said, stammering some.

"Do you hunt, Private Pabst?" said Doane.

"Yes, sir," I said. It was true. I was a good hunter and I had fed my family a lot of venison, ducks, and geese.

"Our post hunter died of typhoid last week," said Gus, "and you are our new hunter. Report to me tomorrow at dawn. I'll talk with your sergeant."

"Yes, sir," I said, saluting. I'd been doing it every fifteen seconds or so since the conversation started.

"Quit waving your damn hand around like you was killing gnats or something. DISMISSED. THAT MEANS GO AWAY," Gus roared. I was already going as fast as I could squelch through the mud of the parade ground. Then I remembered I'd got up off the steps of *my* barracks. I went back through the mud, wishing I was a goose far above, headed north.

I sat there and watched Company "C" march and drill around until it was time for them to quit. We had cooked food for supper, and the stew was just awful, a mess of old spuds and beets and gristle. There was a good-sized swamp not a quarter mile from the gates of the stockade. So I asked around until I found Gus and threw a salute that knocked the glass he'd carried outside off into the quagmire along with the whiskey in it.

"Jaysus Kay-rist, Pabst," said Gus, rubbing his eyes and coughing to keep from laughing in my face.

So I told him that as idle as the troops was, if they went to work pulling up cattails and I got some decent meat maybe they wouldn't look so starved and peckish and watery.

"Cattails?" said Gus.

I nodded.

Early the next morning I give a demonstration of how to cut the good out of a cattail stalk, and then I started out in the meat hunter business.

3

hat with the war ending, everything was even more chaotic than normal and pay and rations sometimes were lost for months. Replacements for the men whose enlistments had run out were a long time coming. A few deserted each week, and they were let go and godspeed.

We was clear out in the far west end of Minnesota, and the Sioux was farther out yet. Game was thick in the bottomlands—whitetailed deer and moose—and I shot only as much as the cooks could use. I only saw the fort about once a week. Two privates with a freight wagon would follow the route I'd leave for that week. I'd hang the game I shot in the cottonwoods and leave a strip of cloth fluttering from a branch.

The settlers had long since fled, since Red Cloud, Spotted Tail, and sundry other bloodthirsty savages lurked just beyond the horizon. Red Cloud, Spotted Tail, and the rest of the bloodthirsty savages would have been content to *stay* out there, beyond the horizon, but we kept moving the horizon in on them and they got mad over it. They'd been treated out of Minnesota and weren't likely to negotiate again.

The soldiers ate about a dressed ton of meat a week, so I had to shoot four moose or twenty deer or a combination of the two. I really wanted to shoot a buffalo, but they didn't spend any time in the bottoms and I was a little chary of heading out onto them plains. That sea of grass is damned big, even from the shore of the forest, and the sky above is bigger yet. The wind would make swells and ripples in the six-foot-high buffalo grass, and it hypnotized me when I stared at it too long.

The stew meat despatched, I would wander the breaks with Doane's shotgun and knock down prairie hens for the officers, and I kept buckshot handy because there were a lot of wild hogs. Once I killed a sow and found twelve piglets in a burrow nearby, they wasn't above two weeks old. I stuffed them in a sack and took them right back to Doane.

Gus was in some sort of quarrel with the captain, and when he saw my high sign he come and listened to the high-noted squeals and he waved to the captain to come listen and he did and they left off the argument. Like all military camps there wasn't a lot to do.

Doane cooked the suckling pigs himself and the officers went and invited me to dinner; I noticed my table manners was better than most.

The officers broached a small barrel of whiskey and gave me some and while they drank and told jokes I puked my suckling pig dinner up and all over the outside wall of the officers' mess, on account of I had to lean on *something*. I staggered off to lie down and when I felt better I saddled up and left to lick my wounds in my own private thicket.

Having that bounty money, I had been gradually replacing my military gear with better clothes and truck. I bought good high oiled leather boots and thick moleskin pants and heavy flannel shirts, and a patented raincoat. I had also begun to stock up on things a feller might need if he were meat hunting one day and got kicked in the head by a moose and woke up a few months later so far into the Rocky Mountains they had to ditch in the daylight. There was sutlers like crows behind a plow. No idea how I got there, of course, and if anybody asked I could roll my eyes and be simple all over their boots.

Doane knew perfectly well what I was thinking—he'd been a schoolteacher for a couple of years and knew my kind right off—and just the very day I was leaving and not coming back he come up to me and said Tibet was that way, too, which sort of tore the hump out of my sail.

"Uh . . . . . . Luke," said Gus, he was a kind man, "I think that the army and you ain't suited. Now if you go right on to Oregon no one will be lookin' for you, because you ain't even old enough to hang, much less enlist. So have a good journey and watch your hair."

I looked puzzled and I flushed of embarrassment.

"I have been transferred to the Department of Texas," Gus went on, "and no telling what my replacement will be like."

"Well, I'll be seeing you then," I says.

"No doubt," says Gus. "Though I hope not in Texas. I wouldn't wish that festering pesthole on anyone."

I went off with my two packhorses and my pinto saddle pony and rode as fast as I could to the cache of goods I'd hid on an island in a nearby river. In that cache there was a big Monarch of the Plains Stetson, creamy white, like the scouts in the illustrated dime novels wore.

When the ponies was all loaded I let out a yell and a whoop, clapped on that ridiculous hat, and climbed up into the saddle. I tugged the leadrope and we forded the river and we was off to the high Rockies and the gold and silver and Indians, grizzly bears, buffalo, and hidden cities of houses with silver roofs and doorknobs of rubies and sapphires.

I didn't even look back.

It was about the early fall, the wind was crisp, and there was a line of black thunderheads on the far horizon. The wind was suddenly sweet with rain and the world was washed new. I was free and found and going where I did not know, but would when I got there.

Well, the I-did-not-know part was right. First off the storm approaching was a hailstorm such as are common in the High Plains, and chunks of ice weighing five pounds and up come down like Grant on Vicksburg, at fatal velocities. I run my stock up under a cutbank and we made it just fine till the hail knocked the cutbank down on us. The storm was passed by then and I was able to struggle free of the sand and grass roots and got my saddle horse and one packhorse free but the other one smothered. This meant I had to leave some of my traps and truck.

Well, I got rid of the folding rubber bathtub and the leather cases of canned anchovies, sardines, tomatoes, corned beef, and tongue, and the folding grille and the wicker hamper with the tea service and cheese planes and silverware in it. Never a feller to know when a nice wheel of Stilton might come poking up out of the prairie like some mushroom, and refined ladies to go with it.

I set three bottles of port down on a stump for some lucky soul. I abandoned the hammock—good thing, too, the next suitable tree was seven hundred miles straight ahead—and the mosquito netting and patented snake stick for the murtheration of cobras and anacondas. I kept all the guidebooks, which I found out later was written mostly by failed poets in opium trances who never got more'n a day's travel from the Atlantic Ocean. I tossed the mandolin in the bushes with heavy heart.

Well, the storm had passed and the sun was down and the stars was out. I took a fix through the patented prismatic engineer's compass I had bought and went west.

It didn't feel like due west, though, so I got mad and figured the compass was broke and pitched it off in the buffalo grass. I found a trail and I rode along under the starlight, my big white hat a good four feet above the grass. The wind was sweet and the stars was bright and I was happy as only ignorant fools can be. Anybody who cared to could see me easy five miles at night and at twenty miles during the day. I rode all night.

The sun come blazin' up behind me and I knew I was headed west. I come on my own horse tracks but thought it was another party on the way west and when the trail forked I went left where the other folks went right. I didn't want to crowd them, you see. I followed the sun.

Just about two hours before it went down I come to a little river all hung over with willows. The clear water wound slow among lilies and cattails and I sang a few verses of a dirty song I knew and then I off-saddled and unpacked the goods I had kept and I fed a little grain to both horses and hobbled them and gathered firewood and started a fire to boil water for to make the imported Turkish coffee I customarily drank. My boots was a little tight—I was stiff, been in the saddle for more than twenty-four hours—and so I pulled them off using the brass and mother-of-pearl bootjack with my initials on it and then I set down with my back against a stump and went to sleep. Had my hot feet dandled in the cool river water, it was just like the dime novels said.

I don't know how long it was fore an ant began crawling on my neck. I scratched it. I opened my eyes. Four pairs of handsomely beaded moccasins was arranged around me. Slow-like, I lifted up my hat.

Right in front of me was a short, squat, moon-faced Injun painted black and white stripes, like a zebra, across his face. To my left there was a tall, scarred customer looked like he et live wolverines without mustard. To my right there was two younger fellers holding sharp-looking hatchets and evil grins. Some polite soul behind the stump I leaned on farted so as not to surprise me with his being there.

My mouth had gone all cottony-dry and I'm sure my eyes was the size of stove lids.

"Whatever do you use for brains, young man?" said Zebra Face, in a plummy Canadian accent, sort of like my aunt Margaret's. "Gopher shit? My young men would have killed you last night but they thought that you were so stupid that you might be crazy, and they didn't want to offend the spirits. What did you have for supper last night? Steamed locoweed?"

All this was God's Truth. My eyes must have grown a few rings.

The scarred booger to my left rattled off a bunch of grunts and wheezes, then laughed heartily.

"Red Bear, my esteemed associate here, wishes to cut off your balls and make you eat them, prior to skinning you alive. He wants a new saddle cover."

Then there was a chorus from the two on my right.

"Unimaginative," sneered Zebra Face, "so I won't bore you with their suggestions."

The one behind the stump farted again, I was glad to see he was holding up his end of the conversation.

Farts-Behind-Stump lifted off my hat. My hair was cut short on account of the lice the fort had.

"Jesus Christ," said Zebra Face, "you call that a scalp? That's an insult to civilized warfare, is what that is. It's barbaric. Put the hat back on," he went on, gesturing to Farts-Behind-Stump.

The scarred one in need of the saddle cover rattled off some more suggestions and Zebra Face turned to him and rattled back pretty hot and sharp.

"Get up!" Zebra Face snarled to me. He made a motion and my hat was jammed down over my eyes. I struggled to my feet. I saw one of my boots and picked it up and pulled it on.

Even in the High Plains far north of where you'd think they would be there's a nasty little yellow scorpion likes dark, smelly places and the one in my boot took offense at being smashed flat and it stung me right in the instep.

"Yaaaaaaoooooooooowwwwwww," I hollered, hopping around on the other foot and trying to get the boot off while the scorpion took a few more stabs. Naturally I fell in the water. There I lay on my back with my right foot in the air, holding a boot and hollering, while my hat floated generally toward New Orleans.

I sat up, water running out of my clothes. There was a good forty braves on the bank, all laughing like loons and slapping each other on the back, except for Scarface, who was scowling and making unpleasant gestures at his crotch with his skinning knife.

"Unbelievable," says Zebra Face, holding his head like it hurt. Well, hell, it was pretty funny even to me, so I started in roaring away, and I got up slowly and staggered to shore. My foot hurt like hell and was already beginning to swell.

"Take off your sock," says Zebra Face. He looked at the welts, nodded, and then he went to the riverbank, pulled a plant up, peeled the root, smashed the white core with his knife handle on a rock, came back, slapped the mush on my stings, and stood up. The pain quit in a minute and the swelling went down in two.

After shaking my boots out thoroughly I squeezed my feet into them and stood up. Some kind soul jammed my hat, full of water and weeds, over my head and everybody laughed hearty at the sorry figure I cut. I offered just no end of amusement.

"Don't try to run and don't try to sneak off," said Zebra Face, "because if you do you'll be two or three days dying and a most unpleasant death it will be. And my name is Spotted Tail."

"Luther Kelly, pleased to meet you," I says, fetching up my parlor manners and sticking out my hand. Spotted Tail looked at my hand like it had maggots in it and stank to boot. He shook his head.

"Luther Kelly," he said, shaking his head, "you are a goddamned fool. I wonder that you could live as long as you have."

"Thank you," I says, meaning it. I figured if a few warriors had found me they'd have rubbed me out and gone on without working up a light sweat.

"One more thing," he said, still smiling. Even with the smile, I *knew* he'd cut my balls off. Especially with the smile. It was one of them smiles. He'd have made a great lawyer. "It pleases me to let the whites think I don't understand English. You will be good enough to not let on? And keep your word. The man who keeps his word, keeps his balls." (And I kept it till now. Spotted Tail is long dead, murdered at the request of a missionary bishop. I'll tell you sometime.) We mounted and rode west.

Up on the High Plains it was the middle of the fall, the weather gets colder the higher and farther north you are. It was time for the great Autumn Buffalo Hunt, to lay up meat and fat and robes for the winter. Spotted Tail's people were Brulé Sioux. (After I got some Sioux I asked him what language Brulé was. It didn't sound Sioux. "It isn't," he said. "Two hundred years ago a Black Robe, a Jesuit, came to convert us to Christianity. He was so eloquent, so filled with the Holy Spirit—so elevating, that we ate him, out of respect, and ever after we were called the

Brulé Sioux. He was, shall we say, commingled with us in a manner not often found with missionaries and heathen. We are still heathen." Same smile.)

There was about a hundred lodges going out to the buffalo country, and maybe five hundred Injuns of all ages, sexes, and sizes. It was like harvest time elsewhere, a joyful gathering for the long, cold, hard winter ahead.

The Sioux and other Plains tribes lived off the buffalo, as us whites do corn and wheat. They gathered roots and berries and killed deer and birds, but the buffalo was the nail they hung their life on. The Sioux made over forty things from buffalo—from pemmican to glue and bowstrings, moccasins to teepees—and so of course it was a holy beast.

My traps and such sort of melted away. It wasn't exactly plundered or outright theft, just someone would take a fancy to something and take it and when they was tired of it they'd give it to somebody else. They was impulsively generous, just like they was impulsively cruel, and by and by I was down to clothes, boots, a hat, and a couple guns. Everything else disappeared and then turned up only to disappear again in the moving shoal of people.

I slept in a lodge with about eight other fellers my age, and I et out of a common pot, puppy stew likely as not, and the worst discomfort I had was missing salt. Hell, I'd *dream* about salt.

The Autumn Buffalo Hunt was about the biggest celebration that they had all year. The medicine men medicined away, painting signs on bleached buffalo skulls and building cairns of rocks to hold them to the sun, and singing and dancing around the buffalo horses. The hunters painted themselves and fasted and prayed.

The band set up the making-meat camp near where the border of the Dakotas and Montana is today. The women commenced into building drying racks to make jerky and sewing up deerskin parfleches to put the pemmican in. A few exceptionally keen-eyed young hunters went out and scouted the herds.

Early one morning, with the frost heavy on the grass, the

hunters took off in a mob to hunt the buffalo. I went along, armed with my Navy Colt and Spencer carbine. I planned to watch the rest of them hunt, and maybe chase down a few cripples or strays. I sure didn't want to get in the way.

Then Spotted Tail grinned that awful, sunny, murderous grin of his and motioned for me to come along with him. We rode on and topped a little rise and looked out over thirty miles of red and yellow grass dotted with thousands of black buffalo, grazing in bunches, not herded up at all.

The mob of Injuns was spread out five miles to the left and five miles to the right of us. I could see right off that buffalo hunting was not what you'd call a heavily organized sort of sport. For one thing, buffalos' eyes are so far out on the sides of their heads that they can't see the same thing at the same time with them. It makes them real erratic runners unless they are in a herd. Unlike cows and horses and most all four-footed animals, they pivot on their *front* legs, and can swap ends and directions so fast it seems magical, when it ain't fatal to the rider chasing them. A bull can swap ends and hook a horse's belly and carry horse and rider a long ways, if the horns has a good purchase up in the horse's guts.

Well, I reined up on a little knoll and folded my hands over my carbine and Spotted Tail turned and looked at me and nodded. He whooped and gouged his horse with his heels and off he went. They was after the young cows for meat and the bulls for robes, moccasin soles, and teepee covers. Some Injuns used firearms and some used the bone and Osage Orange bows, double-curved things of enormous power. Unless they hit bone, one of the bows would send an arrow clear through a bull's chest, to bury itself in the earth. (When the settlers plowed the plains they found thousands of arrowheads, these people must have been hunting here a thousand years. We killed most of them off in about ten years.)

Whooping, the Injuns chased the buffalo and the hooves drummed in the earth. I had a good view. I watched for two or three hours and then all that was left were the black dots that was dead buffalo and the warriors starting to skin the bulls. They did this by hitching a horse to the hide and then they slashed while the horse pulled.

And that is all they did. The men get to hunt and make war, and the women do anything that looks remotely like work. Not a bad life. The braves whooped back to camp with buffalo tongues to roast on the coals, and they sat there for the next three days telling lies about how many they had killed and what great and impossible shots they had made.

It was pretty much like any hunting party I've ever been on—Injun, white, or European.

There was a few more hunts that fall, and I took part in them, finding that it was easiest to use the pistol on the cows and leave the bulls for the braves. The carbine couldn't be aimed much from a moving horse.

I still rode a saddle though I was chaffed a lot about it—an easy thing to bear when you don't know the language so well. I picked a lot of good points up—how to find water and feed in the winter, and the saltweed that keeps horses close. Later on, when I was hunting down the Injuns, knowing where the saltweed was stood me in good stead.

The life was good. I didn't do much but eat and sleep. Once in a while I'd get a twinge and think I ought to maybe write my mother and let her know I was all right, but I was a long ways from a postal box. A couple pretty women started slipping into my robes—I found out later that goddamned Spotted Tail floated the rumor that my dick was so long I had to tie knots in it to hold the tip off the ground where I'd step on it, and though my anatomy proved a disappointment they did keep coming back.

I was growing again, getting what would be my full height, and I shot up visibly if you stared overlong. It was April now and the rivers were starting to full up with ice and water and there was some green on the ridges—the little pasqueflowers all rowed in their hundreds, and snowdrops and little crocuses.

Spotted Tail come one afternoon and he give me a letter to someone he called Big Throat, way on over to the west.

I was to leave the next morning.

All that evening this or that Sioux stopped with a gift for me. One woman brought a pale doeskin shirt all worked in colored porcupine quills. They brought bags of pemmican and moccasins and robes and soft underclothes made of deerskin. One gift that I was purely dumbfounded over was Scarface give me a scabbard for my Spencer, made out of rawhide. (As I lashed it on my horse the next morning I glanced at the back and saw MOTHER and two hearts entwined on it. Well, the thought was nice, so I kept it.)

Next morning I headed to the south and west, trying to find the Emigrant Trail. Big Throat lived on it somewheres, in the mountains.

Spotted Tail rode with me for a few miles. He was smiling and whistling and happy, no doubt thinking of especially satisfying past castrations.

"If you need to," he said, when he stopped, ready to turn back, "you can ask for Big Throat by his white name, Jim Bridger."

"Oh," I says. I'd been reading about Jim Bridger and the Mountain Men since I was a pup. And now I was going to meet him. I commenced into thinkin' on what I would say.

I put heels to my horse. Him and the pack pony broke into a jog. Down there with the Black Hills on my left and a lot of badland between, there was the Bighorn Mountains, and Bridger lived right near the southern end of the range.

Nothin' to it.

4

Well, the ride I thought would take a few days took me a month. I had no way of knowing how big the land was out here, and it was unnerving to ride toward a mountain range all day and have it seem no nearer at dusk than it was at dawn. I drank only from springs had green in them—there's arsenicals all over the West; cold, clear water in absolutely clean rock pools. If you drink it you die of convulsions an hour later.

I sure as hell knew it when I come to the Emigrant Trail. There was a litter of trunks, chests of drawers, pianos, tables, rocking chairs, and such piled deep on the sides of the trail, where the wagon wheels had in some places cut a foot down into stone. All the metal had been stripped off the furniture, of course, since iron was as precious here as silver back East. It was far too late in the season for any trains of Conestogas, and I thought of the thousands of people who had come by here. Some of them stayed, under a grave marker cut from a wagon board.

I'd run on to solitary freighters a couple of times and asked if they had seen Bridger or knew where he might be. 'Course they was all great friends of Jim, and swore he was in Hawaii, or up in Canada, or in Mexico, or "kilt and skelped." This last came from a pair of pustle-gutted loafers riding the sorriest nags I ever seen. They had a bald-backed mule carrying a couple small kegs of whiskey, and that and their overhauls and greasy hats was their outfits, along with a couple of rickety trade muskets. They eyed me and my gear hungrylike. Fortunately they was pretty whiskeyed up and when they invited me to camp I wheeled my horse and took off. A musket ball follered after but came nowhere near me.

I made a dry camp and was giving myself the congratulations when it occurred to me that that pair was going to kill the first folks they come to wasn't loaded and aiming at them. So I got my carbine and Navy Colt and little derringer all tucked up good and tethered the pack pony and went back on my pinto. I could damn near smell the bastards fore I could see 'em.

They'd throwed together a big fire—too lazy to cut the wood—and they was chawing on some raw bacon and drinking whiskey out of a tin cup.

"That little shit give us the slip I liked his gun," says one of them, reaching out his cup for more redeye.

"Be nother'n," said the other.

"No, there won't," says I, squeezing the trigger on the carbine. The slug went through the man's skull and into his partner across the way. The brainshot one stood up and walked till he fell in the fire and the other looked at the big hole in his chest and then the blood started to come out his mouth.

"You've come a long way, Luther," I says to myself as I rode back to where I'd left my traps. "You just killed two men because they needed it." I wasn't too happy, but I couldn't think of another thing to do. Leave them alive to slaughter anyone weak in their path?

If you wanted anything done out here you damn well had to do it yourself, even if it was things you'd hang for in New York. I began to take especially good care of my guns and my horses. Got to be a little tetched on the subjects and never come out of it.

I knew vaguely that Bridger had been drove out of his home on the Salt Lake Trail by the Mormons.

He had a place somewheres around the foot of the Bighorns, near the Wind River, wherever that was. I went west on the

Emigrant Trail, figuring I'd run on to someone, somewheres who would know.

Late in the afternoon of the next day I looked west and saw the dot of a rider moving pretty brisk. I pulled off figuring it was a courier or something.

Pretty soon the man come up close. He was riding a great big Thoroughbred, which he slowed to a bare walk. From where I was you could see five miles down the trail.

He was a weathered, whip-thin customer wearing two Colts tied down on his hips and he had two more in scabbards either side of his saddle horn. The handles was ivory polished by much use. A long gun's stock hung out from under his right leg, looked to be one of the Sharps buffalo rifles, .45–90 or .45–120.

"Good evening to you," I said, touching my hat. His eyes flicked over me and he smiled and nodded. We begun to chat about this and that, the War, what pretty country it was. He got off and gave his horse a little water, and then checked its hooves. He swung up.

We was both looking down the trail, at a blob of dust over a rise. Several riders were coming, hard. The gent with all the artillery took a pair of German binoculars out of his saddlebag and looked for a long time at the party coming this way. He put the field glasses away and checked his tack and girths. His horse could run to Chicago paced right.

"Well," he says, "much obliged for the talk. Name's Black. Those gents down there and I have some differences and I'd just as soon not settle with them, it only makes it worse."

He clucked to his horse and they took off at an easy, ground-eating lope. He seemed to not have a care in the world.

About an hour later some horses near blown bearing sweating soldiers come on up, led by a lieutenant. They reined up and the men started to walk their mounts to cool them, but it was too late. Black could outrun these mounts on foot, never mind that magnificent horse he was on and taking such good care of.

"Did that murdering bastard talk much?" said the lieutenant.

"No," I said.

"How was his mount?"

"Oh, looked like it just came from Kentucky and ate corn all the way. You'll never even get near enough to see his dust," I said—it was true.

"Shit," said the lieutenant.

"Do you know where I might find Jim Bridger?" I asked.

"Thirty miles ahead at Fort Laramie," he said. "Mount up!"

The soldiers got on and away they went, the fools. From what I'd seen of Mr. Black they was smartest *not* to catch him.

"Who'd Black kill?" I asked.

"Two gamblers and a sergeant," said the lieutenant. He led them off east, with no hope of catching Black.

I decided to go down to water and camp and go on into Laramie in the morning. I found a spring looked reasonable and unpacked and hobbled my horses and put my bedroll out to air some.

I was tired of jerky and pemmican so I thought I'd go shoot a rabbit.

As I walked softly through the sagebrush I saw a flash of white off to my right and whirled and fired at the same moment the skunk did. I got both barrels at a range of about ten feet and a good batch in my eyes. It burned like hell, I was coughing like a one-lung donkey engine, I was blind and staggering, and I felt my way around looking for water to wash my eyes with. That meant that I fell over bushes and rocks and I pretty well beat up everything the skunk didn't get.

Damn, what a fine night that was. I fell in the cactus and I found out later I had teetered on the edge of a thirty-foot drop and finally I got one eye to where I could see with it a little. Of course it was dark and I couldn't see well enough with it to find my possibles, and that's where the matches was. So I shivered and cussed all the damn night—the skunk oil sure burns your eyes—and finally I got to my kit and water.

It didn't help worth a damn. I smeared some fat from a bag of pemmican on my eyes and face and that helped some. I thought I'd catch the horses and go on into Laramie.

The horses didn't want anything to do with me. They ran and whinnied and crow-hopped and tried to kick me and rolled their eyes and finally the pinto got hung up in a sagebrush and I got a halter on him—him screaming the whole time—and little by little I got everything together and the other horse packed and made tracks down the trail to Laramie. I come on to the fort in the late afternoon. It had a scattering of tents and teepees around it and wagons parked a ways from the log walls.

The sentries at the gate let me in, nodding politely, until I got past when they commenced guffawing and coughing. It was not a dignified way to meet these folks.

God, was I ripe. I hadn't had a bath for months and the skunk on top of that. A dog come out to me leading my horses and he was wagging his tail till he got a noseful and he run off howling.

I was desperate for a bath and clothes—new clothes—and I saw this tall gray-haired feller in a checked red and black shirt and doeskin pants tucked into leggin's and moccasins walking along the promenade deck of the officers' quarters. I turned my feet over to him and hallooed.

"I need a bath," I said. He nodded, not even sniffing and coughing.

"Bathhouse is down that way," he says, pointing toward a raw board building.

"They sell clothes here?" I asked.

"Outside," he says. "Peddlers." He'd come down off the porch, keeping well upwind of me. I noticed a huge goiter under his chin. The goiter was the size of a small melon. It hit me sudden who this was.

"You Jim Bridger?" I asked.

He nodded, and I told him I had a letter from Spotted Tail for him, and he got a real interested look on his face. I fumbled around in my saddlebags and found it, stained with horse sweat and the dye in the saddle leather. It was a longish, soft tube, something written on scraped white doeskin.

"Mr. Bridger," I says, "I have money. I'd pay a lot for some clothes to make me presentable. If I don't get a bath pretty quick

I'm going to lose my hide. Could I give you some money? And could you go buy them while I try to soak off the skunk?"

Bridger looked at me—he had shrewd blue eyes and a smile almost beginning on his lips all the time.

"Go wash off the stink," he says, "and no, you can't pay me. But I'll get you some clothes and canned tomaters. Onliest thing takes the stink out." He took hold of my horse's reins and he pointed to the bathhouse, sort of wrinkling his nose and coughing a little for appearance's sake. Well, I was young and whiny and he was trying not to hurt my feelings, I thought.

There was nobody in the bathhouse but me, and there was big copper boilers full of hot water and a slab of yellow soap near a cedar washtub six feet across. I moved a hose from a boiler to it and filled it and got in and commenced lathering the hell out of me. That damn soap was so strong I could feel about the first six layers of skin come off and it burned worse in my eyes than the skunk oil had.

A woman shrieked and I looked blindly toward the noise. I couldn't see a damn thing. The water in the washtub was so soapy I couldn't use it to clear my eyes, so I just stood up and felt my way over to the boiler and I got in that and tried to wash out my eyes. When I stood and walked there was a lot more shrieks and the sound of feet moving away, and swishing skirts. I sloshed around for a long while and got the soap out of my eyes. The boiler was deep and I couldn't see over the rim—I'd been dog-paddling and treading water—and I grabbed the lip and lifted and looked out and what I saw was this huge sergeant damn near flaming from his nostrils come stomping in the door.

"Wottinell's goin' on herabouts!?" he roars. I let go of the rim and sank beneath the waves.

A couple post guards come hotstepping along, and the upshot of all this is that goddamned Bridger had sent me to the washhouse instead of the bathhouse and a lot of enlisted men's wives who worked as laundresses to fluff up the sixteen dollars a month their husbands was getting had come back from supper to find this naked feller sloshing around in their washwater, when he warn't waggling his privates in their direction. The guards goosed me out of the boiler with their bayonets and flung a blanket around me and tossed me in the filthy, dank guardhouse. I was sitting there thinking on how much of a problem I was going to be to Bridger commencing when I got out of this.

Finally that pumpkin-throated son of a bitch had got his guffaws for the moment and he got me sprung. I still reeked of skunk, so he hauled me behind the barracks where there was a tub of canned tomatoes and fresh clothes. The tomatoes took the scent right off and I toweled off and got into some good, heavy, cheap clothes and boots. There was a brand new hat and a wide leather belt in the britches with my gun and knife already on it. Bridger was always like that, he'd drive you about half-crazy but never clear into the ground.

He fetched me as I poured the last of the tomatoes down the jakes. I squeaked along beside him, my new boots complaining at the work and my shirt and pants stiff with sizing.

He took me to the stables and showed me where my horses were—they was fat with water and had had their hooves trimmed and oiled.

"I'd nary spend a night under a roof," said Bridger, "if it ain't winter. Got a little camp nearby, if'n you'll join me."

I slipped off the nosebags and put my gear aboard the horses with Jim's help and then I follered after him. His big bay horse was waiting for us at the gates. Bridger swung up on him—I saw he used an Injun rein, a loop knotted on his horse's lower jaw. (I was to find out later that the horse came when Bridger whistled, if told to stand would stay there and couldn't be spooked off, and that he'd let a stranger mount and wait until he could buck him off and stomp him, too. Jim trained all his saddle horses to do them things and if they wouldn't he'd sell 'em. I was to adopt the same ruthlessness.)

Bridger had dossed down near a little spring and built a little firepit. He always used the least that would do, and when he selected a place to bed down you could be sure just at evening a breeze would start up and blow the bugs off. He'd been out here now for more than forty years, and he knew so much he didn't have to think about it anymore.

I slung my bedroll off to the side and unpacked the rest of my gear. I hobbled my ponies in a place with good grass and water, and went back to break up wood I gathered on the way. There was a cast-iron pot of stew bubbling on the fire and bread fresh-baked he'd got at the fort. I hadn't had bread in a year, it seemed. There was a big blue tin coffeepot full of coffee, like I hadn't had in months.

I et and went to sleep on top of my blankets. Some after midnight the cold woke me up and I burrowed under. I'd never seen stars this close.

5

eing Jim Bridger's apprentice was a lot easier than you'd expect. He didn't really, so he said, get no pleasure out of tormenting me, and I wasn't very cocky what with Spotted Tail, the skunk, Oneida, the army, and all the rest of it. I'd been living mighty hard and fast but I was only fourteen and about ten times a week I felt like going home. *Let* them hang me.

I minded my manners around Bridger—it was hard, he could rasp on you so, and I watched everything that he did hard. He was a grand storyteller—best ever till I heard Charley Russell, the painter—and if he hadn't come out with Ashley and stayed I'd easy bet he'd have turned a good hand to anything he done. He never wasted a motion or missed a shot all the time I was with him. He was a good blacksmith—been apprenticed in his youth—and for years he had repaired emigrant wagons at his little fort, till Brigham Young pestered him shooting his stock and firing his crops to where Jim just packed up and left. (Young kept sending them damn missionaries out to bother him, and Jim would make fun of him and of them, subtlelike, and the one thing no religious quack can stand is to be made fun of. It sends them purely crazy.)

Now he was contracted to the army to find a good site for a fort to protect a portion of the Bozeman Trail. So three days after our introduction we went north from Laramie, supposed to find a right place for a stockade.

Now Bridger could draw them a map of all the Rockies and "X" the spots that would be good sites for stockades. His sketches was the most accurate maps of that country until the ordnance survey the army made in 1910, but that ain't the way the army worked. They couldn't pay him for what he knew, they'd pay him for going to look for what he damn well knew was already there.

I was gratified in my apprentice position and hoped I would be able to work my way up to scout. It seemed like regular work, and Bridger was being paid for a day what a lieutenant made in a month, and the absence of your employer while you were doing your work was a grand recommendation.

Jim was a quiet feller, set easy in the saddle. His eyes never stopped flicking here and there, here and there. He avoided places that might conceal someone. He noticed everything, both the things that shouldn't be there, or the things that should but weren't. So I watched *him*, not the country, since I figured that I couldn't see it anyway, and besides I could tell it got on his nerves. I warn't brimmed with the forgiveness for what he done to me at Laramie.

One day we crested a long rise and Jim got down and looked for sign, sort of grunting to himself. Then he stared off into the blue distance, counting the mountains.

"Wul," he says, "there ain't much point in this."

"Beg pardon?" I says.

"Wul, I'll tell 'em fifty good places to put a fort they'll find another ain't got nothing to recommend it 'cept I didn't. Red Cloud and Man-Afraid-of-His-Horses and them will be raisin' hell no matter where I put the damn fort, and the army will try to fight 'em like they's Confederates and so the army will lose. I get weary of this time to time."

I looked off to our left and damn near jumped ten feet straight up. There was three Injuns in red trade blankets strung out on a ridge a couple of miles away, sort of headed toward us. I choked and spluttered and pointed.

"Oh, them's been with us the last ten miles," says Bridger, unconcerned. "Oglalas by the looks of 'em. Think maybe Yellow

Hawk's the first one, Old Smoke in the middle thar, and Bull Waller on the far point."

"What are they doin'?" I said, checking my guns.

"Wul, they's waiting for a chance to lift our hair."

"Are there others?" I said. My face got hot. I was some flustered, like a young turkey the day before Thanksgiving.

"Wul, there's the six we been follerin', sort of. They's riding ahead, good way to trail a man, stay ahead of him."

Bridger swung up and on we went, me so scared my teeth were clacking. I fell behind, my mind whirling. Then I goosed my horse a little and come up alongside of him.

"What was in that damn letter," I says, sort of screechy.

"Wul," says Bridger, "my wife was mortal fond of Spotted Tail and she used to make this here beaver tail stew that Spotted Tail was mortal fond of and he has writ all polite like to ask for the recipe."

"Shit," I snarled, dropping back behind. (Actually, I had opened the letter and unrolled it, it was covered with stick men and horses and sun symbols. Recipe. Shit.)

"Aren't you going to do something?" I yelled. "Let's get forted up, fer Godsakes, 'fore they all get here." Bridger reined up and waited till I got up to him.

"Wul," he says, "we got three to the right and six up front and three to the left . . ."

"We got repeating rifles," I says. "They won't make it to us."

"And about two hundred and forty-two right behind," Bridger went on. "So I guess forting up wouldn't do us all that much good. I'd admire to do it and I think the suggestion is excellent. Lessen you got a hot-air balloon in yer kit there I think we oughter wait and see what they want. So. 'Sides, scramblin' into a hole ain't dignified and they would think the less of us."

I screamed and bellered and cussed for what seemed an hour while Bridger kept looking over the land, as unconcerned as if we was in Boston and in church.

We went on and down through a little gap in the stone wall

of the breaks, and when I first come round the corner behind Jim I saw a sight burns in my mind to this day. Oh, I was to see lots worse after this, but it was the first.

There was three white men—you could tell only by the boots and the litter around them—and they was hanging by their feet from rawhide ropes strung up to the top of the cliff. Their heads weren't but a foot or so off the ground.

The Injuns had slit them around the beltline, pulled the skin down like taking off a shirt, and tied the skin off over their heads. They cut holes for their mouths so they could get air. The blood was all clotted but red rivulets still ran down one of them. He was making a very faint eeeeeeeeeeing sound, as high-pitched as a glasscutter's tool on a pane.

Bridger slid off his horse, pulled out his pistol, and shot each man once in the head. He turned away, still chewing his tobacco, while I puked up my guts after falling off the horse. I finally got up to one knee and was trembling on it, running with cold sweat. I had a grip on the stony ground so hard that when I looked later my fingernails was broken.

"Wul," says Bridger, "seems to be them three sneaked round the fort tuther day, headed for the gold fields. Wish 'em had stopped in, I'd have mentioned how it would likely end. Last shortcut they'll take, I believe."

For a cold moment I wondered how I had pulled the luck to stay alive. This was hard country and these was hard men. I started crying. I'd run from home, joined the army, been captured by the Indians, and now I was in the Rockies like I always had wanted to be (or the South Seas) with a man I had been reading about since I could read at all. And I wanted my mother. And nothing else. I sobbed some.

Bridger paid no more attention to me than he had to the three poor bastards he'd just shot. "Wul," he says, "there's a good place to camp up a few miles. I'm getting on hungry."

I staggered up and hauled myself up to my saddle. My two horses were getting snuffy at the smell of blood and my fear.

"Hungry?" I wailed. "Ain't we going to bury them?"

"Wul," says Bridger, "I always thought I'd rather be et by

birds and coyotes, myself. This here ground's stone. Take blasting powder to dig a grave and I'm fresh out." Bridger slid down and walked over to the hanging corpses and quickly slashed the rawhide holding them up. They flopped down like so many sacks of guts. Bridger casually flipped an arm off his boot with his toe and then he remounted, riding in that slaunchwise way the old-timers favored.

Bridger rode past me and I followed, trying not to fall out of the saddle as I blubbered and blew snot and tried to wipe my face and I shook like a scared pup.

Bridger ignored me. He went on and I followed, and always his head kept moving as he flicked them pale blue eyes everywhere. By the time we had come to the campsite I had pulled myself up some. I felt thin and glassy, but I tended the stock and then I fetched some firewood and started making a fire in the three-stone pit.

"It can get purt near rough out here, time to time," he said. "But she's a purty place, that she is. Air so pure that meat don't spoil. Water so clear ya cain't tell how far it is to the bottom and the stars hang down so low at night you can lean up in your bedroll and light a seegar by 'em."

He was tryin' to cheer me up without much effect. For one thing, calling this vast place, this damn endless ocean of mountains and water and grass and blood and death "her" didn't fit. At least then it didn't. Course, over time, I learned that blood makes the grass grow green and fast and that this land *was* like a woman's heart, big, mysterious, fold warm around you and make you suck in your breath with the beauty of it, and then turn cold as a black north wind in winter and leave you fighting for your life without much hope but a lot of habit.

I chewed some jerky and dried fruit in a peckish way and had some coffee. I was beginning to relax some and sweat a little less when three Injuns appeared like the damn air froze into them and one of them threw a knife underhand across the campfire. It buried itself in the log beside me with a nice, solid chonking sound.

Something in me snapped and I damn well heard the crack.

I come up to my feet and jerked the knife from the log and made for the Injun that had throwed it at me. I was in a blood rage and no mistake. I was sick of being frightened, and sick of being lost in a place I didn't know, and sick of being picked on.

I still had my gloves on and I scooped a handful of coals up and threw them in the Injun's face. He'd gone to a crouch and started for me and he got one in the face and one down his collar. I made a quick slash for the hand he held his knife in and I made a grab for his topknot. I swear I was going to scalp him first and *then* kill him.

My knife hand stopped like a tight vise had shut on it. I looked and saw the beaded gauntlet and looked up at Bridger. I cussed him good and tried to jerk my arm free but I might as well have had a horse standing on it.

"Wul," says Bridger, "I'm full of the congratulate fer you but I think that mebbe you best stop."

"Why?" I screamed. "The son of a bitch was trying to kill me. Let go of my wrist, goddamn you."

"Wul, no I won't," said Bridger. "They was just funning with you to see if you had sand. Last time you didn't and they hoped for improvement. And there's three hundred of 'em close enough to drown us if they all spit at once. Do your own figgering since you had such good schooling."

Just about this time my feet told me they was awful hot, almost in flames, and I looked down and saw I had been standing in the cook fire all the time I had been arguing with Bridger.

I dropped the knife and commenced to hopping around and yelling and whooping and pulling at my boots. This got a whole round of laughter I did not much appreciate from a whole lot of folks I could not see but who could see me just fine, thank you.

(This ridiculous moment led to my being named for all time Stands-in-the-Fire-and-Argues. As you can see it had nothing to do with personal bravery or all them rude things I was to say to congressional committees and the like later.)

Once I had got rid of my smoldering boots and hopped a bit more my feet quit hurting. I stood there, fuming, trying to recall when I had been this happy.

"How come they ain't killed us?" I says to Bridger.

"Wul," he says, "if'n I'm alone but for a child or a couple friends they won't bother to kill me. If I'm leading soldiers they'll try real hard. They like me all right and I signed that you were a retarded nephew, to explain all of that vaudeville act you put on just now. They appreciated it and think you are worthy of a few more days of life."

"Look here," I yelled. "You crazy miserable balding old bastard fart I ain't yer goddamned . . ."

"I know I ain't the quality folks yer used to fer parents but 'less you want to be slow roasted and fed yer balls and dick while yer dyin' I think ye'd best go along with muh little joke for . . ."

"All right, uncle," I says. "I have been rude to you and I apologize to you, uncle . . ."

"SHUT THE HELL UP YA LITTLE SHIT OR THE INJUNS ALL BE THE LEAST A YAR WORRIES . . ." Bridger bellered, being even less fond of the idea of me for a nephew than I was of him for an uncle. "If it's any consolation," says Bridger, "it hurts me as much as it does you. Prolly more as I'm older and got better taste."

Then Bridger set down and so did some of the two hundred Injuns and a lot of them went off somewheres silent as slow water. Spotted Tail's moon face beamed at me suddenly from the right.

"Good evening," I said, and remembered and nodded while my balls gave a little hop. Spotted Tail looked blank and stupid.

I had pretty good Sioux now—it's the prettiest spoke language there is, and damn the Frogs—to follow what was being said, which was that the Injuns was prepared to kill all white men on the Thieves' Road or anyplace else on their hunting grounds or anywhere near the Pa Sapa, the Sacred Black Hills.

The Bozeman Trail run right through their pantry, and they had been promised that this would never happen so long as grass should grow and rivers flow and the sun shone and they were concerned that the Great White Father (No Injun I ever knew called the occupant of the White House that. What they did call the President was . . . . . . oh, never mind.) anyway, maybe the Great White Father and his Sons had forgot that the grass was growing, rivers flowing, and why didn't all these white sonsabitches go back where they came from and eat shit and die of the bellyache?

Bridger told them that white women bore four children at a time, and so the whites, who were beyond number now, would soon be thick as grasshoppers in a wet summer. (Unwittingly, Bridger condemned a lot of white women to abduction, the Injuns being as eager to have bigger litters as any Mormon, and the funny thing about it is that very few of them women wanted to go back if they stayed even a month with the tribe.)

Bridger explained that he was just up here trying to help his son (me) learn about the country and such, as I had got into trouble in town, a sad and sordid incident involving a goat and several other medium to small barnyard animals. Bridger went on in that vein till he glanced over my way to see what I was adding by way of sign language to his narrative. He nodded once at me and we quit the contest.

Then he started in in a dialect I couldn't follow, and in order that the joke not be lost on me Spotted Tail came over and interpreted for me, describing my prowess with frogs and ducks. The audience was hooting happily. I took it all in good part, not wanting to be three days dying over hot coals and privately I was swearing that this pumpkin-throated old bastard was going to pay a very heavy price as soon as I figured up the bill and the coin.

There was one feller in a plain dark blue blanket sitting next to me, and he never moved or uttered a word at all. He was light-skinned and had light brown hair—common in the Plains tribes—and while everyone with him was painted and quilled to the last patch of skin he had no decorations at all but one eagle feather in his hair and a small medicine bundle behind his right ear.

The palaver ended and everybody got up, and the feller in the blue blanket flowed up off the ground like a cat after a butterfly.

He spoke then, sadly, that they must fight with much bravery to defeat the numerous whites, but that was the business of warriors and would be till the last of them rode up the Star Trail—the Indian heaven is at the end of the Milky Way, a place of mild weather and good water and game and war. It sounds a lot nicer than the whiteman's heaven, which seems forlorn and vengeful and noisy, what with all them seraphim and cherubim bellering hosannas day and night. (Wild Bill Hickock said that the whiteman's heaven had always sounded to him like a third-rate hotel at Saratoga Springs in the off season, with locks on all the doors. You couldn't get in to any place you wanted to be, or out of the others.)

Our guests melted into the night, I heard the sound of unshod Injun ponies moving away.

"That feller spoke last was Crazy Horse," said Bridger, who was wadding cheap trade tobacco into his pipe.

"He don't look like an Injun," I said.

"Spend some time with him," said Bridger. "You won't think that he's even human."

6

Having passed my entrance examinations—failure would have meant my slow and painful extinction—Jim now commenced to throw his fifty years of experience at me like a man tossing hay with a damn big fork.

In order to stop me from daydreaming, which every youngster does practically all the time, he commenced into whacking me with a stick any time my mind wandered away. In order to make me wary of alkali bogs, for instance, he suddenly challenged me to a race to the ridgetop. He swung wide round a boulder and seemed, to me, to be taking an uncommon long, dumb way to the top. I joyfully spurred my horse right on to one of them damn flat yellow-white patches and the horse sunk through and me right behind him, down into blue, thin, burning mud, sticky as glue. I jumped off the horse and tried to struggle to dry ground and was in above my waist in no time.

Bridger took an uncommon long time to even come to where me and the horse was sinking out of sight, and after he got there the son of a bitch set down on a handy flat rock and began asking me questions about some of the stars in the night sky, the various colors and patterns the warrior societies painted their arrows, how ducks fuck, and other such vital matters while me and the horse sank an inch or three.

"I cain't stand to watch an animal suffer," Bridger said. He tossed a loop over the horse and backed his big bay away and pulled my pinto out pretty easy. He took the saddle off him and patted his neck and checked his hooves good and hobbled him and the animal went on down to the river.

During this here rescue I had lost another couple inches of freeboard.

"What's the poison hemlock look like?" says Bridger, back on his rock and *whittling.*

I called him a lot of names and I made a lot of threats, and I was shaking with so much rage I slid down in the bog another couple inches.

"Very good," said Bridger. "You are getting handy at cussing, and I'm proud of how far you've come. Now how do you know it's poison hemlock?"

"If the roots is joined at the base, otherwise it is cow parsnip," I says. "Would you let me suffocate if I couldn't recall what hemlock looks like?"

"Course I would," says Bridger. "Cain't learn quick and good you'd just die out here anyways. I got a responsibility here. What if you was ignorant and guiding troops?"

"To water hemlock?" I said.

Truth to tell, more pioneers died of water hemlock, death camas, and nightshade than died of any Injun arrow or bullet.

He'd about had enough fun—good thing, I was about neck deep and my neck wasn't near as strong as a horse's. I suppose he'd thought of that, too. Anyway he tossed a loop over me and I got it under my arms and the horse pulled me out. The blue mud made a loud sucking sound and I left both my boots in the bog.

"If'n you just lay down you can roll out a them easy," said Bridger, as I lay there on firm earth wheezing. I got up after a bit and went down to the creek and washed as much of the blue mud off as I could. When I went back to the bog my boots was floating, sort of, on top of it. I rolled out and grabbed them and rolled back.

Bridger hadn't stopped whittling or moved off his rock.

"I'm sorry," I said. "I'll pay closer attention."

"Damn right you will," he said. "Go wash up and I'll make us up some grub."

I hoped that things would sort of calm down. They didn't. He still had that infernal stick, and I'd leave off paying attention to where the stick and him was and get a good whack across my shoulders or ass. I cordially wished gophers with dull teeth would chew on his piles and other dangling things through all eternity. He thanked me kind enough. The most maddening thing of all of it was his good humor and fine manners.

A couple days later it just stopped. Oh, the practical jokes we amused ourselves with went on as long as Bridger was alive, all of us back then enjoyed them, even if the victim was maimed for life, but the whackings with the stick and the bog lectures stopped. I wasn't cocky enough to think they were over, but I could at least afford to hope.

"Wul," says Bridger, "we'd best waste a little time. I knowed where the fort should go first off they asked me, but they'll make their own decision. Just want me to make the decision so they'll have something to fight over. I'd admire to see the Tetons anyways."

So that's where we went, backtracking a few days and up over Two Ocean Pass, coming to the Tetons by a seldom traveled trail. Two Ocean Pass is divided by a stream, one mouth of which goes to the Gulf of Mexico and the other to the Pacific. Streams have two mouths about as often as calves have two heads and live.

No one ever forgets the first time they see the Tetons rising blue in the distance. They ain't got no foothills, they just start up and keep going. We wandered around them for a few days—it was cold and there was snow on our blankets of a morning—and then we headed back for Laramie, swinging far south of the wagon trail and then cutting north to go over Happy Jack Pass. It was named for a feller so full of glee he never stopped laughing, which made folks sort of avoid him. I never met him, he froze solid with a smile on his face in '62, during one of them cold snaps so deep that when you spit it goes *pop* before it hits the ground.

Colonel Carrington was waiting at the gates for Bridger, and the two of them stood off a little ways talking, Carrington real earnest and gesturing with his hands, and Bridger yupping and noping and scratching himself.

Damned if we didn't leave the very next morning up the trail, Carrington to pick one of the sites that Bridger recommended, and some three hundred soldiers and civilian contractors to build it.

The whole and usual and customary blend of incompetence, foolhardiness, just plain stupidity, and all other military virtues was constantly displayed from the morning we left the gates clear through all that followed after. The military idiocies I had seen heretofore was mild, on account of how the practitioners was mostly amateurs and they lacked the sheer professionalism necessary to true strategic and tactical imbecility. You have to go to West Point to get that. I wasn't overfond of the military even then, and to this day after Big Piney Creek the sight of *any* uniform makes me want to laugh and run at the same time.

Carrington was all right, actually; he knew his business and he had a level head. But he had the worst subordinates I ever seen all piled together in one place.

This expedition had some cavalry, though not enough, some infantry and artillery, and three days behind us two hundred teamsters and contractors and the wives and children of officers and men. *That* wagon train was two and a half miles long. They had one blacksmith where they could have done with ten—the ground was stony and hard on horseshoes and the iron rims of the wagon wheels. The wheelwright didn't even have the tools to make the hallies with, and they left the spare ammunition for the whole detachment on the last two freight wagons because those wagons was heaviest loaded.

We even had six magazine correspondents and a couple photographers.

This sorry mob made, on a good day, six or eight miles. The Injuns, if they'd a mind, could have started at either end of the train and chewed the whole thing up like a string of sausages. They didn't recognize the opportunity, thank God. Injuns stole horses every night, but the sentries and wranglers never saw nor heard nothing. Bridger shrugged and said that was a sure sign of Crows.

'Bout a week up the trail we found what little was left of a small wagon train. The folks belonging to it had been trussed up like chickens, scalped, and tossed into the burning wagons.

"Musta been in a hurry," says Bridger. "Wonder what over? It ain't usual for them to work so fast and sloppy."

Carrington's infantry buried the bodies, breaking pickaxes on the stones and sweating to get graves two feet deep to hold the bodies. They piled big rocks over them.

On we went. The equipment that Carrington had gathered for his fort had necessaries like a forty-piece brass band, one whole wagon full of flagpoles—patent brass ones that screwed together—a sixteen-pipe organ for the chapel, hay rakes and mowers, huge cast-iron cookstoves, and a two-thousand-volume library. (Bridger remarked that him and the other trappers was saved by being so ignorant, if they'd *knowed* what they had to have to wander the Rockies they'd have been too heavy loaded down to leave St. Louis.)

"Oglala'd admire to have all that nice soft paper with winter comin' on," says Bridger. "How'd I ever manage to stay alive out here so long. Luck, I guess." He was funning but there was an edge to it, no mistake. A military disaster has a *smell* about it, I was to see a lot of them. This one was my first and I could nose the high odor but I didn't know what to call it.

Bridger had recommended a site way the hell and gone to the north, on the Tongue River, where there was ample water and wood, a good clear view for forty miles, a grand defensive position for the stockade, and plenty of fine grass for the stock. Colonel Carrington, with that eye they give you at West Point for good spots to make Last Stands in, chose a site that could only be improved by being in a narrow canyon with lots of big rocks up top for the savages to toss down.

He found a nice spot on a hill overlooking the Big Piney Creek Basin, with lots of higher hills around it so all the Injuns in North America could be crowded together out there and you'd a never knowed it, so it wouldn't disturb your sleep. The wood and water was a good five miles away, and it was sixty miles in one direction and a hundred in the other to the spots where Injuns would likely attack wagons. Oh, it was a real good kind of defensive position, but in order for a real good defensive position to work it has to be someplace the enemy will have to or want to attack it.

By the time the troops Carrington sent out reached the spots of trouble even the maggots would have got wings and flown.

Every man jack in the expedition was put to work digging trenches or cutting and hauling logs for the palisades, except me and Bridger.

"My back hurts," says Bridger. "We'll go look around a little bit here. For weeks." That last was muttered but I caught it. (That's what he was paid for, and he was payin' me, sort of, and you know Jim never went back. He said later he was afraid that when it happened he'd lose hisself and say something unkind that would haunt him of nights, as he hated to hurt folks' feelings. Soon as we were away from the fort he started bellering "DUMBSHITS," and he didn't quit for a long time.)

While we was gone for the rest of the fall and into the winter an average of a man a day was either wounded or outright killed and scalped. A photographer died of having shards of his glass plates pounded down his throat. Two magazine writers was hung upside down over slow fires. Soldiers was gutted like sheep. The woodcutters refused to go into the timber until the artillery had shot canister into the trees. It went on and on.

The Injuns burnt up the hayrakes and mowers. Carrington's poodle wandered outside and the skin was found nailed to the gates the next morning. Sentries was found dead with their eyes open and alert, dead of an arrow in the throat or head.

I wasn't there but I got told later one November day close on to the end of the month a short, blustery little captain name of Fetterman showed up to his new post, and hadn't taken his coat off before he started bellering that if he had eighty men he would ride through the whole Sioux nation.

Captain Brown wanted to scalp Red Cloud himself.

Lieutenant Grummond felt the Sioux were the poorest cavalrymen he'd ever seen.

I never met any of them, but I was to see them die.

Bridger and me had wandered west. He'd been paid up and he gave me half of it, even as I protested that I hadn't earned it and I didn't need it anyway.

"Wul," says Bridger, looking out in the distance, "you been an endless and amusing comfort to an old man, kept me from boredom many a time. Ain't laughed so hard since I cain't remember. Arful good for my kidneys and digestion." I assumed he meant the twinkle and little shake of the shoulders that signified Jim Bridger was having a hard attack of mirth.

"Thank you," I said, hefting the pouch of gold coins. "I don't know how to repay you but I will have something occur over time. You can count on it. I promise."

"No doubt," says this lovely old goat. "I'll be watchin' fer it."

The Wind River Range was high on our right. We come to a huge village of Shoshones, and Bridger went on in with me behind, and we come to a teepee had a big old man with long white hair and a smile like half the moon. We slung down and Bridger and the old man commenced to rattling back and forth in English, chaffing each other over a hundred bygone misadventures. I'd never heard Bridger laugh loud, but he done so now.

Finally, Bridger put a hand on my shoulder, and he commented that I was learnin' the scout's trade, that Bridger had never seen anyone so dumb learn so little so slowly, that I liked to fuck turtles, that there was warrants for me back East for this or that felony, that when I robbed banks I dumped the gold out of the sacks to lighten 'em so as not to hamper my escape, and that any warrior would likely kill me with a rock 'thout taking his mind off serious matters, but the Bible says love the hopeless and Bridger had never seen a challenge to compare with me.

The tall old man twinkled through all of this. Then he stuck out a big, gnarly paw and shook my hand.

"This here's Washakie," said Bridger, introducing me to one of the greatest men the world has ever known, "and this is Luther. He's even less than he looks."

"Big Throat has great regard for you," said Washakie.

"I don't know how I survived that there regard," I said.

"Ya get old in yer dotage and ya get merciful," said Bridger. "It's sad but there's no escapin' it."

"My wives have supper for us," says Washakie. "We can lie and eat, too." He led us into his lodge.

I shoveled buffalo stew in my mouth and listened to these two old monsters most of the night.

7

ashakie was close on to seventy when I met him, maybe ten years or so older than Bridger. He was a good six inches taller than Jim and broad-shouldered and he moved hale and graceful as a strong man of thirty. Just how hale the old bastard was I would find out shortly.

We crawled into his lodge and spread ourselves out on buffalo robes and Washakie tamped a long pipe's bowl full of tobacco mixed with sweet herbs and he and Bridger passed it back and forth. It was obvious that they held each other in great esteem and they spent about an hour remembering particularly hilarious times they had enjoyed as wild youths running around the mountains looking for beaver, both kinds. I found it uncommon dull and I fidgeted and yawned and finally allowed as how I was going to stretch my legs and rest my ears, which had been taking a windy beating. I did not fail to appreciate all this that they were saying and I marveled at its truth, I went on, and I would stay but for some reasons goddamned lies made me sneeze. I sneezed a couple of times to make my point.

I knew I'd set these two old buzzards to hunting for a way to play a joke or two on me and I was just mad enough to make a fight of it.

Bridger allowed as how it was a splendid idea I go for a walk and I ought to do it in such a manner as the horses was all cared for and all our gear ended up in the next lodge over.

It took me a couple of hours to curry the horses down and clean their hooves and such. The lodge we was assigned to was a big one, full of robes and thick with the scent of burning sweet grass. There was a nice kettle of dog stew bubbling on a low fire of aspen coals and a bowl of wild strawberries all cemented over with cheap pale brown trade sugar.

I et some of the stew and chiseled out a few chunks of strawberries and sugar and sort of scratched myself reflectively and thought that I'd last had a bath in the summertime but I couldn't recall exactly when.

I fetched some clean possibles from my bags and a chunk of lye soap and I wandered down to the river and up it, looking for a private place to bathe. I must have walked for three or four miles. It was a late and very hot summer day—hard to believe it had been snowing up high in the mountains just a couple weeks before—there was dragonflies clacking past over the water and blackbirds gargling away in the cattails.

The water was cold, and I shivered a bit in it and stood up and lathered up good and scrubbed my body and then my face with a rag. I rinsed off and stood up, my eyes prickling, and the sun warmed me pretty good and quickly.

In most of these tales this is where the beautiful Injun maiden shucks her clothes off on the bank and comes paddling out to disport herself with the brave scout, on water and on land. Hear Jim Beckwourth tell it he couldn't take his clothes off without some fair maiden leaping passionately upon him and entwining her slim limbs with his whereupon they flatten the grass and knock over small trees in the heat of their passion. After several hours of reckless landscape gardening she takes him home to Daddy, who promptly resigns the chieftainship and hands it over to Jim, who to hear him tell it was chief of a whole lot of tribes at the same time, even if they'd been happily cutting each other's nuts off for centuries.

Now, all that's wrong with that story is that most Injun maidens is as shapely as paving bricks, and damn few tribes had or wanted a chief. Injuns was true democrats, couldn't get the same opinion from three of them two times running and most war councils was about as orderly as payday at the post saloon.

Luther Kelly's luck was holding steady and some different from Jim Beckwourth's, for when my eyes cleared I saw two grim-looking gents packing up my clothes into a bag, which they then set on.

"Good afternoon, brother," said one. "This here's Elder Olson and I is Elder Olsonson and we is here to bring you the word of God."

Beckwourth gets a piece of tail, I get the goddamn Mormons.

"Much obliged," I says. "Now if you'll be so good as to get yer asses off my clothes then we'll chat while I'm dressing."

"We all has to stand naked before the Lord on Judgment Day," says Elder Olsonson.

"I don't got to stand naked before a couple of fools in August," I snarls, stalking up to the bank. I picked up a handy club.

"Please just listen to us," says Elder Olson, whipping out a handy Navy Colt.

"Can't think of a thing I'd rather do," I says.

"How much do you know about the word of God," says Elder Olsonson.

"Not a damn thing," I says, "but being from a good Catholic home any time God wants to drop in and speak his piece I'll listen if I ain't too busy doing something useful."

"We's the Mormons," says Olson. "And we bring you the work and word of our prophets Joseph Smith and Brigham Young."

"My grandfather Teignmouth knew Joseph Smith and he said he was a ninny and a man couldn't go to town without that fool busting in the house and knocking holes in the walls looking for treasure. Grandfather Teignmouth took a poor view of the man and marched him to jail twice."

"Hunnnnnh?" they said.

"Smith about ruined half the houses around. He was

famous for it. After a while, he started looking into his hat and he claimed he found gold plates in it. I did a little arithmetic and figured his hat weighed eight hundred and twenty pounds. I'd have admired to see his shirt collar if he actually wore it . . . ."

"We are wasting our time," said Elder Olsonson, the brighter of the two. "This one is past saving."

They got up off my clothes and I dumped the things out and handed them the sack.

"You'll need this," I says. "Your best bet is to kidnap infants and make sure they never learn how to read."

A bright and evil light went on in my brain.

"But I know a feller who has much trouble in his life and who said just this morning he longs for the Word of God," I says.

Well, you'd have thought I had just come up with a six-hour sermon and a hard bench to set on while listening to it. They looked hopeful.

"Even the heathen may bring some folk to the light," says Elder Olsonson. "Where is this wandering soul."

"Over to Washakie's camp," I says.

(Washakie was always very nice to the Mormons. He told me they was such pitiful damn fools that no grown man should treat them any worse than you would other congenital idiots. "They must belong to the Great Spirit," said Washakie, "and I wish He'd come get them.")

Well, you may well imagine how good I felt leading this brace of morons back to Washakie's lodge and shoving them in the door. I then lit out like a fox with its tail on fire because I suspicioned what was going to happen next. I was a good two hundred yards away by the time Olson and Olsonson's narrow little eyes opened far enough to see the convert.

"Bridger the Antichrist!" they bellered, loud enough to blow the hair off a passing dog.

They come boiling out of Washakie's lodge, looking one way and another for me, and both with their guns out. The world ain't seen such devoted missionaries since Cortes slaughtered half of Mexico.

Right behind them come Bridger, bellering, too. "WHEN I FIND YA YA ROTTEN POXY PIECE A SKUNK SHIT I'LL FEED YA TA THE GODDAMN ANTS. I'LL MAKE A CAP SACK OUTA YER BALL BAG." I figured he was talking to me.

The Church Militant was splitting up the better to cover more ground and the West's Greatest Scout was staring hard at the dust reading my sign and it warn't three seconds before Bridger was loping down my trail, even though there was thousands of footmarks to choose from.

I whipped off my boots and ran back to the edge of the camp, carefully keeping a lodge between me and Bridger, who was listing at the top of his lungs all the horrible things he was going to do to me and sounding damn earnest about it, too. His temper weren't being helped by the Elders trying to convert him as he stalked me.

The din was something. I was proud of it, if I got away.

I dived in the door of a lodge two down from the one we was staying in, hoping by sign language to explain my presence, but it was empty and so I burrowed deep under a pile of buffalo robes. I was tired and I decided to take a nap.

How long I slept I can't tell. I was woke up by someone sitting on me. The someone didn't weigh very much, and then she began to sing. She had a lovely, clear voice, and the song was a Scottish lament I'd heard as a child.

I thought I'd leave about then, and when I slithered off I caused her seat to drop about eight inches, suddenlike. She gave off a little hum, rising at the end to a question, and commenced peeling back the robes.

She peeled back the last robe and saw my face grinning up at her. Most girls would have shrieked—white ones, that is—but she just smiled and put her hand to her mouth and laughed. The light coming through the doorway was behind her, and her hair gathered the sunlight. I thought she had the most beautiful face I had ever seen.

She started rattling away at me in sign, telling me that Big Throat was very angry with me. Good, I signed back. Sour Faces mad, too, she signed, dogs bit them.

We talked with our fingers for a long long time and I'd have been happy to go on till dark. I couldn't take my eyes off this girl.

She went out for a bit and came back and come to me. Where's Bridger?

Left hours ago.

"What?" I said. For truth to tell I hadn't made any plans other than follering Bridger around. I wiggled out under the back of the lodge, pulled my boots on, and went looking for Jim. He was gone without so much as a wave. I sat down, stunned, and I sniveled and thought I'd catch up to him and apologize. I'd beg him not to leave me go, is what I'd do.

Once, some years later, I come across a grizzly cub—year and a half old, maybe—digging roots with his mother in a high meadow. The mother stood up and looked at Junior like she's never seen him before. She started walking away and the little bear ran after her and she half turned and whacked him ass over tip about sixty feet. The little bear was more puzzled than hurt and he chased back to mother who gave him a roundhouse would have broke the neck of an ox. The little bear tried a few more times and it sunk in that he was unwelcome. The sow went over the hill, and the cub sat on a log at the edge of the meadow and bawled.

I sat on a stump in the brush and cried and sniveled and drowned in the sorrowfuls for my poor self. All right, goddamn these treacherous shitheels, I'd show 'em. I'd go get my traps and ride north where the varmints could eat me, and to hell with them.

Here I was, on the run from the law, a deserter from the army, in a camp full of Injuns I didn't know, halfway to hell and I could see it from here if I climbed a tree. I'd put up with these treacherous, overbearing turds and I had at all times been respectful and . . . . . then it occurred to me that I seemed to be handed off from one adopted uncle at fairly regular intervals, and there was a small possibility that I was such a pain in the ass that they had had all they could stand.

But I was going to damn well leave. I walked back to the

camp and full of the woe and perplex I hauled my saddle and such out of Washakie's guest lodge and got my horses and commenced slowly to pile all my goods on the packhorse. My tail had one hell of a droop to it, I am remembering.

While I was checking the ties I almost sobbed. I turned and took a step and ran straight into Washakie, who had drifted over silent as smoke.

"Stands-in-the-Fire-and Argues," Washakie says, with as infernal a grin on his face as Spotted Tail's. "Do you think of leaving? Of running? I would not have thought the son of Big Throat was so fish-hearted."

"That old bastard ain't my father!" I snarled, my voice busting so the last part sounded pretty soprano.

"Yes he is," said Washakie. His black eyes were twinkling. They were the most intelligent eyes I had ever seen, or would. I thought that those eyes knew things about me I couldn't even guess at.

"Where will you go," Washakie asked, sounding concerned, his soft deep voice on my young ear like home.

"Jackson's Hole, maybe."

"Pretty place," said Washakie. "Lots of snow. I don't think you'd better go there. Maybe you should take your fish heart east and grow turnips. Turnips don't have teeth and they can't run or fight."

"I am not a farmer," I said, big and brave, my voice cracking and my dignity crumbling like a cutbank in the spring.

"Some of my young men called me an old woman last night," Washakie went on. "They want to go to war. The young men always want to go to war, and when they do some die and the others come back much older. After that first time they don't want to go to war so badly."

So Washakie would take his young men off to fight somebody, I thought. It ain't anything for me.

"Your father said I should teach you to make war," he went on. "So we will go off and fight the Crows and Blackfeet. Big Throat said you weren't much. Let us see how much."

"That pumpkin-throated son of a bitch," I yelled. "He . . ."

Washakie hit me sort of casual-like on the top of my hat with his open hand, driving my hat down to where the brim was on my collarbones and most of my neck down in my lungs. My feet was swept out from under me and when I put my hands out to catch myself as I fell I just grabbed air till I hit. There was a light touch at my throat. Washakie's foot. The foot went away and there in the prison of my Stetson I reflected that if this was a real fight I'd have a crushed windpipe. I'd be dead. Washakie had put forth about as much effort as he would swatting a horsefly.

I got my hat off finally, though the silk lining had been torn away from its moorings and hung haybellied out from the sweatband. My ears had lost skin and the wind stung them. I looked at Washakie, white-haired, old, standing there smiling with his twinkling eyes.

"A warrior would kill you with his hands," said Washakie. "A warrior would not waste a *rock* on you. He wouldn't take your weapons, he wouldn't take your scalp, he would not spit on your dead body. Big Throat was drunk when you found him, yes? He'd eaten bad mushrooms? His horse threw him on his head? Shit."

My eyes started leaking tears. My lower lip was trembling and I was about ready to bawl. Then I felt a sudden hot flush of anger in my belly and it ran out to my fingertips and the soles of my feet in no time. I could feel myself swell.

"I don't know nothin' about it," I said to Washakie. "But I learn quick and believe me I'll pay right close attention." I wanted to go for this old monster's throat with a part of me, and a part of me wanted his nod.

"I ain't very old," I hissed, "and my education's been a bit neglected in some matters. Right now, I'd study hard enough just so I could break your goddamned neck."

Washakie threw back his head and laughed and laughed and bellered and bellered till the tears run down his face. Each time his eye fell on me he went off into another fit. I must have cut a sorry, scrawny sight, though at the time I couldn't see it.

"You want to play a game?" roared Washakie. "Run. Take all your guns and run for a day, and I'll follow with only some salt from the Bitter Lake, for the rabbits I catch with my hands. Who lives, wins. Well?"

"Why waste all that time," I says. "Just kill me now, Bridger would enjoy that."

"I have things I must do," said Washakie. "When they are done, we will go and make war."

"What do I do while we wait," I snarls. "Braid the tails and manes on your horses?"

"Hum," said Washakie, "I think you better chase that little piece you met when you hid in the lodge."

"Huh?" I said.

"Slight a Shoshone girl, she'll cut off your balls," said Washakie.

I slumped down and sat on a nearby rock with my head in my hands and stared hard at a black beetle struggling through a grass thicket near my boot-tips.

Washakie went off whistling sunnily.

I was to sit on that rock for a half hour or something, and in addition to my complete ignorance of the proper methods of blood and slaughter I was somewhat mystified at the thought of courting any girl. The Bishop's daughter and the Sioux maidens hadn't exactly polished me for smooth talk. Bridger had given me a lot of knowing about the country and I had a shivering sense that war school with Washakie was not going to be restful.

These savage Injuns likely courted by bringing the girl a sack of grizzly hearts or something. I got up and walked back to the camp and dropped the gear off the horses and then took them out to the big meadow and let them go.

When I got back to the guest lodge all my gear was gone. I thought Washakie had tossed it inside and I thought not much of it. I wandered off and found the spring the camp drank from. It was a huge spring, twenty feet across, and the water rose out of it swiftly, and made a good-sized creek that ran into the river a half mile away.

I drank long and deep and cooled my face—the sun was hot and there was thunderheads gathering to the west, they always sort of formed up there and when there were enough, on they came. A little black and yellow canary trilled at me and a pair of magpies went mad when I come near their nest on the way back. I thought I'd take some sleep and see what the morrow would give over in the way of humiliations.

I crawled in through the door and peeled off my boots and laid out. The teepee had been rolled up a little so there was a cool draught on my forehead.

I was ready to turn over and sleep when I saw a flash of light across the teepee from me. I squinted into the darkness and saw a woman kneeling. She didn't have a stitch of clothing on.

It was the girl who'd sat on me earlier, when I was hiding from Bridger and the Mormons.

8

fter all these years has fallen off me I have decided that women decide things and then they have a big wedding so men, who are pretty thick, know a point has been made even if they ain't never sure what it was. It warn't no different there in Washakie's camp. I'd been chose and that was that.

Well, boys, I sat on her and there you have it.

I asked her in sign language just what in the hell she was doing here and I got back the hand over the mouth and the giggle. I was some distracted that she didn't have a scrap of anything on and she was purely beautiful. I finally made a grab for her and she popped me a good one in the nose with her little hand. I lay there reflectively holding my whacked snoot and wondering why I was here at all. She started in on the buttons of my shirt and as soon as I was naked she lay down beside me and at it we went, started slow and clumsy and then the pace picked up.

"HHaaaahhhhhhh!!" someone screamed five feet away. A squaw tossed off the buffalo robe she'd been hiding under and went out the door and I could hear her bellering the news at the top of her lungs to all in hearing, and that meant everybody.

A considerable crowd gathered outside singing and there was a lot of advice shouted that I could understand only by sensing the shift of intentions on the part of the girl. It was a most strenuous afternoon.

We was lying there, spent, and then the girl got up, put on her dress and moccasins, and came back to me. I smiled and she damn near knocked my teeth down my throat. She scuttled out the door and there was hoots and cries fading off in the distance toward the river.

I pulled on my clothes and boots and went looking for Washakie, and I *was* a tad worried that I had somehow offended the little minx and this was her way to get her father to cut off my balls. I wondered who her father was. I was getting a little jumpy of women, what with the Bishop's daughter and this slender charmer in my lent lodge, and how all tales seemed to end with Luther gelded and such. It can make a feller peckish, a life as hurried and confusing as mine had been these last couple years.

Washakie was nowhere to be seen. I walked toward the bluffs behind the camp, past the big spring, and I found a cleft with a trail good enough for a goat so I went up it and come out on the top. I could see fifty miles or more south of me and behind me there was a faint blue haze on the horizon where the mountains was. I sat up there pitching pebbles over the edge and hearing them thwock on the scree.

An eagle sailed in and hovered right in front of me, not a hundred feet away, moving his pinion feathers to catch the little winds. He was looking down at something. Then he decided it wasn't interesting and banked away, whirling up till he was so high I lost him.

I wandered back down to the camp and asked about for Washakie, and got told he was in council and couldn't be disturbed. I could hear his big voice coming from the council lodge, so I waited nearby, hiding behind a rack of drying jerky. I crouched sort of protectively over my balls, feeling much put upon.

He come out after the pipe-smoking and I fastened on to him like a bulldog and asked him to do something before my balls was sawed off by this slender girl had just attacked me in the guest lodge.

I got the fatherly diatribe to end 'em all because the girl, of course, was Washakie's. What in the whiteman hell did I think I was doing complaining to Washakie, father of Eats-Men-Whole, a young woman of virtues I was too coarse to appreciate. Wasn't she good enough for me? Not good enough in the robes? Had I et of her cooking. How lucky I should feel that this woman would find a worthless paleface jackass stripling attractive. She saw good things in me that Washakie couldn't see at all. I looked to him like I'd been raised in the dark and fed magpie shit. I was so stupid horseflies wouldn't bite me, afraid they'd forget how to fly. I was the lowest form of whiteman scum and the only thing he could think of to recommend me at all was that I warn't a Mormon.

Washakie's great friend Big Throat had asked Washakie to take Luther and make him a warrior. Biggest challenge that Washakie had ever faced, but he'd do it, and Washakie had always observed that a warrior was lots more efficientlike if he had a nice hot piece at home to think on while shooting and stabbing and scalping. But if in my white jackass ninnyhammering pride I wished to fling his lovely daughter, the pride of his decrepit old age, fling her back into his ancient lap he, Washakie, would bear no ill-feelings at all forever and the matter would not be brung up by Washakie again.

I'd heard speeches of this nature from my uncle Angus, on different subjects to be sure, but I'd heard them.

"Like hell you won't do anything you bloodthirsty goddamned old pirate," I yelled. "You won't have to, that daughter of yours will cut off my balls. Eats-Men-Whole, was it? Nice name, you musta thought for days on that one. Well, I think she's beautiful and I'm honored to be a part of your family. Has any one in it died a natural death for the last three centuries?"

Washakie's smile would have blinded the moon.

"Big Throat said you had sand," he said, "if one dug enough. Now, Eats-Men-Whole, when she was a little girl, would go to the traders with me, and she loved the gingerbread cookies that the traders sold. They were in the shape of men."

"My only regret is that Big Throat ain't here to be at the wedding," I says. "He gets so little amusement of his life."

There is a particular shit-eating grin that some of my good friends has worn from time to time, when they has gone and got me in a fearful and embarrassing tangle and can now set and watch as I claw and wiggle my way out of it. Some of them spend *years* in the thinking up of these traps and the sheer joy they pump out their pores when they finally got me up a stump runs kneedeep and sticky. (Of course, I do the same thing.)

Washakie was as pleased as he could be. He'd got his last daughter all married off and out of his old gray and white hairs, to some kid Bridger had flung at him like a weepy booby prize.

Washakie also had an apprentice to make miserable, which would fight off boredom and such. Washakie was a shrewd judge of character, and he knew that Eats-Men-Whole would have me in a constant state of confusion that was the best foundation for a marriage. If the old bastard had been a college professor he would have taught something useless and complex.

Washakie was pleased as a dog in a field of fresh cow shit, and he took me by the arm and marched me back to my new home, the one complete with bride, dog stew, warpole, robes, and a priceless family heirloom, the dried head of a Blackfoot Washakie had taken a particular and deep dislike to, so much that Washakie had killed the man and cut out his heart and et it, and then slow-smoked the feller's head after scalping him.

This treasured souvenir was hauled out of its verdigris-green buffalo hide case on ceremonial occasions, when Washakie would piss on it while making nasty comments on the Blackfeet in general and this here specimen in particular.

Eats-Men-Whole was standing demurely by the door of the lodge, wearing a white doeskin dress and leggin's and beaded moccasins and she had an angelic expression on her face, which did not match the bloodthirsty old pirate she had for a father or her considerable left hook. The two of them embraced touchingly, ignoring the dolt of a husband she had decided to take.

Washakie joined our hands in his huge paw, sang a short song, burned some sweetgrass, and then beamed happily at his children. Especially his son-in-law, and for some reason his smile did not warm me.

Eats-Men-Whole waited a decent interval, upwards of a minute, and then she grabbed my hand and led me off to our lodge. A good-sized crowd had assembled and was shouting instructions and all manner of encouragement while Washakie stood there grinning. I wished I had a cannon plumb full of grapeshot. Eats-Men-Whole near jerked me off my feet when she dived through the door. I sort of fell through it and covered the hole with a robe hung there for that purpose.

Eats-Men-Whole shucked off her dress, leggin's, and moccasins and stood there in the creamy light, all soft curves, smiling. She had very long legs and high breasts and she'd been born sassy. When the pace I was removing my clothes at didn't please her she started tearing my shirt off, and the sound of ripping cloth was hailed with loud cheers outside where the crowd was.

We went at it with great enthusiasm, and after the fourth time I'd shot off I was so winded I couldn't even lift my head from the robe. (A few years later I happened to be out on the Smith River, at the end of the salmon run. The salmon die after spawning, but before they die they float for a time belly up, fins wiggling in faint jerks, head downriver, too far gone to care. They wait and hope on death and it is received gratefully. Them salmon always put me in mind of my honeymoon.)

The next morning I managed to crawl to what was left of my clothes, signing that if I didn't piss I'd begin to leak everywhere, streams running out my ears and what a terrible sight and all. I slung my rags about me and pulled on my boots and crawled out the door, to find about two hundred Shoshones of all ages, my dear father-in-law included, ringed around the teepee.

I didn't doubt but assumed that they would shortly tot up the scores and I'd get a cheer or a hissing. I stomped off and found a tree and stood behind it pissing for what seemed like half an hour. I checked my dick for blisters and spur marks and it seemed to be all right. One more night like the last one and I'll be all paralyzed for life anyway. I walked to the spring and fell in it and drank deep of the clean cold water and thought about drowning.

When I come out of the spring Washakie was standing there looking so pleased I thought I'd vomit.

"Eats-Men-Whole hopes that she has pleased you," Washakie rumbled, "and wishes to tell you that she now believes the lies she heard from the lodges of the Brulé Sioux are lies."

"Lies from the lodges of the Brulé?" I said, thinking on just screaming for an hour or two. "So let me guess. I'll just bet any money you care to name that Spotted Tail is a relation of mine."

"Spotted Tail, your uncle," said Washakie, "who you respect and honor."

I nodded. I thought I could have stayed home and gone into the law or graverobbing or something honorable like that.

"Your cock seems to be big enough and if you will go back to the lodge she will have new ways to please you."

"New ways to please me . . . . . ." I said, with all the bright enthusiasm I could muster. I think my voice broke.

"And if you don't go back pretty quick she will think that she hasn't pleased you and she will be hurt and she will probably . . ."

"Don't say it," I said holding up my hand. "Please. Please don't say it."

"When I was a young man we always took two wives at a time," Washakie observed, looking at me like I was an order gone wrong from Sears, Roebuck. "Men have lessened lately."

Well, as a young feller with the blood rising I couldn't stop thinking about screwing and now it seemed I was going to die of it. Sometimes the only thing worse than not getting what you want is getting it.

A beautiful doom, though, a beautiful doom. Just thinking about Eats-Men-Whole and my balls began to heat up, she was a lovely woman, aside from her choice of fathers and uncles.

And as Washakie no doubt planned, my interest in going off on a war journey increased as my dick sanded down.

Eats-Men-Whole would stop from time to time to force various vile concoctions down me, chased by big bowls of dog stew to keep my strength up and she painted my face with symbols that was easy to read as to their intent. While I tried to catch my breath she would think up new approaches and after a week I looked like a feller dead forty-eight hours of the consumption.

The only resting time I had I got when she was off stocking up on fresh suggestions from older women. When she had techniques enough to last all night she'd come back.

On one of my infrequent crabwise forays out into the wide and vertical world I run on to my father-in-law and I allowed as how I needed a rest in a desperate way so could we go kill and scalp a few hundred folks. Tribe and race no problem, anything he might want for his warpole. I wanted to wade up to my hips in blood.

"I'm down to half a pecker and a moan," I said. "I never was much up to blood and slaughter before but damn if it don't seem to sound restful-like. I've only killed a couple folks and that hardly counts."

"We have to build a sweat lodge and refrain three days from women before we go," says Washakie.

"Where do you want this here sweat lodge," I says. "How 'bout right over there? Lots of saplings about. I'll just hotfoot it back to my traps and get a hatchet and . . ."

"Yes, my son," said Washakie, laughing.

Eats-Men-Whole took it all in good part, and she threw herself into preparing foul potions of mallard guts, bat hair, and frog eyeballs to give me strength, wiliness, luck, and courage.

Washakie and me took frequent sweats in the lodge, pouring water over hot stones and singing holy songs and telling dirty jokes. And Washakie told me his life, what he cared to have me know. He'd been born around 1800, up in the high Wind River country, and fetched up between the Great Salt

Lake and the buffalo country to the east, on the Republican River. He went to work as a trapper for the Hudson's Bay Company around 1815, and trapped till the beaver were gone. Around 1840 he had taken to guiding pilgrims over the Oregon Trail.

"I took the Mormons to the Great Salt Lake—Big Throat asked me to—thinking that it was such bad country they would go on and die in the white deserts on their way to California. But they *liked* it. Jim and me, we stayed drunk a month on that mistake. Life is not all victories." Washakie poured more water on the hot stones. I was beginning to feel a little less pale and wan.

Washakie talked of his buffalo hunts and the mountains and waters. There were so many whites, he knew, that the Indian was doomed, doomed to vanish like the snow in spring. So he got along with the whites. They were crazy, and there were a lot of them.

"What would you do if we weren't so many?" I said.

"Kill all of you, even Bridger and the Rope Thrower." He smiled after he said it, but when he said it his eyes were hard.

We slept in our lodges, of course, and now that we were getting ready to go and had to abstain from fucking I fell into one of those traps that had been there all along. I was signing to Eats-Men-Whole and fishing for a word when she got that sunny smile on her face, giggled, and said, "I speak English and write it, too."

I'd been the fool so often and so long I just sort of goggled at her and didn't say anything at all.

We would be leaving at first light and I had to get some rest. There I lay, my mind racing, and then I dropped off and pretty soon I was woke up by my bladder—that's how Injuns rise early, they drink a lot of water the night before.

It took time to get the war paint and war clothes on and pack the horses, and the sun was near up when we went off down the trail, each of us riding a leggy horse for the fast work and leading a strong, stock one for our traps and loot. We both had repeating rifles and revolvers. Washakie was real sour about these whiteman inventions, he felt they give fools and dwarfs advantages they should not possess and the art of war suffered accordingly. Why, he said, when he was young a warrior would often jam his hand down an opponent's throat and rip out his lungs, disdaining even the using of a knife.

"What'd ya do with all the lungs?" I asked, getting a scowl as reward for not being awed enough.

"Wiped them on our arses," said Washakie.

"Must have made yer arses slippery," I says, "no wonder the Shoshones is thought such lousy riders. The 'feet likely call you Greasy Butts or something like."

Which in fact *is* what the 'feet called the Shoshones, and Washakie didn't like to be reminded of it. He spent a fair time grumbling about how Bridger had seen some promise in me but he, Washakie, even though he had give up his favorite daughter and had unwisely brung me along on this scalp-taking expedition, was beginning to think Bridger was full of shit and his daughter could use a good spanking.

For, Washakie went on, he was a good friend to Big Throat and he had out of friendship taken on this task but a man can't make bear stew out of bear shit. Washakie was old and tired and trying to do his best but hadn't much to work with. There was some good in all this but he was having trouble seeing it.

I let the old fool maunder on as it was plain that he'd gone and accepted me—out there back then partners never had a good word to say about each other at all.

We fringed around the edges of the Crow country for a couple of days and found sign that a village had moved through and so it wouldn't be far off. We went careful after that, never showing ourselves on a skyline or watering from pools where our tracks might show. We finally seen the village, on a long sloping hill that went down into the Bighorn River.

We went in the middle of the night to the cover of a grove of aspens maybe two hundred yards from the camp. Washakie went silently into the darkness, flitting from shadow to shadow. I stretched a light, thin rope in front of me and the horses, looping it around the trunks.

The war ponies had been trained to silence and they were no trouble. Of course, my first time out on one of these little romps I was sure every bird call and sound was a whole war party just about to jump me and leave just a little greasy spot where I went down. Washakie was gone maybe an hour, and he come slithering up to me with two fresh, bloody scalps and thirty-four more he'd pulled off the chief's warpole. He had taken a shit in front of the chief's door, so when he went out to piss he'd step in it.

"Where'd you get the scalps?" I said.

"Their watchers not much good," said Washakie. Of course, not so much as a dog had barked over there. Chills ran over my hide every which way.

While he was telling me this in a whisper the chief of the Crows must have stepped in it good because all of a sudden the camp come alive with people hollering and shots being fired and fires blazing up sudden.

"Hah," says Washakie, "very quick are the Crows." We made tracks for the high country where we had left the packhorses.

I had expected that we'd hightail it but Washakie shook his head and told me that he always left a calling card, a black feather from a raven, stuck to the bloody skull where he'd scalped his victim. It was his calling card and tended to make the Crows and Blackfeet not overzealous in their pursuit. I could hardly blame them. Crow mothers scared their kids into good behavior with Washakie's name, and down in Wyoming there is a place called Crowheart Butte, where Washakie killed the best warrior that the Crows had in single combat and then tore his heart out and ate it.

Washakie told me the story, laughing. "But I can't remember his name, it's terrible, eat a man's heart and then not remember his name. I am ashamed of myself." And he laughed and laughed and didn't sound all that ashamed to me.

Washakie sort of liked the Crows and only kilt and scalped a few now and then for appearance's sake, but he had a mortal hatred for the Blackfeet and with our first raid on them I wished to God I was home having my brains screwed out by my lovely little wife.

Washakie changed from a sort of dutiful, funny scalper of Crows, only doing it because he didn't want to hurt the tribe's feelings, to a methodical cold-blooded killer, and I found the change as frightening as the war work following. Say what you will, it's the laughing ones with the easy smile that are the worst of killers, I've seen it so many times.

We moved only by night in the Blackfeet country, and off the trails, hidden in the lodgepole pine. The horses made terrible crashing noises breaking sticks and small tree trunks, but so did the bull elk, and no 'feet was interested in bull elk meat, or the noise they made either.

When Washakie found fresh Blackfeet sign we bound the horses' feet in leather boots and went to sneaking full time. The pack animals got left a good ten miles back, each footed to a whippy sapling, with rope enough to graze and water. There ain't a lot to moving silently other than being careful and in no hurry.

We smelled woodsmoke and tied the war ponies in a thicket, and smeared our faces and hands with charcoal. We slithered off through the brush and watched the camp pretty close, marking the lodges only had one or two Blackfeet in them. I'd been lugging Washakie's medicine bundle for him, it weighed about thirty pounds and I'd have had a smart question for him except that I was so scared my mouth was dry and stuck together.

He unrolled it and there was this double-barreled sawed-off shotgun in there looked to be about a two-gauge, and a dozen shells two inches in diameter and six inches long. He whispered that if he came back running I was to fire low. The idea was to blow as many legs off as possible and to hell with the scalps. "Further," he hissed, "no matter how tempting, wait till I am out of the field of fire. You'd never make it out of here alive."

"Shit!" I managed to whisper.

Then I reflected that it would leave me bringing up the rear. He was almost seventy, I'd pass him in ten seconds. My nostrils was all flared out and I was breathing deep and my senses seemed to have got better. I heard everything, saw everything, and smelled the woodsmoke from the cooking fires.

Washakie moved into the shadows when the moon was up good and I watched the Blackfeet warrior riding guard around the camp move into the shadow of a big black spruce and the horse came out with no rider on it.

A squaw come out of a lodge and moved off into the tall grass and she squatted and tipped over backward. A big shadow went into the camp.

Something had gone wrong with our counting, for the lodge the woman had come out of suddenly gave off terrible high screams just cut off like that, and then Washakie came boiling out the door and straight toward me.

I heard horses behind me and whirled around—there was four 'feet there, a hunting party come in late maybe, and they had come up behind me and if one of their ponies hadn't nickered they'd have been on me before I would have knowed it. I let my breath out and pulled the trigger and a pound or so of lead, rusty nails, bits of strap iron, rocks, and glass shot out in a black cloud and lifted all four right off their horses. The horses fell over next, screaming, too.

When I whirled back round I saw Washakie maybe fifty feet from me, running low to the ground and covering a lot of it, and two 'feet warriors behind him. All of a sudden Washakie stopped and whirled round and shot the lead warrior and the one behind him stumbled over the corpse and went down and Washakie's war club broke his head open like a smashed melon.

We mounted and rode hell for leather. It would take them a little time to sort things out but the 'feet was a brave sort and they have the worst tempers in the whole of the Injun nations. We bent over our horses' necks and I wished we'd never come.

Washakie suddenly pulled off the trail into a stream and doubled back, which was the last damned place I thought we ought to go. He reined up behind a curtain of willows and grabbed the shotgun and jammed two more shells in the monster—they was the goddamn size of bitters bottles—and with that in one hand and his war club in the other he waited.

Only he didn't wait until they was past. He spurred his war horse out when they was maybe fifty feet away, eight of them running close together, and Washakie charged right at them, firing the shotgun once—which cleared off the front four or five, and the others went down in the horse wreck that followed.

All but one who managed to rein off to the right. I yelled, all rage and fear, and went straight at him, firing my pistol when I got close and I don't know if I hit him with that but by God my big horse just went right up on his and I smashed his face in with my revolver barrel.

I was hollering whatever came to mind, being short on the personal sort of war cries (I settled on "Fuck the Irish," later, and it stood me in good stead) and mine were heavy on the aarghs and yyyyaaaaaahggggs, and for some reason the Twenty-third Psalm's "shadow of death" popped out pretty regular. I saw one 'feet struggling up from the mess—Washakie was already down in it scalping away—and I rode at him and pulled the horse up and shot him in the face with the muzzle of my gun no more than a foot from him. The powder flames scorched his hair and the stink come up quick.

Washakie had the 'feet all pelted out and he got on his pony with a big boo-kay of them scalps in one hand and he leaned over and said we'd best fly, we'd have hundreds of them after us at daybreak.

We rode for two days, getting off every few hours to rest the horses, feeding them grain we'd packed on the stocky burden horses, and going on. We went over passes that were there then and I have looked for them other times and not found them. We even doubled north at one point and then east. I never saw a 'feet and I never saw fresh sign. Washakie was always ahead of them, and me, too, and I wanted to know how he done it.

I was full of the admiration for the old buzzard, and we was headed for home.

9

arriors, I learned, throw up and keep going. Blood makes the grass green and long and rich. Killing is neither a horror nor a pleasure. It's a chore, our work, what we do.

The 'feet was tenacious and they'd started catching up, and it was all like that first time. I learned from that fierce old man to strike when we warn't expected, hit hard, and run. The old bastard *liked* being outnumbered, the crowd spoiled each other's footwork. If he was like this at seventy, I wondered what he was like when he was twenty-five. He also never got cut, or shot, or kicked by a horse.

He come back without a mark on him. All the marks was on *me*. I come back belly down over a horse, on account of a barbed arrow in my arse. Washakie'd dug it out right away—the 'feet poison their arrows with a green gum they get boiling the bulbs of pasqueflowers, but it's a slow moving poison. I had cuts and bruises, a hell of a slash across my cheek, and some broken toes I got kicking a 'feet's throat in, the treacherous bastard was wearing a brass medal heavy as a fry pan across his windpipe.

A couple of the young warriors who had been saying Washakie was a fish-hearted old woman carried me to my lodge, taking good care not to jar me.

I was set face down and Eats-Men-Whole fluttered about and fetched me hot tea and ashbread—toss a lump of dough on the coals and then when it's cooked eat the center part—and she had a hundred questions all of which I answered with grunts. I was sore-assed, exhausted, and if I'd close my eyes I'd get the wim-wams right off, seeing one or another batch of mean Blackfeet bearing down on us.

My education was just ripping right along.

Washakie was too much the showman to haul all of the scalps out at once. He put up ten, fresh-salted ones with blood in the hair, and then every morning and evening he'd add more. Since we was so busy staying alive we often hadn't the time to lift topknots, so the scalps he lifted from the Crow chief's warpole come in handy. Washakie was an honest man, he only cheated by three or four scalps as to the numbers we killed. He was an awesome and terrifying fighter, in battle he'd glow with an insane light. And like I said, he come back without a mark on him.

Here I am, I said to myself, as I laid belly down and my wounds itched, white child of good family, married and murdering. We was back and safe and I had the horrors every night, feeling like I was stuck in glue while I tried to run from howling mobs of Blackfeet. Eats-Men-Whole tended me gently and sweetly and I healed up pretty fast, though the worst scars was on my heart and soul. I was changed forever and I knew it. I was a stranger to myself.

Washakie had sewed up my arse and cheek with thick thread, and when the lips of the wounds had joined good he jerked out the thread. Some of the stitches had got infected, Eats-Men-Whole put hot compresses on them and they drained good.

My scars was still flaming red, but not painful, when one day a letter come from Bridger, sent by military courier. The Oregon Trail wasn't even a day's ride south of us—one of the spike trails come almost to the camp itself.

The letter was dictated by Bridger who was sick and thought he'd go home to his Missouri farm to recuperate. He had a cough wouldn't stop and he was too sick and weak to scout. Would I come to Fort Phil Kearney—that was what the army was calling Carrington's useless stockade—by early December. I wanted to hide the letter and claim that I never got it, but I owed Bridger and so I sent back a note saying yes. They didn't need me till then as all the Indians was off hunting buffalo.

Red Cloud had seemed to me to be the sort of feller who would attack right when all the whites thought he was off hunting buffalo, which was foolish on my part and a continuing misreading of Indian politics by all us whites that didn't result in more than a couple hundred thousand deaths of Injuns over the latter half of the nineteenth century. In statecraft, that's small change, but we was a young country and not as good at it as England.

Bridger was absolutely right, and the reason for it was that the Indians *was* all hunting buffalo, and though Red Cloud could start a war anytime he chose, if he wanted company he had to wait till his warriors were through hunting buffalo. When we started signing treaties for whatever land we was going to steal anyway, we'd sign one with Red Cloud and three or four others and them five would abide by it but the rest felt that it meant nothing at all, which it didn't really. The Canadians never did fight an Injun War, they let smallpox, measles, and trade whiskey fight for them, and it did every bit as well.

This was a modest beginning for me in scouting for the United States Army and I was, due to bad luck and my weak character, to go on scouting far too long.

Wul, as Bridger would say, I spent what was left of the fall spawning myself almost to death. Eats-Men-Whole did show a little more respect for me since I went on the scalp-taking vacation with her father. One day she announced we were going to have a baby, and she cuts off the screwing just like that. Washakie called it the time of coyote love, when all you do is sit by the hole and howl.

I headed toward Fort Phil Kearney the first of December; the fall had been so mild the leaves was mostly still on the trees, the cottonwoods and birches in the river bottoms and the aspens on the hillsides. I wasn't in any great hurry to get to Fort Phil

Kearney, because I was sure the tribes was off east hunting buffalo.

Fort Laramie wasn't much out of the way, and I figured to stop at it and I did, coming in on a bright crisp day to find a band assembled out front of the stockade, tootling and thumping away. I was most gratified that my fame had come before me. I pulled in casual-like, halted my horse, folded my hands on the saddle horn, and nodded along with the music.

The music trailed off and a strutty littler feller with major's rank on his shoulders come hotfooting over to me.

"Goddamn it," he hollered. "Git yer trampy ass out of the way! We got important visitors!"

I allowed as how it being the Christmas season and all and an old family custom decreed that I wear a large sprig of mistletoe on my shirttail in this blessed holiday season and he could pucker up and lunge anytime he'd a mind to.

"Who in the goddamn hell are you?" he screamed.

"I'm the scout filling in for Bridger," I said. "If I offend you so goddamn much I could just go back home and you could hire somebody else, or do the work yourself."

Bridger's name calmed the little major right down. "Would you *please* get out of the way," he pleaded. "General Custer is coming in."

I had been hearing rumors of Custer for some time, and I gathered he was famous among the tribes for killing women, children, the lame, halt, blind, and old. Washakie spat before using the name Custer, and after, too. Washakie wasn't averse to the taking of human life, for sure, but Custer's slaughters really stuck in his craw.

So I set my horse off for the parade ground where the troopers was all lined up, and got behind a gaggle of civilians and sat on my horse quietlike.

"Here he comes!" someone hollered, and the troopers snapped to attention and the civilians muttered with the excitement of it all.

Custer come in the gates wearing buckskins and his blond

hair down to his shoulders. His wife was riding sidesaddle, a little behind the man of the hour.

He had a gaggle of hangers-on and lackeys following him, and one feller in particular stood out—a tall, brown-haired galoot in a blue leather coat with the suede side out all worked with tiny beads and enough silver on his saddle and bridle and spurs and hat to make up table service for forty.

Just my luck, to see Custer and Buffalo Bill Cody on the same glorious day. Behind the three main attractions there was a ragged assortment of newspaper correspondents, without which he never went anywhere. Why, Custer even had a couple at the Little Bighorn ten years later. They made their deadlines, so to speak.

The strutty little major sought me out after the carnival was over and invited me to dinner in the officers' mess that night. He also apologized for his "fit of rudeness." I said I'd had them myself.

I thanked the major and accepted the invite and I give my horse to a hostler and went on in behind the newspapermen. I had a little time, and Custer and Cody was such ridiculous and inflated specimens I really wanted to see more.

Now, who should be the Officer of the Day but big old Gus Doane, escaped from Texas. We shook hands and he looked at the scar on my cheek and shook his head. He was on duty for another hour, we'd meet later.

The newspapermen was hollering questions at Cody and Custer, and it wasn't much amusement, so I strolled out the main gate to buy a few things from the sutler's wagons. Things generally cost less in the raw-board, false-front business district, but the sutlers was more interesting.

Which is how I met Klaas Vipsoek. I look back on that black December day when I met Custer, Cody, Doane, and Vipsoek and though all of them was to cause me trouble Klaas was a real special case.

He had his wagon opened up and his wares displayed in piles here and there. Pants, thread, needles, whiskey, patent medicines, pans of gingerbread baked six months before in

Chicago with glycerine in the recipe instead of water, vermilion for the Injun trade—all that kind of truck. The proprietor was missing. There was the sound of a hatchet thunking softly behind the wagon, ripe curses in a heavy Dutch accent, and blatts and pops and explosions, which was Klaas farting, which he did all the time. (His Injun name was Father-of-Bad-Winds.)

It was downright musical. Thump gaddumph focking fraaaappp blunk splash Rphreeeebipbipbip sinofabotcher whack blaaaaatttt and so forth.

I peered round the wagon, my eyes and nose was assaulted with a fearsome stench, and I hurried upwind to watch this here interesting spectacle.

Klaas had on a bright green Robin Hood hat with a filthy feather—might have been ostrich once—hanging down off it, a yellow-and-red-checked coat that was fairly new on account of you could still *tell* that it was yellow and red, green-and-white-checked pants, high yellow leather farmer boots, and a twisted pair of spectacles upside down on his nose.

He was one of them big men looks fat but isn't. He had twinkling bright blue eyes hid back of rolls of fat red cheek and one or the other or both of the cheeks had quids of tobacco in them. Tobacco juice flew off in any old direction, faithful as a leaky faucet. His beard and hair was blond in some places, except where the tobacco juice had dribbled down or he had wiped off some black axle grease in his hair.

"Focking sonopitching blaaattt phreep whonk," him and the hatchet said variously. He was hauling what appeared to be clean sausage casings out of a gut tub and cutting them into lengths about a foot long.

Making a note not to buy no sausage, what with this big old scabbly hound pissing on the pile of cut casings, I set down to watch an artist at work. I'd no idea what he was doing, but whatever it was he was good at it.

The guts slithered out of the tub and become lengths, which made no sense at all, since you stuff sausage in the whole gut and *then* tie it off.

Klaas stopped to catch his breath. He introduces himself, as did I, and when we shook hands a glob of fatty soap come off on my hand. I wiped it on his wagon cover, and I was not the first.

"What the hell are you doing?" I said, pointing to the piles of cut guts.

He tried several explanations in his fractured Dutchy English, accompanied by farts and gestures, and the last couple gestures I figured it out and laughed so damn hard I fell on the ground.

Klaas was makin' French hoods for the soldiers. Cock covers. Tomorrow was payday, and the boys would first run for a few stiff drinks, and after that the whorehouse. Them fifty-cent whores was poxy as hell, and the soldiers could protect themselves some with Klaas's wares.

I'd spied a medium-sized glass barrel out front with a few of these gut lengths floating in it, but it hadn't remarked much to me. Klaas finished up chopping the guts and started tying an eight-inch piece of stout thread on each one. Feller could slide on as much as he needed, tie it off, lay it on the table and whack off the overage with a bayonet or axe. I was impressed. The West is full of unexpected delights.

Klaas wiped his hands off and come round to the front of his wagon and took my money for some few possibles I'd found. There was a banjo stuck in a sheepskin case by the driver's seat and Klaas hauled it out and proceeded to make the godawful noises them things do. Klaas planked and twanged and farted and between the noise and the stench I made my escape right smart.

His wretched banjo music followed me all across the wagon camp, fading, finally and mercifully. On the way I stopped and bought some new duds—Strauss denims from San Francisco and a heavy wool shirt and a bright yellow silk scarf to needle the cavalry boys with. A hatter put a wooden sizer over my head and then he steamed and poked a new custom Monarch of the Plains to my every size. I bought some seegars and a tooled leather case for them. I'd smoked a pipe or two of tobacco and sort of liked it.

The officers' mess had white linens, silver, china, nigger

waiters, and fresh flowers for the grand occasion of having Custer *and* Buffalo Bill dining with them. I didn't amount to spit but I was grateful for the entertainment.

But Gus Doane caught me on the porch and we got to talk before the hysterics began.

"Saw an ad in the Omaha paper for a Luther Kelly," said Gus. "It said all is forgiven, whatever that means."

"Oh," I said.

We went on in to dinner. The food was horrible, fresh flowers or no, like army food everywhere or food anywhere in England. Boiled, bland, tasteless, and sort of True Regulation Gray.

I really wanted to leave and send a telegram to my mother. Then I thought suddenlike that it could be a trap. Be easy to put an ad in the paper, for the law.

"I can see those wheels turning," said Gus. "I'll check on it for you. Okay?" I nodded, thankful. Well, I didn't know.

After the godawful dinner there was godawful speeches, and the worst was Custer's. He was the most overblown actor ever carved from a hog's butt. I was embarrassed to even watch, but me and Doane seemed to be the only ones present who weren't just moved to tears by him. We also were probably the only two men in America who knew his generalship was of the same high order.

After we toasted the flag and the seegars came out I tried to bolt and would have made it but for Gus who had a grip on my arm like a bull terrier. He hauled me outside and Gus being Gus I found myself volunteered to guide Goldilocks and his wife on a buffalo hunt. Some had been sighted near the Little Cheyenne River.

"Why don't Cody take him?" I said.

"Bill's got two bad teeth he's havin' out right now by the post surgeon," said Gus, "and he ain't going to be in any shape to do anything but lay back, drink whiskey, and wait for his gum to heal."

Well, I owed Gus a lot, so the next day Custer, his wife, his teenage cousin Boston, a few soldiers, and me took off toward the northwest. A herd of journalists followed, George would have been uncommon lonesome without them.

Custer dashed here and there, looking noble, while I hoped his horse would find a prairie dog hole. By God if it didn't, shattering a leg so it had to be pistoled. We had a few spares with us and Custer had the soldiers strip the tack off the dead horse and put it all on another. Up swung our brave soldier, and the horse looked back at the rider and wrinkled his lips and bucked like a raw, mean old wild horse. I liked to think that the sight of this ridiculous ass caused the horse to do this. Anyway, George landed hard in a rosebush and the horse bucked on away. While the soldiers caught it, Mrs. Custer plucked thorns from George's parts.

Then someone up ahead hollered that there was buffalo in sight. George dropped to his knees and begged his wife for her horse. He would shoot a buffalo in her honor, with a pistol. I kept a respectful distance, trying not to throw up.

Well, this wet-brained clotheshorse took off on his wife's expensive Thoroughbred mare, and he was easy to see on a long rise over a little creek, chasing after the biggest bull in the herd.

Now, buffalo can swap ends faster than you can blink, and they are damn hard to foller and hard to get up beside so you can take a good shot. George got close in and gaining, and me and the scribblers were close and watching him when he suddenlike aimed his gun at the dodging buffalo and blew the brains out of his beast.

The one he was riding, I mean.

George flew in a long arc down to the yeller prairie grasses and he plowed a deep furrow for about forty yards with his nose. Many would have been spared much if he'd broke his fool neck, but luck warn't with us that day.

I galloped up quick to him and could have run my killing blade into his throat—he was bleeding so bad no one would have noticed—but I didn't and it shames me.

There was life in the body, so I turned it over and poured

out my canteen on his face and he coughed and spluttered and
sat up looking even more stupid than he usually did.

"Bloody hell," he said. He was in one of his British moods,
it often happened, I'd heard, when he'd done a lot of heavy
labor with his face.

"Did I get him?" said George, eyes lighting up.

"No," I says. "You did manage to blow the brains out of
your wife's horse, though."

"Do I know you?" he said suddenly, peering at me suspi-
ciouslike.

"No," I says, standing up. I watched his wife dismount and
run to him, uttering little cries.

I loped on back to the fort and told Gus the thrilling events
of the day, snarling that Custer hadn't the brains of even so low
a form of life as a soldier. Gus took it all in good part. He'd sent
a telegram and received one and said I had no warrants out for
me in New York.

"I'll see it soon enough," I says. I'd promised to take over
from Bridger, and so I would.

I headed north, wishing to get as far away from Custer and
what passed for civilization as I could.

The next morning, when the sun had got up high enough
to warm the air a little, I come by three freight wagons down in
a creek bottom. The lead wagon had a broken rear axle and the
three teamsters was setting at a makeshift bar they'd put together
out of battenboards from the wagons, flour barrels, and a bright
red-and-white-checked cloth to give it some high-type class.
They had a small keg of whiskey in a stand.

The West owes a great deal to drunken mule skinners, I will
have you know.

I climbed down off my horse and nodded to the three.

"I'll buy a round for the house," I says, putting a ten-dollar
gold piece on the tablecloth.

"What'n I tell you," says the mule skinner behind the bar.
"An'plass in this beshitten territory's good fer a saloon. We only
been here an hour an' we got a custom . . . er."

One of the fellers in front stood up. He was dignified, like drunks get just before they fall over backward.

"I'm Bart and that's Pete," he said, pointing, "and the barkeep thar is Mulebreath."

I got handed enough whiskey to pickle Mrs. Custer's ex-horse, and I sipped it slow. I'd not much experience drinkin' whiskey or much of anything else.

"Luther," I says. Bart's eyes rolled into his nose and he fell off the stump he'd been setting on.

"Ya got no manners," said Mulebreath, "ya Yankee pismire."

Mulebreath still proudly wore the rags of his Confederate uniform. He could have been one of the shoeless men in that damn stockade I'd soldiered around.

"If we hadna run outa whiskey we'da won," says Mulebreath proudly.

"No doubt," says I.

Mulebreath started tapping on the whiskey keg, and then he marked where the level of the liquor was.

"We'll be a week late ta Kearney," he said, smiling.

They'd hobbled their mules who was grazing in a meadow maybe a hundred feet away. The mules got jittery all of a sudden, and a whiff of the wind from the trees near the creek brought me a scent of bear.

"Come on out to the medder and fight like a man ya goddamn skulking hairball!" Mulebreath yelled. "I'll rip yer balls off an use 'em dried fer buttons."

Mulebreath staggered toward the mules and the meadow.

"Sergeant Mucklebreech to the rescue," said Pete. He wasn't drunk, just laughing.

"Mucklebreech?"

"Of the West Georgia Mucklebreeches."

We looked up toward the meadow where Mulebreath and the bear was now squared off. The bear would take a swipe at Mulebreath, and Mulebreath would take a poke at the bear.

"He do this often?" I says.

"Yup," said Pete. "Only usually there ain't nothing there that anyone can see but Mulebreath."

The bear was a good-sized black, but it was showing signs of disbelief turning to fear. Finally it run off, Mulebreath staggering after it hollering for it to come on back and settle this once and for all.

I said my thank-you's and left three seegars for the teamsters.

Mulebreath was waving his hat when I looked back.

10

I got, as you see, real disenchanted with the military early on and this is a very good thing for a young man. Oh, we got to have armies and navies, but you'd best remember that the leadership is drawed from them as likes to take orders so that someday they can give them. George Armstrong Custer was last but one in his West Point class. He made general faster than any of his classmates. I rest my case.

Still chuckling from time to time at the remembered happy sight of Custer plowing up the prairie with that monstrous hooter of his, I ambled on up the trail to Fort Phil Kearney, wondering why they wanted a scout at all. The whole idea when you are fighting primitives is you get them to attack you at a place of your choosing, and mow 'em down with massed volley fire. Most of our soldiers couldn't hit the wall of the mess with their dinner plates, let alone shoot straight.

I was damn sure that all the Sioux and Cheyennes were off making winter meat, so I whistled as I rode careless down the trail. Well, there was several hundred warriors watching *me* as I dawdled along, admiring the last touch of fall and how handsome my shadow was and like any true fool I had a guardian angel. This here angel was the unlikeliest one imaginable, my chum Spotted Tail of the Jesuit-gobbling Brulé Sioux. (He told me later that day he spared me only because he wanted to see

Bridger's face when he described how easy his apprentice had been caught.)

I wandered here and there and found a pleasant place to camp and smoked a seegar even though they still made me want to puke, and I lazed back against my saddle looking at the stars coming out.

First inkling I had that something was amiss was eight or ten people dropping on me out of the damn sky. They grabbed me by the arms and legs and then they rolled me up tight in a buffalo robe with just my head sticking out. They propped me up against a convenient tree so I could have a full and uninterrupted view of them chopping a soldier up into bloody rags, which they tossed off into the bushes.

All of a sudden Spotted Tail's zebra-striped face appeared in front of mine, smiling that warm, horrible smile, like he'd just et twelve nestfuls of live baby bluebirds.

"I'd shake hands," I granted, "but I'm a bit tight."

Spotted Tail's smile disappeared and he stuck his nose about a foot from mine and spat in my face.

"I have a use for you," he said, "but I should kill you for being taken so easily. Big Throat would be shamed. You learned nothing from him."

This was the very last spot in life when I ever trusted the land I was moving through again.

"You are a complete bastard," I says, getting hot and not caring. Several of his chums unrolled me and then tied my hands behind me tight to the point of gangrene.

They jerked me upright. One foot had gone asleep and I hobbled around trying to make the feeling come back to it.

There was this mean murderous little runt called Little Big Man who was hollering that I ought to be served just like that poor soldier, and all whites should suffer the same death. His whole family had been massacred at a meat camp in the Sand Hills, and I couldn't really blame him, but I still wasn't overfond of his suggestions.

Him and Spotted Tail yelled at each other for a while, and

finally Little Big Man went off, there were tears in his eyes. All of this was a dirty damn business and no mistake.

"You have some books in you, Stands-in-the-Fire-and-Argues," said Spotted Tail, "now tell me what did the Iceni do when they defeated an enemy?"

"They always left one alive to tell the tale," I said. They left that there messenger without hands, feet, eyes, or nose, and I sure hoped whatever translation old Tail had read had been deficient as to footnotes.

"Tail," I says, "I may not live much longer. Where in the hell did you get your education?"

"My father and grandfather who were also called Spotted Tail presented me with a beautifully erudite English governess when I was four. I got her days, and they . . ."

"I see," I said. "Where is she now?"

"Making meat with the Brulé. Living in the clean air. No corsets, no boredom, no hateful shrews or stuffed shirts. Sleep with my grandfather and father, the line is well-hung. Women are lawless, Stands-in-Fire. They tolerate us men. We amuse them. But don't ever be so foolish as to think you know what they want."

Well, that explained the old blond squaw with the pince-nez I'd seen in the Brulé camp. I thought of Eats-Men-Whole and a hot green flame of jealousy run up my spine and set my ears to smoking.

Spotted Tail spun me around and slashed the thongs away from my wrists.

"You owe me your life," he said. "You will not run. If you try you can become like the soldier." He looked at me for a long time, and then he said, "Shit," and walked off. I knew how he felt.

We moved north pretty rapidly, and no one paid much attention to me and I suppose I should have tried to run. But I owed my life to so many people I was feeling overbought.

After three days' pretty hard riding we come on to a wide valley about ten miles to the north and west of the fort. And all them Indians Carrington and everyone else thought was out on the plains hunting buffalo was there, nearly three thousand of them. For their war leader they had chose Crazy Horse, and that eerie, quiet man had a plan that was simple and soon to be put into effect.

The fort was in such a terrible position it sort of passed belief, to those who hadn't much experience of the military, and the siting of the fort led to all that came after. To get firewood the woodcutters and infantry detailed had to be protected by artillery and cavalry.

It was better than five miles to the timber, and the cannon fire had to rake through the forest before the cutters would even go into the shadows of the trees.

Even this considerable expenditure of taxpayer's lead did not make it safe. The Injuns would wait until the cannon stopped, and then they'd come back into the trees silent as rising water, and wait. So Carrington lost a soldier, a woodcutter, a teamster every so often, a steady bleeding, and it played hell with the men's minds.

They also knew what winters was like here when they came so they had to have that firewood.

The Injuns cropped off a few correspondents, too—one reporter from *Harper's* got pounded full of his own pencils and slathered with fat and burned alive. Soldiers all over the world feel the same way about correspondents, you may depend upon it.

A couple days after we arrived I rolled out of a robe stiff with frost one morning and found Crazy Horse standing near, he'd been looking down at me.

He told me to ride with him. We went up a long ridge to the end, where it broke off into a sheer fall of gray rock. There was a flat spot there, and a big brass spyglass like the artillerymen use to spot their fall of shot. The fort was easy visible in the distance. Crazy Horse put his eye to the lens.

I heard a screeching above and looked up. It was a sparrow hawk, flapping his wings so as to stay right above us. Crazy Horse looked up and smiled.

"They come twenty-two times a day," he said. He took a

small medicine bundle from behind his ear and unfolded the blue leather. He had what looked to be a sapphire. I reached for it but he took the stone away. It does not do to have an enemy touch your magic.

"Ah," said Crazy Horse, looking on the fort, "there he is, the fool who will come to kill me and die himself. Who is he?"

I couldn't tell at this distance, even with the telescope.

"He is very stupid and has a terrible temper," said Crazy Horse. "He beats the horse he rides with his saber. I cannot imagine that, to do that to the horse your life depends upon."

Well, I thought, you'll like Custer, too, he blows their brains out.

"Come," said Crazy Horse. We walked back down the ridge to our horses and mounted and rode north, past the little camps of ten or twenty warriors, piled all together to war on the whiteman for the first time.

Another sparrow hawk fluttered overhead and then it shot away, and shortly another came, or perhaps it was the same bird. Crazy Horse whistled a harsh greeting each time.

"I cannot be killed save by a Oglala with steel," he said. "When I fight the bird flies above and the stone behind my ear pushes the bullets away. Do your people ever keep any promise that they make?"

"Not to you they won't," I said.

"I thought so," he said. "We are many and brave. We will teach them a lesson and then your people will stay out of our lands."

Not much I could say to that, but I tried after a while.

"You are brave and when you got to fight what do you fight with?"

He patted the stock of his rifle.

"You cannot make them or the bullets. So when those are gone the whitemen will sweep you aside like a man sweeps a cloud of gnats from his face."

Crazy Horse pulled his horse up, and I stopped mine, too.

"What you say is true," he said, "but we cannot lie on the stones and die happily. We must fight."

I looked up and there was another sparrow hawk.

"But we will win this time," he said. "And perhaps a time or two again."

Well, there wasn't nothin' I could add to that. We rode on and come to a couple striplings cleaning out a deer they'd caught in a snare. The deer's front leg was scraped to the bone—they had used stolen telegraph wire—and the boys offered us fresh steaming raw liver with a dab of gall on it. I et mine hungry, I hadn't paid any attention to food the last few days. The blood was sticky and I wiped it off on the yellow grass, then went to the creek to rinse my hands.

The blood went away in dark red threads.

"Bravery will be enough," said Crazy Horse behind me. "It is all that we have."

Well, that and enough rifles and ammunition should see them through, I thought, all the way to noble deaths. Their wives and children and old folks can starve to death, which takes longer and makes no songs.

When I looked to the west I could make the distant peaks out and each one had a gray line topping straight out off it. Sign of snow for sure. If the line is *black*, that's a blizzard and a bad cold wind, and take cover. Just snow, but how much?

Crazy Horse stood at the edge of the trees looking west, with his hands held up and his eyes closed, praying, with the sparrow hawk skittering above. He prayed for a long time, and when he was through he nodded.

We rode back to where he was camped with Spotted Tail and Red Cloud, for the three of them were the war leaders. Even Red Cloud deferred to Crazy Horse.

That afternoon they held a war council, and each man recited the names of the enemies he had killed and numbered the horses he had stolen. It seemed childish to me, but they was happy with it and my opinion warn't asked for.

"We fight tomorrow," said Crazy Horse. "I have had a dream. I will lure the little angry soldier, and when he and his men come past the crest of Big Piney Ridge we rise and kill them. Rise and kill them. The snow will make them hungry for wood. No one has gone near them for days. Perhaps they will be foolish."

Crazy Horse had been waiting for the dream. Even with all the men in the circle, outside the sparrow hawk fluttered above him. He moved like a cat, he flowed, and I think he really could see not only the victory tomorrow, but much other death, too, his tribe's and his own.

The scouts had been pulled back and no one had taken a shot at a sentry in days. I thought them fools down there in the stockade was probably about thinking the Injuns was gone. If they did think that, they was about to pay a big mistake off in bloody coin.

The Injuns had been edgy, but now as I walked about the camp they all seemed tired and contented, sharpening their knives and cleaning their rifles, without any of the usual brag on what would happen tomorrow.

We et good of stew that night and I went to sleep early. I woke up when the first snowflakes touched my face. It was a light snowfall and would quicken and stop and quicken. It warmed up a little. My bladder was full, and I rolled out and folded the robe to keep the warm in and went off toward the bushes.

Crazy Horse was sitting in front of a low red fire, his eyes closed and motionless as stone. He seemed larger in that light, heavy, as though he might slowly sink into the earth.

I pissed and made my way back and went to sleep.

He was still there in the morning. A sparrow hawk shrieked over him, and his eyes flew open, and he stood up quickly and walked off toward the horse lines.

I saddled up and waited to go where I was told to.

11

The day of the Fetterman massacre was a clear cold one in the morning, but the wind was still hard and steady from the west and it smelled of snow.

The warriors kept well back, and had been forbidden to peer over anything for fear they would alert the troopers who were in the corner block towers with binoculars.

We heard a few bars of reveille and maybe an hour later the gates swung open and some teamsters and their wagons come out, with the woodcutters and a few soldiers to guard them. I looked for cavalry and the artillerymen, teams, caissons, and cannons, but the gates swung shut and on the little party came, maybe all of twenty men.

It took the teamsters well over an hour to come up on the trees that had been girdled in the summer to dry them up for winter firewood. The woodcutters moved off with their saws and axes and the guards lounged around the wagons.

Crazy Horse was standing by me. He had his hand out, palm up, making pulling motions toward the wood party. When the men went to the trees, Crazy Horse shut his hand and raised the fist and tapped his left shoulder with it.

He swung up on his war horse and raised his rifle, one of them brass and steel lever-actions, and his picked men, just twenty of them, come riding to him. They took off and when the guards saw them they threw up their guns and fired to no effect.

Crazy Horse's men were after the horses pulling the wagons, three teams of four, and they come on fast and shot down some in each team, panicking the others who went purely crazy from fear and broke themselves up on the traces and crosstrees. The cutters and teamsters and soldiers took such cover as they could find. Crazy Horse's men came back. Other Indians on foot kept up a steady sniping at the men pinned in the wagons.

I could see some of it, and it warn't long before I figured out that the Indians wasn't *trying* to hit anyone. Keep the bait alive, I thought, and the fish will be along presently.

In half an hour the post gates swung open and two double lines of troopers come out. The soldiers was followed by a few civilians on their own mounts, coming along for the fun. All I could do was nod. Fun, indeed.

I walked forward so I could see better. The aimed fire at the wagons picked up, and this time in earnest, and men was falling or seemingly slammed down by a big fist. The cavalry was coming on, and just as it crested the rise and could see the wagons Crazy Horse and his little party flashed in front of them. The troopers halted and then the man leading them pointed his saber at the retreating Injuns and on they came, going right past the woodcutters and straight up toward the ridge that I stood on.

Suddenly I was grabbed from behind by several pairs of hands and hustled off to a dead snag of fir had a fine view of the bowl behind the ridge. They tied me to it hand and foot.

Spotted Tail's striped face hung grinning in front of mine for a moment.

"Just remember," he said. "So you can tell the others." He was gone as quick as he come.

Crazy Horse's band went by far to the right of me, and they broke up and took their ponies dodging through the boulders all scattered through the bowl, and right behind them come the cavalry with that ass and his saber out front.

Crazy Horse stood up across the bowl, on a big gray rock, and I could see that strange hawk above him. The troopers were making right for him when every boulder in the bowl had an

Injun resting his rifle on it, and the fire sounded like cloth ripping. A huge mass of mounted Injuns come in from my left—easy a thousand of them, and several hundred more cut across the open country on my right that the soldiers had just rode through. They was all caught and to die.

Hard to tell how long it was from the time the troopers came over the ridgetop to the silence after the battle—I'd say no more than five minutes. The warriors checked the dead to see if any was shamming and I heard a couple shrieks cut off in gurgles, and then the Indians just melted away, leaving only me to tell the tale. The silence after a fight isn't like any other, it has an emptiness that's black.

The Injuns were in such a hurry to go they didn't even take the sound horses. The animals jingled when they walked, of the tack on them, and they nosed the bodies looking for their riders.

I was trussed real tight to the snag and the chill was coming on fast. If someone didn't cut me loose quick I thought I might lose my hands to frostbite. I strained away at the rawhide but I had no luck.

I saw a trooper way off, riding real careful. Of course, they would have heard the firing at the stockade. I hollered and yelled till he looked my way. He went back to where I couldn't see him.

Perhaps twenty minutes later an officer suddenly appeared in front of me, and he was looking at me mighty hard.

"Who are you," he said. His eyes was mistrustful. He looked at my worn clothes, which was a mixture of Injun and white.

"Luther Kelly," I said. "I was captured four days ago. They wanted me to see so I could describe it. I don't know why."

"We wondered what happened to you," he said. He took out a Barlow knife and cut the rawhide thongs. I chafed my wrists. My hands was just cold. I thought upon how low my stock must be in the scouting business, and I thought of other possible lines of work.

The officer was looking at his troopers who were riding in and out among the boulders.

"There ain't going to be anyone alive," I said.

"How big was the war party?" he asked, civil enough.

"Near on to three thousand."

"Jesus," said the officer. He turned to me. "Fetterman said to give him eighty men and he'd ride through the whole Sioux nation. Guess he didn't make it too far, now did he?"

I hear a nicker behind me. My horse had been tied to a scrub pine. All my gear was on him. I walked slowly back to him and rubbed his nose. We'd just been riding up the trail and been taken past where we were going. I looked back at the bowl where the battle had taken place. Soldiers lay here and there, loose-limbed, like a kid's doll after they'd gotten angry over something and stomped on it.

Hours later we come to the fort and the big gates swung open to us. We were bringing back thirty of the bodies. The others would have to wait until light tomorrow.

The officer was a captain named Tenedore Ten Eyck, a tall feller with a black beard and a slight limp from some wound he'd got long ago. He beckoned to me and we went to see Colonel Carrington.

Carrington was drawn and white. Fetterman had got himself killed, and Fetterman had fallen and torn Carrington's career down with him. (He was to spend the rest of his life defending himself about those ten minutes at Big Piney.)

Ten Eyck saluted and gave a brief report. The men he'd been sent to rescue was all dead, so there wasn't much to say.

Carrington was a civil gentleman for all his worry, and he motioned me to a chair and got one himself for Ten Eyck and then he asked calmly if I would mind telling him what happened.

Fetterman run after Crazy Horse and hauled everything and everyone along with him, I said, and it was over in five minutes. There was eighty soldiers and civilians, and three thousand warriors.

Carrington was slamming his fist into his palm and he was growing angrier by the minute.

"I ordered that bastard not to go beyond the ridge," he said, "and that was all of it right there. But I can't bring it up strongly even in my official report. It would look like I was blaming everything on a dead subordinate."

But the blame, I thought, is yours. Fetterman was an idiot, and you must have known that.

"And how did you come to be there, and the only living witness?" Carrington said, angrily.

So I described how I'd been captured, and the killing of the soldier.

"Sergeant Price, a courier," snapped Carrington. He got up and paced back and forth behind his desk.

I went on to describe the battle, though there wasn't much at all to say, with them odds.

"I thought that they would all be off hunting buffalo," said Carrington. "If you had been here perhaps my intelligence would have been better."

I doubted that but stayed silent, and I wasn't thinking on the numbers of Injuns.

"And how did you come to be spared?" Carrington snarled.

"Injuns is unpredictable," I said. I thought it a poor time to claim Spotted Tail for an uncle.

"And what will they do now?" he asked.

"Go home, sing songs, tell the story of the battle a hundred times, and winter out of the wind."

There was a knock on the door and Carrington said come in and his adjutant opened the door and stomped across the puncheon floor. He handed me a bag, a leather one worked with quills. There was a tag of thin leather on it and "Luther Kelly" printed in flowing, copperplate script.

"This was just thrown over the gate," said the adjutant. "It is snowing so hard no one saw whoever threw it." The wind suddenly rose and rattled the windowpanes, and snow struck them like shovelfuls of sand.

I undid the thongs and dumped out the contents of the bag between my feet. There were two blond scalps complete with ears, a worn volume of the writings of Plotinus, a catlinite pipe with a six-section red alder stem—slotted to line them up right—and a photograph of Spotted Tail in full war regalia wearing his I-just-ate-my-fill-of-live-baby-bluebirds smile. The photo had been taken by the F. Jay Haynes Studio of Mankato, Minnesota.

"Are those *yours?*" Carrington hissed, pointing at the scalps.

"Nope," I says, tossing them on his desk. "You can have them."

Ten Eyck got up and picked up the scalps and walked out with them. He wasn't gone long, and by the time he got back Carrington had gone from white to purple, which I took to mean better health.

"You know who this is?" said Ten Eyck, pointing at the photograph.

"Spotted Tail," I said, "Brulé Sioux. He was there." Oh, my beloved uncle, no doubt skinning someone alive at this very moment. I was going to say virtually nothing about him, by God, I liked my balls hanging right where they was.

"I still don't understand why you were spared." Carrington snorted.

Not anything left to say, so I went out of the office, leaving Carrington and Ten Eyck to mourn the late Captain Fetterman and by the by figure out a way to break the news gently to General Sherman, who was nobody's fool.

I have never seen a harder blizzard than the one that was roaring out of the Bighorn Mountains. There was a lot of snow falling and a hard wind behind it, and drifts was building ten feet deep in no time at all. On a hunch, I climbed the sentry ladder and walked round the guardwalk. On the north and west sides the snow was building by the minute. If the Injuns were to attack on snowshoes they could walk right up the drifts and have the further advantage of the soldiers firing into the wind while their eyes was stung by the windborne snow, and that wouldn't help their aim much.

Back down I went and across the parade ground to Carrington's quarters. I told his adjutant about the drifts and left. Little did I know this would panic Carrington utterly and cause much discomfort, especially those dependents who had lost a husband or father at Big Piney Creek.

Not ten minutes after I had told the adjutant of the danger Carrington ordered all of the women and children put in the post magazine and left a detail to blow it and them up if the Injuns should scale the walls. Now, them savages hadn't been killing women and children except for them "accidents of war," which was a term used to describe mistakes in which many lives were lost. *We,* the whitemen, had been slaughtering Injun women and children anytime we could find them, which was another reason the tribes was so fond of us.

Red Cloud, Spotted Tail, Crazy Horse, Rain-in-the-Face— they was all of this country and smelling a big storm they'd know that they wouldn't be pursued till late in the spring. So it was a good time to get out of the wind and screw and tell lies and make war again when the weather was better.

You couldn't see ten feet in the swirling snow—which meant the Injuns couldn't find us either, probably, but Carrington was running scared and he quadrupled the guard and swore any man he caught asleep or not looking out to the wind would be court-martialed summarily and shot.

Next he come to me demanding that I ride hell for leather for reinforcements. Now, no one but a dead fool would try to ride in this goddamned blizzard and the reinforcements couldn't ride neither and I was damned if I was going to perish of chilblains because Carrington had his head up his butt. Which is what I told him and he screamed about insolence and insubordination (my only real talents, the years would prove) and made threats. I coldly told him I wasn't a hero, and I warn't going to collect troops that warn't needed for an attack that would never come till late in the spring.

Finally I resigned my job of scout and told the jackass to go piss up a flagpole and climb the ice.

Carrington had now got to the whining stage and he leaked streams full of sorrow over the injustices of life. All he had to do to forego Big Piney Creek was throw Fetterman in the guard-house on charges of imbecility and forget to feed him. On he went dragging in a lot of horrible English poets like Tennyson and I'd had enough vileness for the week and I thought I'd go find some whiskey.

There was a few wagons parked off on the parade ground and one of them had a cheery yeller light in it and when I got close I could hear banjo music and when I got closer yet I could hear some drunk singing along with Klaas, or at least that might have been the idea that they had.

I scratched on the tenting canvas the wagon was covered with and in a bit Klaas's round head poked out, still with the glasses upside down on his nose.

"The whores iss all gonk," says Klaas.

"I don't want a whore, you stupid Dutch bastard," I says. "I need some whiskey."

"Skelly?"

"And not the goddamn Injun whiskey." Case my specifications here mystify you, all whiskey was dubious, but safer than the Injun whiskey, the recipe for which was one barrel of water, six gallons of alcohol, four plugs of tobacco for flavor, half a pound of cayenne for punch, and four ounces of strychnine for the blind staggers and howling horrors. Man had a skinful of Injun whiskey you could shoot him in the brain *and* heart and he wouldn't die till he sobered up.

Klaas had one-star, four-star, and eight-star whiskey, I combed out of the stream of Dutchy English flowing out from under his moustaches, and priced accordingly. Also canned and pickled delicacies such as buffalo tongues, oysters, turkey gizzards, and lobster thermidor. Hearing Klaas tryin' to pronounce thermidor was sort of like setting a paralytic on fire to see if he could dance. I got all pitying and told him to shut up, I'd just read the labels. Ortolans in vinaigrette. Lichi nuts.

Lord, how that man could fart. With them tight, green-and-white-checked pants I wondered why he didn't blow his boots off. He took my money and climbed back up in his wagon. I stood there, while he motioned me to come on in.

The wagon bed would have been crowded with just Klaas in it, and by the light of a hurricane lamp I could see someone slumped against the wagon box, in the back. Mulebreath Mucklebreech, by God, and to look upon him was to know why the South lost the War. Klaas gathered the wagon cover around him to keep the snow out. He looked like the dolt in the circus you try to concuss with the wooden balls.

"Injuns nearf," says Klaas. "I haff nice cabink but can't go."

I explained in slow English that there warn't an Injun within fifty miles of us and tomorrow they'd be farther away yet. So we hitched up his team and struggled out the gates—the drifts wasn't too bad yet—and went to Klaas's cabin. He had a big canvas tent for the stock.

We hauled Mulebreath in and stacked him gently in a corner.

I settled in there for four days, and in time Klaas's farts diminished their toxic effects. The goddamn banjo and the high tenor mule skinner was another matter. The music Klaas made with that goddamned banjo was a primitive Dutch backwoods sort called "blugerss," lamenting foreclosures and the deaths of especially worthy and virtuous hogs. Klaas's *farts* was a lot more musical.

Time to time I thought of just shooting that Dutchy gasbag and riding into the storm, but on reflection I thought the holes in him would release enough gas to blow us all and the fort clean off the map and to Ohio, so I let the matter drop.

Mulebreath spent his time drinkin' one-star whiskey and explainin' to me how us damn Yankees had actually *lost* and I got dragged through all the battles Mulebreath had enjoyed. I kept remarkin' that a diet of catfish, grits, and swamp greens shrank the human brain to the size most birds carry. This happy conversation carried on until the rasp of the snow against the wagon cover slowed and in the middle of the night I stepped out and looked up and smiled at the bright stars in the sky.

I give a map of where I'd be to Klaas and Mulebreath and they said they'd see my sorry Yankee face soon.

There was still a lot of wind in the morning, and I was most grateful for it as it would over time scour Klaas's vapors off my clothes.

Eats-Men-Whole was at the end of the road and I was free in all respects. Washakie would be glad to see me and I him—ain't often anyone gets a chance to know a giant.

It was cold and snowy but I owned the world now, all of it I could see.

I was a most happy young feller all the way home.

12

I came back to find Eats-Men-Whole in her grave and our child dead in her belly. I stood by her bier while the wind took her spirit. I felt like there was a hot spear in my chest and I wept tears and wished they were blood. I tried to will my heart to stop but it would not. My life was in that bundle on that platform. Something in me would be maimed forever. Rage swelled up in me, I tasted copper in my mouth, I wanted to strangle every god in heaven.

I tied the yellow silk kerchief to one of the poles. My father-in-law, Washakie, had refused to answer my many questions until I had come to wish her a safe journey to the Star Trail.

We went back toward the camp, walking slowly, our arms across each other's shoulders.

"It was the sick belly, the cholera," said Washakie. "A wagon party came through and the disease after them."

"Who were they?" I screamed, stepping away from him. They were all dead. I would find them.

"I don't think they brought the cholera as a gift," he said, "and the whites don't like to bury their children and women and fathers. There are many graves up the trail toward Salt Lake. If you want to kill, go kill Crows and Blackfeet. The Blackfeet killed my first wife and two little boys, killed them very badly. I was away, trapping for the Hudson's Bay Company. I have been killing Crows and Blackfeet for fifty years. It doesn't help, I still see them in their blood, my wife and boys, and many others that I loved. If I could kill all the Crows and Blackfeet maybe it would help. Killing hundreds hasn't helped."

"Why kill Crows if the Blackfeet killed your family?"

"Killing Crows is a duty, Shoshones been doing that for a long time. Killing Blackfeet is a pleasure, as well as a duty."

And God help us all, I thought. If there had been a church nearby I'd have prayed in it. I couldn't even get drunk. I was afraid of what I might do.

But, Washakie said, a warrior must have a heart as bright and cold as a star. In my rage and sorrow I would make mistakes.

Another train of Mormon converts come along and their guides had died of some lung congestion sweeping the plains, and they asked Washakie for help. So he come to where I was staring out a hundred miles and told me to take them on to Salt Lake. I wasn't too happy about having to guide folk who had already gone and declared themselves complete idiots by converting to Mormonism, and I rode out in a sour mood and damned if I wasn't wrong.

They was Norskys and Swedes and Finns and they was so hungry for land of their own that they would have tattooed their arses blue and worshiped with the Sea Dyaks of Borneo for a few hundred acres and a deed in their hands. Warn't it some French king, who was Protestant, who remarked that Paris was worth a mass? (My kind of man, that king.)

Anyway, the Scandihoovians and I laughed a lot. At night they would bring out musical instruments and dance. There warn't no danger from much of anything, so I hadn't much work to do. The worst was the poisonous things—springs, plants, and some of the small, pale brown spiders had a bite like nothing I'd seen or heard of.

If a fiddle-backed spider bit you the flesh around the bite went white, and then gangrenous black, and the poison worked on so in some folks there was nothing to do but amputate the hand. I had to caution the children and mothers about reaching under anything.

Winter was harsh but there wasn't much snow and wouldn't be until we come to the Wasatch Range, between here and Salt Lake City.

One day I was idly setting on my horse watching the train go by when I thought I heard a banjo back on the end of it. More infernal twangs come to me, and pretty soon here come Klaas on the seat of a big Conestoga had all sorts of advertisements for patent medicines and "aids to young mothers." The Mormons are first of all a well-run business and the more Saints there were out busting hump and making money and tithing the more missionaries can go out. It is a most interesting church having all the best attributes of a novel written by one of them ladies with three names and a pyramid stock swindle. I didn't know how the Saints would take to Klaas, because whatever his other faults Mormonism warn't one of them.

The weather was warm for January. I shot antelope and deer for camp meat and the trail was so well worn once a wagon got its wheels into the ruts it was a hell of a chore to get 'em out again and nobody could get lost. The pasturage right by the trail was played out, but there was good wild hay on the back slopes and cutters with a light Cape wagon would cut and pile hay enough at the next camp.

These Scandihoovians were pure quill. Their English was so bad—even worse than Klaas's—that we couldn't make a point one to another.

They'd pause of a Sabbath morning and their leader, a tall, curly-headed dark feller name of Hansen, would rattle through some sort of service and then "bear testimony" to his conversion, which had come about after a visit by missionaries and some sort of near-fatal accident with a tree. Hansen was concussed for days, and he'd swear, "Dat I peer intuuueee Da Great Behind and see tha trut of tha Vurds of tha Buek of Muermon," which made me very fond of him because he was twinkling all the time.

Paris is worth a mass.

We stopped for a couple of days to do repairs to the wagons that couldn't be put off no longer, and since the Scandinavian land measure ain't got nothing to do with an acre I paced off a half-section and put tall stakes at the corners, to show 'em what the size of their holdings would be. They looked on dropjawed, and then I told them there wasn't water, and they'd have to dig ditches unless they planned to raise horned toads for the novelty market.

There wasn't anything in Scandihoovia looked like the animals and plants of the desert. (I've always thought that the State Motto of Utah should have been "I bain don't tink this luek like Sveden.") There was even some who had brought nets so they could set up shop as fishermen. The only thing that could live in the Great Salt Lake was a little critter sort of like a sowbug. I'd never seen it, but Bridger knew it well, and any suspicions he had of Mormon stupidity was confirmed when they lighted there and stayed.

The wind howled steadily down out of the northwest, so if you stayed away from the left rear quarter of the wagon train Klaas's farts and banjo doings were blown on toward Texas, and I can't think of a more deserving place.

By the end of February we had come up to the last of the bad salt-sage country and all that remained was to get through the Wasatch and down to the Great Basin floor. The Saints had set up skids and sledges and was plowing the snow with twelve-ox teams. My job was over.

Hansen came to see me with a bag of gold and silver coins—probably about all they had among them—and I refused to be paid for the work, telling him truthfully that I'd never been here before and I enjoyed seeing new country.

"Never been here before?" he said, looking kind of sick.

"You got here, Mr. Hansen," I says. "Trust in the Lord."

With just my horse I was able to work my way down the steep canyon far ahead of Klaas's farts and plunks. I blessed the air.

Salt Lake City was booming even in the dead of winter. There warn't any snow on the ground at all. The Mormon part of town was orderly and clean and about as much fun as a rubber rose, while the Helltown built out past the north shore of the Great Salt Lake was like any other little Western town of the time—raw wood and rough folks.

There was forty or so saloons each one cruder than the last, bedraggled whores working out of canvas cribs, restaurants that served rotten food where the only healthy things in the pies was the maggots and weevils, who'd died in the oven. (Years later, when I'd get roped into listening to speeches about our valiant pioneer forebears, I'd think of all the riffraff and scum what done the original work. Riffraff like me, scummily hiding out here from the consequences of misunderstandings with folks back East. We seemed to be greedy of gold, but if any of us made money we fair threw it away.)

Course, Helltown being Helltown and folks being folks the population after dark was about half male Mormons looking for a drink and a seegar and some dance-hall fun. The steady diet of sermons and hard labor didn't provide them with that feeling of satisfaction so necessary to all men: I done something bad and I'm proud of it.

Some dour fellers in them shapeless Mormon black felt hats was follering me and I didn't know why they would, so I pushed on past Helltown and went out a few miles onto the salt flats to get away from the stink and the bugs. I hadn't but about rolled out my bedroll when they come riding up in a group and the leader got down and shined a lantern in my face, blinding me.

"Brother Brigham wishes to speak with you," says this sour bastard.

When I asked what in the hell about, I got told Brigham kept his own counsel. Fine, says I, let him keep it and I hope each of his sixty-seven wives has a litter of six.

"I got nothing to say to the man," I finished. Various pieces of artillery appeared, and I suddenly recalled one or three items of interest to both of us. Maybe even four. Matter of fact, if Brother Brigham wanted to read me the entire Book of Mormon and do running commentary on it I couldn't think of a way I'd like to spend time more.

My levity was wasted on these fellers. They packed up my traps and we rode off toward Salt Lake City. I couldn't for the life of me figure out what in the hell this tinhorn prophet wanted from Mrs. Kelly's darling son.

We clattered through Temple Square, where a large crowd had gathered to watch the streetlamps flicker, the fastest entertainment in town, and soon we come up to Lion House, Brigham's home. The Prophet's tastes in architecture was as atrocious as his taste in Scripture.

I waited an uncommon long time for him to appear. I supposed he was busy with whatever wife was on the calendar for that night, and, annoyed, I lit up a seegar. Two of the gents who had fetched me there wandered over and inhaled deep at the tendrils of smoke. Me being a generous soul I finally asked if they'd like a couple and that flustered them up a lot. They set off a ways and glared greedily at me.

Brigham come in finally, wearing a silk bed-jacket, and he was frowning at what I took to be a checklist of room numbers.

Two big kerosene lamps threw a warm yellow glow on the old pirate's face as he sat at his massive, carved desk. Brigham's face was like the old rock of the deep canyons. His close-set eyes was shadowed. When he spoke his voice startled me, it was high and reedy, like Lincoln's.

He motioned all the guards out, sending them through a passageway and locking the door behind them. There was two more sets of such doors, with alcoves, and he checked those and then poked all of the drapes and tugged at the windows and then he dropped to the floor and checked under the sofas.

"I'd be happy to leave you want to make sure that there's no witnesses," I says. "You have only to say the word and unlock one of them sets of windows or doors."

"I see the marks of that bastard Bridger on you," says Old Brigham, "and I can't tell you how much it pains me to have to ask a favor of someone even as little connected to him as you are."

"I'd hate to think of you suffering embarrassment," I says,

pulling on my gloves, "and I can't watch, it gives me hives, so I'll leave."

Brigham came round his desk and grabbed my kerchief. His blue eyes glittered at me for a moment. He had presence, for sure, and a fierce will.

"You insolent pup, if you wish to be buried out on Antelope Island and pickled in brine at that, try my patience a little more. Now give me a goddamned seegar and set down, I have need of . . . . . I have a difficulty."

He lit up the seegar and puffed happily and put his feet up on his desk. I moved my chair over and put my feet up there, too, and we smoked companionably for a few minutes.

Brigham was obviously enjoying his seegar hugely. He had the expression of a man finally found what was itching him and scratched it good. He sighed and farted and beamed happily up at the ceiling.

"You don't believe any of this, do you?" I says.

"You mean this ridiculous faith I am the prophet of? Of course not. The banning of alcohol, tobacco, tea, and coffee merely saves my sheep one-third of their income and a lot of difficulty."

I laughed quietlike, for Brigham was a very canny, very dangerous man.

Brigham looked at me shrewdly. "I'm sure that the theological maunderings I find necessary to a Mormon state are of little interest to you. They have a use. If a prophet speaks, he don't get backchat. It's lies and stupidities, and very necessary. If you would be so stupid as to quote me, my devout followers would no doubt cut your throat, all the way back to your spine, as the Word tells them to do."

"Interesting," I says. "Which angelic being told you that particular piece?"

"A bird in my ear. I sent a few of my finest and most intelligent men off to silence a misguided soul. They shot him six times but he lived. So I had a revelation—my fools may not be able to follow simple instructions, but they are hell on Scripture."

He pulled a long inhale on his seegar, blew out the smoke, rubbed his eyes, and began to tap on the desktop with a thick forefinger.

"My daughter Palmyra is kidnapped by the Injuns and I want her freed," says Brigham, "which is what I say to my followers. Actually I married her off to Elder McMullin, who turned out a bastard and she run off and she's over somewhere in the Colorado Territory with a renegade band of Utes. It's embarrassing."

I didn't do anything but look at him, bored. He'd told me lies and about a fiftieth of what I'd know before long anyway.

"I'm wasting our time," he says. "She's got a batch of Joseph Smith's letters, stolen from me. She did not want to marry Elder McMullin."

"And them letters is what you want?" I asked. I wasn't going to kill a woman for this lizard.

"Ten thousand in gold and the Prophet's blessing, no small thing, Mr. Kelly. Even better, I'll baptize you myself, should you be successful."

"Them gents dragged me here," I says. "Why don't you send them?"

"Unfortunately," Brigham said dryly, "this Church I built up don't attract folks with brains. They never do. It's one of the tragedies of the business I'm in. Bridger and Washakie recommend you highly."

"Well, why don't Bridger and Washakie do it?"

"They've been asked. They volunteered you."

I run on unflatteringly about my two teachers, and hoped that grasshoppers would gnaw their parts forever.

"Washakie said you were just young, stupid, and ignorant enough to look harmless," said Brigham, picking up a Colt from his desk. "You may either accept my offer or die on the spot."

"Half in advance," I says.

"Done," says Brigham.

"And what about Palmyra?"

"Palmyra, the ungrateful little bitch, may rot where she is. I am fond of her, and the simple fact that she would do such a

treacherous thing tells me she is the child of my bowels. I am not
overly worried about her. I am worried about the letters."

"What makes you think I won't just take the gold and run?"

"Curiosity," says Brigham. "Any sane man would have run
from either of those two scoundrels who have more or less made
you what you are today. They did have a candidate fully ripe for
corruption, tis true."

"I'll do it," I says.

"I knew I didn't have to load this thing," said Brigham. "I
hate Colts. I got my goddamned thumb caught in the hammer
once, I was hopping around like a mad fool and my followers all
fell on their knees. They were sure I was wrestling with the
Lord."

I left then, taking my horses south. I'd asked for directions,
and gotten a jerk of the prophetic thumb.

13

ul, as Bridger would say, I thought the firstest thing I ought to do was find Elder McMullin. That turned out to be easy. I come up on some freight wagons, the long two-ton-load ones called "Democrats," and asked the driver of the lead one where the good Elder McMullin might be.

The driver, a Mormon with one of them tall black hats on, spat a stream of forbidden tobacco juice on the rump of his off ox and snarled, "Straight south mebbe three hundred miles, ter Elder McMullin's little kingdom." I thanked the feller and made tracks.

I was traveling light, except for my guns, gold, and pride, and needed some things built for the country. I come on a Mexican freight outfit was taking stores south, too. They had one wagon full of high boots like you see in pictures of the conquistadores. I bought a pair to fight off the thorns with. That was some country. Farther down I went the drier it got and the meaner the vegetables, and the insects all chawed on you with one end and stung you with the other. About the fourth day out I come across my first Gila monster.

This fat black and pink critter was waddling across the trail, and it was so silly-looking that I pulled my horse up and got off and walked up closer, it was a most amazing sight. It come closer, staring at me. It decided it didn't like me one bit. So it waddled over toward me and I whipped out my Colt and fired twice, missing clean, and the lizard opened his mouth and bit on my ankle. The conquistador boots was real thick there, no doubt for just this purpose, so it got its fangs stuck, and this just made it madder, so it flopped and clawed and chewed while I tried to shake it loose. (I was to see this same sort of witless determination years later in Tennessee Claflin.) I finally got my knife blade under the roof of its mouth and pried it off. It sat there panting in the dust and then it shrugged and walked away.

When I swung up again I heard a faint breeze overhead when there wasn't no wind, so I swung right down again and about the time my boots hit the dirt the rolling boom of a buffalo rifle rocked back and forth in the canyon. I used the horse for cover and made it to a dry wash. A slug hit a rock ahead of me and shattered it, sending bits of stone everywhere, and one stung my cheek.

Now, I felt for certain that whoever was shooting at me was someone who I hadn't been properly introduced to. It always makes me mad as hell to have someone try to kill me when they won't even give me a chance to talk them out of it. I was dressed poor and how could they know about the gold. So I thought I will kill these bastards and never think on it again.

The buffalo rifle went off a couple more times, the damned fools, because they'd no idea where I was and the plume of smoke from their Winchester told me exactly where they was. I started up a dry wash and then went from boulder to boulder, and finally pulled myself up a steep wash by grabbing the bushes. Then I was on a flat layer of stone, and above them.

I made my way quiet till I was just above and behind them, and looked at them for a moment. They had on them high Mormon hats, which they'd take off and belly forward a ways to look down and see if they could spot me.

So I waited till they was back and one of them was looking down the rifle and the other sort of staring at the canyon, like he did not know what else to do.

There was a little series of steps, almost in the rock, and I come down them quietlike until I was maybe twenty feet behind them. I shot the one sighting the rifle in the back of the head. The slug picked him up and carried him over the lip of the cliff and shortly we heard the thump and clatter as he and the rifle landed on the rocks.

"Git them hands up!" I yelled, my Sharps on a line to his belly. "What in the hell are you doin' shootin' at me?"

He was holdin' his arms so high his shirt had come out of his pants. He was shaking and he'd fouled himself. I marched him down and yelled at him to take me to his horses, they was tied in a grove of cedars. They hadn't off-saddled, which sure burned me. Someone had told them I was coming, and they hadn't been up there long.

I got the shaking, smelly apprentice bushwhacker up on his horse, setting backwards in the saddle, and I tied his hands behind him and then cinched them up good to the saddle horn. If this varmint wouldn't tell me anything, I'd go find someone who would.

Figuring to get an explanation soon I led my prisoner down the trail, and we'd gone maybe four or five miles before I come on a roadhouse. It was just a place for the freighters to get likkered up and eat a plate of beans.

The proprietor was a dirty gent with one eye and one arm who greeted me cheerily enough. I paid for a whiskey and sniffed it and it seemed to be good old raw alcohol, the kind comes of fermenting the mash in open barrels so there was a little added tang from all the critters that had fallen in and drowned. It warmed me up considerable on the way down, blew off three toenails, and left me short of breath.

When I was finally able to croak out a few noises, I got the barkeep to come outside and squint at the gent I had ass backwards on his horse. I explained that he and his partner, unfortunately deceased, had been shooting at me with a .45–90 and did he know this stupid bastard?

"Hit's one of McMullin's sons," he says. "Bunch of scorpions."

"How many sons does McMullin have?" I says.

"A hunnert and fourteen full growed, more on the way," says the barkeep.

That worthy flew to his shanty, scooped up his gunbelt, a shotgun, and what money he had and he saddled his mule so fast I thought he'd like to cut his hand on the buckles. He swung up and grabbed for the reins.

" 'Fer you," he hollered, "I'd light out and I wouldn't stop till I got someplace ain't no Mormons."

I couldn't remember when I had been so happy. If I took for the tall grass and just left I'd have Brigham after me, and he had a damn long arm I was sure. He'd have me killed, shaking his head of sorrow at the young folk these days. And on the other hand, I had just trimmed down Elder McMullin's own personal army and he was likely to be none too pleased with me.

"Paw's gonna skin yer Jew Gentile ass," says the captive. Well, God knows I am a patient man, but times was rough. I untied the fool's feet from the stirrup leathers and cut the thong that bound his wrists to the saddle horn, and knocked him gently off with the butt of my rifle. I pulled his face out of the mud in front of the horse trough, jerked him to his feet, and shoved him into the green water and held him under till his squirming went from all frantic to feeble. Then I pulled him out and let him retch and breathe.

"I'd better start hearing things make sense," I says, "or you want another bath here?"

"We's just told to shoot any single riders on pinto horses!" he babbled, still about half full of water.

Well, this here apprentice bushwhacker spent many an unpleasant moment down there under the mosquito larva, till finally he was sobbing so bad and the same story three times running at that, that I cut his hands free. He had deep, bleeding slashes where the leather thongs had cut him.

I kicked him hard enough to crack ribs, just to get his attention, and then I snarled, "You tell your old man I'll be along presently, on business from the Prophet. Brigham ain't going to be too happy you tried to kill me." Actually, I thought

Brigham either wouldn't care or he would be positively delighted.

I needed to figger some badly so I headed up into the mountains. The ranges here is like islands in a hot rock sea—the tops of the mountains was green with firs and pines and about a third of the way down from the top the desert took over. It rained damn seldom in this country, but up high the peaks caught the snow and milked the thunderclouds of water.

There is foolish mistakes that I have made which even today cause me to blush and cuss. I've done many stupid and fool things for which my friends has bought me large drinks and then sat and said, "How was that *exactly?*" Up there above all my follies, in a class by its own self, uncomplicated by bad luck or poor weather or slippery stuff underfoot, was my going up into some pissant south Utah mountain range—an *island* range—having just shot one son of a man who had one hundred and fourteen of the bastards and God alone knows how many sons-in-law.

Night come and I et and slept the sleep of the just, having killed one man and tortured another, mostly working off my fury at the death of Eats-Men-Whole.

I'd thought of sending Elder McMullin a letter, asking just why he wanted me dead, but Mormons are notoriously thin on reading and writing, dangerous habits that Brigham felt might lead to apostasy and correcting his spelling errors.

The wisest course seemed for me to mope on over to Colorado and see if I could scare up Palmyra without further truck with Elder McMullin and his vicious brood. Replacement sons was no doubt popping every day, and in a week or two the good Elder's wrath would have cooled.

I had my coffee and a seegar and packed up and found a trail down the mountain headed east, and I come out of a little fringe of timber and suddenlike noticed there was an uncommon large number of them black Mormon hats sticking up from behind rocks all over the damn place.

I loped quick back up into the timber and commenced a quiet sneak to the north, spotting only a couple of dozen on that trail—I was beginning to seriously dislike them hats—and the south and west trails was liberally coated with 'em, too.

Well, not having a single thing better to do I rode around about three times and noticed that the hats kept moving up in my absence. Clearly I would have to make a death-or-glory charge, or nobly stick my Colt in my ear and cash out, or do the cowardly and unforgivable thing.

"I SURRENDER." I hollered from the shadow of a large boulder.

Much silence.

"I SAID I SURRENDER, GODDAMN IT!" I yelled.

Remembering that these was Mormons and "surrender" is a mortal long word I tried another tack.

"I QUIT I GIVE UP DON'T SHOOT I QUIT!"

One of the hats raised up enough so I could see the face, looking over the sights of a rifle.

"Go 'tother side of the mounting and give up to Pappy," it said, aiming the rifle at my guts. The hat sank back down.

So I wandered over to the other side of the mountain and I hollered and yelled and whistled for a while.

"Put down yer guns and walk out with yer hands up," screeched a squealy voice, sort of like a hog on a hook.

I set down my guns and walked slowly out, hands high. There was about forty various firearms all pointed at my vitals, and all wobbling with the excitement of it all.

"DON'T NOBODY SHOOT! I WANT THAT GENTILE JEW SON OF A BITCH ALIVE. DON'T NONE A YEW WITLESS WUTHLESS WHELPS DARE SHOOT!"

Must be dear Pappy addressing his sundry offspring, I thought.

I walked on down the hill. The skinny little bog-Irish bastard clumb out from behind a rock.

"You Elder McMullin?" I says.

"Yerp," says he. He was about five foot tall, had on a set of one-gallus overhauls and farmer boots, and a thick silver watchchain hanging out of one of the pockets.

"Brother Brigham sent me to fetch back Palmyra," I says, in

hopes that the name of the Prophet would do me some good.

"Ya brung that poison?" he says, leering at me.

I couldn't remember when I'd been this happy. The prisoner of a Mormon whose roof wasn't shingled.

"What poison?" I asked.

"FER MUH TEA," he squealed, drooling some.

"Nope," I says. "Ain't got no poison."

"We'll go to muh house and talk."

I was given back my horse and allowed the place of honor in this shoal of McMullins and whatever had married into the tribe. They come in all shapes and sizes and colors of hair, I supposed from the different mothers. I wondered how many wives this weasely little shit had.

Elder McMullin's house covered about four acres, a warren of lean-tos and log cabins flung together any old way. There was a big passel of women carrying babies and what seemed to be hundreds of small children playing in the dusty yard. What it mostly looked like was the hovels of the shanty Irish on the outs of New York towns, all jammed together as the cedar houses built for purple martins.

I follered him in a door made of old seed sacks, through a long hallway lit by holes in the roof, and into a small room had a log-and-rope bedstead and a pile of dirty clothes on the floor. The place stank thick with old sweat and sanctimony. An old packing box served as a bed-table. It had a candle holder and a leatherbound book on it. The book must be the Book of Mormon, I thought.

Elder McMullin picked the book up and sat down on the bed and squinted at the book. He held it tenderly.

"Read the Word of the Lord," he says, handing me the thick and heavy volume. The cover was unmarked and the gold on the spine was all rubbed off. I opened it. It was a morocco-bound volume of plays by some Frog name of Corneille. I couldn't read Frog very good, try as I might, so there I sat thinking as fast as I could on a way out. Elder McMullin was illiterate and insane, but he didn't have all these folks bowing down to him because of the charm of his countenance.

"Read the Word of the Lord!" he screamed. He was drooling a little and his eyes was on fire.

I paused to make a note in that black part of my brain where the list of folks I am going to kill someday is, moving Brigham's all the way to the top and underlining it in red. This done, I commenced.

"The angel La Gomba come unto the place of the festering altar and he said unto Nephritis what, pray tell, are you doing to that poor goat? It pleaseth the Lord not to get seconds. He delighteth in the sacrifice of oily Herberts . . ."

Elder McMullin sighed with pleasure and listened, eyes abrim with tears, to the Gospel According to Luther.

14

A whole lot of perfectly good Mormon theology made right up on the spot by a desperate character went by the way on account of there not being a competent secretary within a thousand miles.

After soothing Elder McMullin's ears with the very best I could come up with in the way of utter nonsense, I still think my tale of how the Prophet Lumpestre done built the irrigation canals once already and how the Prophet Lumpestre said they would be buried by time and feathers, and that in the latter days the seed of a "deranged, drooling, misunderstood dwarf" would uncover them in the time of the new Coming of Zion.

As night began to fall Elder McMullin began to snort and paw some and he took off into this tenement he owned in search of a wife that warn't pregnant at the moment.

Apparently he had failed to give simple instructions to his sons as to what to do with Kelly, because when I staggered my way out the front door my horse was standing there, saddled, rifle in the scabbard, and my gunbelt looped over the saddle horn. The packhorse was there, too. They both had nosebags on, and the headstalls was over the hitching rail. So I walked over bold as brass and put their bridles on 'em and swung up and rode off. Incredible as it may seem no one raised so much as an eyebrow. They'd caught me and forgot me.

132

Elder McMullin had got it into his head that a man on a pinto horse was coming to poison his tea. I'd killed one son and busted up another and he'd dragged me back to his hovel and then just forgot I existed. More I thought about it, the more sense it made. Still, I rode like hell all night long, to the east, and I smelled the piney scent of mountains on the night wind.

At this rate, I figured, I'd be a rain god on some South Seas island before I was old enough to vote. I wasn't old enough to grasp that my cocky feelings always arrived just before a disaster. (In my age, if I wake up feeling good I get the cold sweats.)

I knew nothing about the Injuns in the mountains ahead of me, other than their high chief was named Ouray. Ouray the Arrow, they called him.

Daybreak I made a dry camp and stared hard about for sign, but there hadn't been anybody by for days. If it was discovered that I'd flown the coop, I thought that I'd still have an eight- or ten-hour head start on them, and so I'd be a fool not to rest. The horses was in good shape, and I gave them some grain and took them to water at a little spring, hobbled them, and turned them loose to gnaw on the cactus.

I curled up in my henskin and went to sleep—the day was coming on hot, even in winter. I wasn't more than half a mile from the trail, and I had taken a branch of sagebrush and wiped my tracks away. Trouble with this country is that you can hide in it easy enough, but tracking's easy, too, since there are so few water holes or ways through the slickrock. (Later, when I was a manhunter, it served me well, this country.)

So it seemed that all I had to do now was find this here Palmyra, toast her toes a bit till she give me the letters, and lope back to the Prophet and collect my gold. I still thought life could be that simple. Well, when one of the players is Brigham Young, nothing is simple.

There was about a half million square miles of country before me, and I didn't know it or its ways. I still swelled up with tears from time to time, crying for Eats-Men-Whole and me, too, and I was a pretty simpleminded youth to begin with.

Such a fine sun lights that slickrock and mountain country.

I swore I could see the tongues of birds at a half mile, waving crimson as they sang. The distances were huge and beautiful and, in a way, mine. I felt so lordly I commenced into whistling. If I'd have had a tuba, I'd have played it.

An Ute kid all of ten years old saw me coming, and being a nasty little bastard he tied a stone to a length of rawhide and the whole arrangement to the branch of a tree and he whacked me right off my horse with a neat head shot, merely letting go of the stone, from his perch. It swung on a long arc of the sort that is favored by pendulums and caught me square in the right temple. At least that is what I got told later. I wouldn't know. The kid run off to fetch his mother and got a hiding from her because the Utes was friendly to whites who was not wearing Mormon hats. Utes is as easily bored as anybody else.

I come to feeling cool water on my head and I had a pain throbbing in my right temple like a steam engine with the safety wired down. Little colored spots danced in front of my eyes.

When you come out of unconsciousness after a whack on the head like that you never remember anything that happened. It's wiped out and gone forever.

The brat and his momma had been out gathering herbs and seeds for medicines. She knelt by my side and bathed my head, frowning with concern.

I rolled over on to my side and threw up.

"Morr-monn?" she said, quizzically.

"Hell no," I snarled.

"Many come," she said, pointing back down toward the west and the house of McMullin.

I stood up right quick and caught my horses. She motioned for me to follow her, and we went around behind a big wind-scoured rock and took shelter in the shade of the lee.

She brushed away the foot- and hoofprints, and walked out to the trail and began to gather leaves from a bush.

Pretty soon the passel of McMullins came and they spoke with her, asking if she'd seen me. I couldn't see, but I could hear fine, and the squaw was a right good liar. She said I had been through six hours before and she had seen pine boughs tied to the tails of my horses to broom the tracks off the trail.

"JUST LIKE A TRECHRUSS JEW GENTILE BAS-TARD!" says Elder McMullin. "I'M GONNA SKIN HIS JEW GENTILE ASS!" To this end, so to speak, the good Elder put spurs to his horse and led his witless brood on.

The squaw come to me and she was laughing and pointing a twirling finger to her temple, Plains sign for crazy. She knelt in the dust and scratched away at the ground with a twig and drew a checkerboard. I didn't see it at first, until she took pebbles and put them on the squares and when she jumped a pebble she took it away. I finally got it.

My head was still ringing and I felt like two halves of me but I did manage to blurt out "Checkers?," which made her nod happily and go to gathering pebbles.

Hard as it is to believe, with about one gross of bloodthirsty Mormon nitwits after the hide of Kelly I spent a most pleasant afternoon playing checkers with an Ute squaw in the middle of a stony desert, and she beat me every game.

She was just waiting to take me on to Ouray the Arrow, as soon as the sun was down. In this country you travel at night. For one thing it gets damned chilly as soon as the sun goes down and moving keeps you warm, for another the night covers the dust you raise. The daylight draws water off men and stock—and you don't feel it go. It is so dry the moisture goes right into the air and you can easy go on feeling fine until black spots dance in front of your eyes and suddenly you are too weak from lack of water but fall over and lie there and wait for the buzzards, who hover over everything like deacons.

The squaw and her brat led me through rocks carved by the wind into the shape of buildings taller than any built by man, and just at dawn we come to a hidden pocket valley. There was a scent of red cedar burning on the air, the sweetest of all perfumes.

It was a safe and easily defended camp. The trail in wound through a narrow channel cut in the living rock and the walls went up three hundred feet, straight up at that. High above a slim band of black shot with stars was all you could see of the heavens, it looked like a stream of silk shot with jewels. One man could hold off hundreds in the trail in, it was a bit more than one horse wide and no more.

Twenty or so laughing brown children shoaled around us and two boys of perhaps seven grabbed on to my spurs and hopped along with the horse, trilling like waterbirds. (Many years later I was to hear that eerie trilling, up in the Arctic, among the Inuit.)

I got down and my horses was taken off by two young men and the squaw led me over to a fire had a pot of dog stew bubbling on it and she nodded at a moon-faced gent in quills and buckskin and eagle feathers who was lounging lordly like against a willow backrest. He had a chessboard set up to his right and a checkerboard set up to his left. He got to his feet and waved to another squaw, who brought me a backrest and a gourd of fruit juice—the cactus apples was in season. It was tart and good and sure cut the dust in my throat. Then I was given a plate of dog stew, which I wolfed down, and when I had belched politely and nodded thanks for another big gourd of cactus-apple juice the gent—and Ouray was above all a gentleman—extended a hand missing two fingers and took mine in it.

"I am Ouray the Arrow," he said. "Do you play checkers?"

"Luther Kelly," I says, "and chess, too."

To home I'd been taking nickels off my uncles at those games for years. Then I remembered that the squaw had taken me every game.

So whilst Elder McMullin and his loathsome offspring beat the creosote bushes for the ass of Kelly, I sat in this oasis drinking cactus-apple juice and playing checkers with Ouray the Arrow. Ouray had three passions in life. Chess and checkers, traveling salesman jokes, and limericks. Now, time to time I have put up with much in life, but worse than any battle ever I was in was that Injun droning on about the farmer's daughters, small barnyard animals, and the drummer's luck.

We was about halfway through a hard-fought game of

checkers in the twilight of the canyon—there wasn't but about ten minutes a day of direct sunlight in it, and a man could dream in that shadowed light. The Ute tales of Creation are as beautiful as the cedar smoke curling up in the pale light.

There was a soft rustle of deerskins and someone had come up beside me. I turned to see a tall, slender woman standing, with the glow of the rim of the canyon behind her. She sank down gracefully to her knees and put out her hand and touched my shoulder.

"I understand that my father has sent you to look for me," she said, her voice was a smoky, creamy one, with something of a faint lisp to it.

I looked at her close and almost gave off a gasp. She was beautiful in a cool Northern way, and her blue eyes were clouded over with white. She was blind of cataracts and likely had been at birth. She'd lived all of her life in darkness. No wonder that bastard of a father married her off to Elder McMullin, that wizened little shit. I was consumed with sudden rage, just at the mere thought of this beautiful woman stuck in that tumbledown sty with that goatish madman. All thought of Brigham's money flew clean out of my head. What I wanted now was his balls, and a few days to skin him slowly.

"Please finish your game," said Palmyra. "I hope you are beating Ouray. He needs to lose." She laughed, and so did Ouray.

"I lost in 1854!" said Ouray, mock horrified, "and a mountain fell down. Do not wish trouble on us, daughter."

Whether Palmyra had distracted him or he thought he'd set me up for more traveling salesman jokes, Ouray had moved a checker to the one spot on the board he never should have. I jumped all of his but one and raked off the pieces.

"Weasel shit," said Ouray.

"You want to give up now?" I says.

"I want to give up two moves ago," says Ouray.

"I'll never breathe a word of it," I said. "I'll promise."

"I promise to tell everyone," said Palmyra, "starting with your wives."

"My wives already know what a fool I am," said Ouray, "don't bore them with more examples." He grumbled and scratched and lit a pipe and sat back against his backrest.

He saw a woman walking a bit away and he called to her and they rattled back and forth pretty brisk for a moment. She went into one of the brush wickiups and come out again with a long quilled buckskin case. She brought it over to Ouray.

He undid the ties and slid a long rifle out, a single-shot Sharps Creedmore. They was worth thousands of dollars. This was a beauty, with a hollow ebony and ivory stock and long ebony and ivory propsticks. Feller knew his business could kill at fifteen hundred yards with this.

Ouray handed the gun to me and I looked it over. It was heavy and the barrel so long it seemed more like an old Kentucky rifle than what it was.

"There's two hundred rounds of ammunition for it in my lodge," said Ouray. "The gun is yours, Kelly. No one beats me at checkers."

I was astonished. I sort of spluttered and said how I couldn't possibly accept such a gift.

"You will need it," said Ouray.

Well, he was right, I would.

15

Ouray the Arrow was nothing if not a gent—rare critters and you are as likely to find them among the Dyak headhunters or Tauregs as anywhere. Ouray up and moved off and left us alone, so as not to hear things he might not want to know. It works both ways.

There was a big tin coffeepot asmoke on the coals and I poured Palmyra some and asked her automaticlike if she cared for milk or sugar.

"There is neither milk nor sugar here, Mr. Kelly," said Palmyra, "but thank you for reminding me of them. I am told that Elder McMullin and many of his odious sons are looking for you, with murder in mind. They have done much murder, Mr. Kelly, directed, of course, by God, who speaks daily to that horrible little man. But the McMullins of this world are dangerous only in numbers."

She went on to tell me that she had made her escape on her wedding night in Salt Lake City, so she had never seen Elder McMullin or the rabbit warren that his family dwelled in. Well, that made me feel like just killing Brigham right off rather than slowly skinning the bastard and feeding him his balls as I scraped slowly along.

Palmyra had a lover, Mountain Jim Cannon, who had cat-footed into the Lion House, put three guards asleep forever, and carried her off and handed her over to Ouray, who took her to the slickrock. Mountain Jim left a good trail for Brigham's killers—the Sons of Dan—and he led them on a merry chase, now and then picking one off to stir them up.

Brigham was in a flaming rage because his Sons of Dan came back without Palmyra, the letters, or Mountain Jim's head. Only one in three did return—Jim killed nine of them—and they wasn't too enthusiastic about a rematch.

"Where's Jim now?" I says, curious.

I'd seen a flash off a piece of glass up high some time in the late afternoon.

"He fled to West Texas for a while," said Palmyra.

"What about these letters Brigham is so eager to get," I asked, wondering how long it would be before Mountain Jim come down to join us. What was up there was him with a buffalo rifle and a telescopic sight aiming at my heart. It's true, I could have been a spy of Brigham's, and in their shoes, I'd have been up there, too, with just that equipment.

"Ah, the letters," said Palmyra. "The letters of Joseph Smith wherein he reveals himself to be nothing more than a half-mad sharpster sure of his right to women by the score and the Throne of God when he ascended into heaven. At one point he speculates that his holy emanations will force God to bring Joseph the throne right down here on earth. He was shot down like a rabid cur by some tasteful soul and tossed in the lime pit with the glandered horses and the cats crushed by wagon wheels."

If you are going to start up a religion make sure that you have it as preposterous as possible, that way you get the folks too dumb to live, and no backchat.

"The letters are hidden at the Lion House," said Palmyra, "and you, Mr. Kelly, are going to get them for me."

"Now just a goddamned minute here," I said, starting to rise, "If you think I'm going . . ." I sort of trailed off right there because this knife had appeared out of nowhere and was ever so delicately pressing the skin right above my jugular.

"Perhaps we should talk about it," I said. "I'm open to any and all reasonable suggestions." The knife pressed just a bit more. "Or even unreasonable ones," I said, lamely.

"Brigham would welcome you if you brought him the head of Elder McMullin," said a deep voice I'd bet gold on was Mountain Jim's. "I don't know what he likes so about heads, but he seems to flat dote on 'em."

So I told them about Brigham's explanation for the throat-cutting, how good help was hard to find, and what he had for hard boys could remember Scripture all right but couldn't think if they was on fire.

Jim pulled the knife away before he started to laugh.

"Well, that blood atonement makes sense for the first time," he chuckled, "as much as any of that trash makes sense."

"I'd just as soon keep Elder McMullin's head for my own self, my father-in-law has a Blackfoot head he pisses on at state occasions." I stopped, I'd thought of my wife and hadn't meant to.

And Washakie had done such a good job on me I thought no more of murder than if I'd have been a goddamn Mormon.

Mountain Jim folded himself down next to Palmyra and took her hand. She put her head on his shoulder. Jim was a big rangy redhead with a lopsided grin under his cookie-duster moustaches and them kind of pale blue killer's eyes that is always froze solid no matter what the heat in the air might be. He'd do to ride with for bad work, I could see right off.

"You understand, Mr. Kelly," said Jim, "that Palmyra and I will have no peace until we hold Brigham hostage to the truths he cannot afford to be known."

I was young and more than half crazy, and with Eats-Men-Whole dead I made about the best sort of warrior. One who don't give a perforated damn whether he dies or not but is cold mad and wants a lot of blood.

I was also more than a little vexed with Elder McMullin on my own account. I was damn well going to kill him on my own tick, nobody had to ask me to do that.

"I'm your man," I says. "I'll go collect McMullin's crazed noggin."

"I'll go with you," says Jim. I could see Palmyra give a little start.

"No," I says, "I'll kill him and his sons won't amount to a hill of ants."

"I believe that you will," says Jim.

He was right then and would be from time to time—I ain't a hero, mind you, my hat size is above five, but there is some things I'll risk my neck on that don't include things like flags and that damned Grace Company I was to get tangled up with later. Well, all those stories in their time.

That nice Creedmore Ouray had given me figured large in my calculations. After a little practice so I knew where it threw I'd be able to shoot and them firing back would be out of range. I'd hear of folks hitting a man's head at two thousand yards. And a little fiddlework on the slug's noses and they'd be explosive.

But I wouldn't use a head shot on Elder McMullin, on account of it being my ticket in to see Brigham, and I was young and cocky enough that I thought I might get close enough for a clear shot at the Prophet his own self. I had death as my vocation then and now I am ashamed a little, but the dead are dead and I ain't so that's all the story, I guess.

I idly asked Mountain Jim what the hell he was doing out here. I was struck by their fine faces in the soft canyon light. Good people. Jim was a Britisher and as a young feller he left home and school—he was the second son of a peer, wouldn't say who—and he come to America to seek his fortune. Kind of like me, he was westering at a young age. He saw the Rockies, and he looked in the high valleys for gold. Didn't find much, but he was curious, and soon he knew the west slopes of the Colorado Rockies pretty good. In truth, like no other man but a few Utes. He'd found the silver where Silverton is now, got cheated out of his claim, shot the cheat, and like so many of us skedaddled from the swift grip of the law. We all tended to be short on temper and scruples and long on imagination and curiosity.

It was coming on dark and Ouray came back with a young man of fifteen or so, called Owl-Walks-West, and Ouray said he would guide me to the camp of the McMullinses and leave me there to whittle down the tribe as much as I liked. The Utes had been so badly treated they daren't be thought of as raiders, or they would be hounded and shot down mercilessly.

When Ouray said that his sadness cloaked him and shrouded his humor.

"When you have lost the McMullins Owl-Walks-West will find you and bring you to us."

"Why don't you just tell me where you'll be?" I asked.

"And if you are captured?" said Ouray. I hadn't thought of that, though it was possible.

I dressed in dark clothes and put charcoal on my face and strapped the long-bladed killing knife to my leg and saw to the Creedmore and my two Colts. Ouray gave me a nice beaded bag full of red cedar shavings for the carrying of Elder McMullin's head.

"The beadwork is Cayuse," said Ouray, grinning. I'd never heard of them, they lived over in Washington, eight hundred miles away.

Off we went, Owl leading. The night was black and a haze of clouds broke the starlight up; we was just two more shadows, with feet. I had long since wrapped all the jingling things on my saddle and bridle, and other than the sound of hooves and the creak of leather we made no sound at all.

An hour before dawn we come up to the edge of the rimrock and saw below the red beds of several dying campfires far below. Owl gripped my hands in both of his, turned, and vanished. Ouray was wise enough to know that we outnumbered his people a thousand to one and we could make guns and they had to buy or steal them. Ouray had lost both of his sons at war and it pained him bad yet. He saw war as the vicious foolishness it is. Plain common sense is as rare as lips on chickens, you ask me.

There was a small spring purling out of a band of yellow rock, good cold water. I gave my horse a hatful and drank deep myself, drank till I sloshed like a bottle, for I didn't know when I'd be able to drink again. The cool wet felt woke me up good when I put the hat back on. I nosebagged the pinto and tethered him good in a dense stand of red cedars. There ain't anything, to my mind, as distressful as needing to make tracks in a hurry and finding your horse went missing. (The few times that has happened to me has caused me to blaspheme elaborately and it is a serious drain on my stores of good nature.)

There was a water channel cut down the face of the rimrock and the left side went out into a horn maybe two hundred feet above the McMullin camp. The walls below that was sheer and I took a good close look around from the top of the horn. It would be at least two hours before the men down below could even make it up to where I was, and two hours in this country of mazes and false canyons was a long head start. And the slickrock country don't take tracks on its face much.

I chewed on a piece of raw bacon and sipped water. I piled up some stones for a screen so that there wouldn't be visible movement for anyone to see who was standing down below.

I slid the telescopic sight out of the hollow stock of the Creedmore and screwed it on. There hadn't been time enough to sight the thing in, so I'd have to see where it threw if I missed and adjust accordingly. I looked through it and followed one of the good Elder's sons as he fed the campfires. It was a powerful telescope, the fire tender looked only maybe seventy yards away.

Sleep came over me. I hadn't eaten right or slept well in days. I had a sudden vision of Eats-Men-Whole lying naked on a pile of robes, and my eyes teared up and I tasted copper in my mouth. I chewed hard on the bacon but the dream wouldn't go away.

The camp stirred about a half hour after sunrise. I saw Elder McMullin come out of his tent with his galluses flapping and his pant legs piled on his boot tops. He waddled to the edge of camp and squatted with his back to me. I put the crosshairs two feet below where I wanted the slug—bullets rise a little if you are shooting down at a steep angle—and I squeezed the trigger and the Creedmore boomed and I ducked down behind the screen and grabbed the binoculars.

The slug had got him low in the back, and he had tumbled forward several rolls and come to rest with his head under his right leg. His spine was smashed and his mouth was open in a scream. I could see but not hear his dying bellers. The wound was mortal and I felt quite satisfied.

My smugness vanished about a minute later when the stone screen exploded to the right of me. No one in the camp had fired, so I whirled and looked up and there was six of them God damned hats up on the rimrock, near to the only trail out.

I rambled on with some elaborate cussing that would have dried out Mulebreath Mucklebreech if he'd been in earshot. I had a fresh cartridge in the Creedmore, and whatever else them boys up there might know I doubted a long killing rifle like this had occurred to them. If the damned Creedmore had been a repeater I'd have made short work of them. Sharps had left the gun singleshot so the barrel would have time to cool between firings. I meant to speak to them about that, if I lived.

Well, I shot three of them just under their hat brims. The last one jumped up after the bullet had furrowed his skull and he run, jerking like a puppet, till he stepped off the edge and fetched up as a pile of bloody rags down below.

That left three still firing and they was getting close. I scrabbled a ways to my right and found a narrow cave opening and ducked inside. I found a miracle in there. There ain't no other way to explain what was in that cave.

A palace. The cave was a low-browed sort of arrangement stained with soot from ancient campfires on the ceiling, and when I crawled in further I found a high and vaulted six-story castle in it, deserted except for the pack rats and ghosts. Water belled somewhere in the dark behind the palace. A shaft of light come down on top of it, and when I got close I saw there was handholds cut in the rock. I had two ways out now.

Life had suddenly gone sweeter, and I knew I could easy hold off them damned McMullins and then slither out or slither up in the night. I fretted some about my horse, and then remembered that Washakie, when we were out of grub or a horse pulled up lame, would grin and say that the enemy had plenty of food and horses and scalps to boot. So I planned to take down as many McMullins as I could—they'd have to stick their heads out, and be backlighted, and I'd kill them till they ran and take what I needed in the way of horses.

I watered myself and washed off some of the dust and then I crept back up to the cave's mouth and waited right on the edge of the shadows and not ten feet from the cave entrance. If they came this way they'd be sunblinded, and the cavemouth, though wide, had only one place to crawl into it from in the mother rock. I counted my cartridges and figured that sixty-two of the bastards would die before I was down to just the Creedmore. That gun was so powerful I'd just hold fire till they lined up, and get ten at a whack.

Not one McMullin came, of course. Mountain Jim was right, with the old man dead—I found out later he screamed for four hours before he died—they'd no idea what to do. The three I'd brainshot was an object lesson, and so these disgusting fools rolled up their dear Pappy in a tent and tossed him over a horse and they took off for their filthy ramshackle McMullinage and so help me Gawd, they got lost. Lost, lost, lost, and a month later less than half of them wandered into their nest, the others having perished of heatstroke, thirst, Gila monsters, tainted food, and rattlesnakes. Dear Pappy had swelled up to the size of two oxen in the heat, so he was inconvenient to pack farther and they dropped him down a sinkhole. Even now when I am mellow with age I am proud of my accomplishment by way of improving the country.

They never even found my horse. He was wanting water, but that was all.

I headed east and north, figuring on crossing Ouray's trail. The third night I was traveling I come round a blind turn and there was Owl-Walks-West. He give me a big grin and a handshake and a pipe and tobacco. I got off and had a sociable smoke with him. He was pleased at the damage I'd done to the McMullins, and told me about them being lost down in the deep desert.

Owl took me by some paths I'd surely have missed, and then suddenly I smelled sweet cedar smoke, and Owl led me into another hidden place.

There was some fuss in the camp. Some of the hot-blooded young warriors wanted to drive the whites back across the Mississippi or something, and when I come on to Ouray there was a lot of ripe criticism of Ouray's manliness.

"Chess?" said Ouray. I allowed as how a nice game of chess was just what I come for.

The Arrow put up with these little peckerheads until the three of them disturbed him as he contemplated a nasty choice—he could concede that I had whipped his ass at chess now or let me do just that about three moves hence.

The lead peckerhead, all six pimply feet of him, ran through his prepared list of Ouray's failings and added "fish-hearted old woman." Ouray looked at me, annoyed, pulled out a revolver, shot the little bastard in the middle of the forehead, roared about how much he hated being disturbed by shitbrains whilst he was at chess, and casually flung the arm of the corpse off his knee where it had flopped during his late critic's death throes.

That sure done put a damper on public displays of disapproval for the peaceful and conciliatory policies of the Arrow, who didn't even look up as the little shit's friends dragged off his body.

"Kelly," said Ouray, "these damned kids try my patience awful. I won't have to do that for six months or so, I guess. 'Nother game?"

"All this murtheration and hot travel had me plumb drawed, so I went off to get some sleep.

Not long after Mountain Jim and Palmyra come in, they'd been off someplace.

They walked hand in hand over to where I lay, looking pink and healthy, so I guessed that they'd been enjoying themselves.

"I don't want to hear it," I says, holding up a hand. "It may be twins and in fact it may be pumpkins but I don't want to hear it for an hour."

They both roared with laughter and went away. I sank into deep sleep right then.

147

16

The letters are in a big jar of chokecherry preserves in the root cellar of Lion House," said Palmyra. "Brigham hates chokecherry preserves, so no one would dream of using them, and he hates waste, so no one will throw them out either."

She was curled up against Mountain Jim's consider-able chest while he stroked her hair.

"How," I says, delicatelike, "did you get these letters in the first place? Sounds to me like any Mormon would have burned them right off upon finding them."

"Brigham kept them," said Palmyra. "When Joseph Smith and his brother were murdered in the Carthage jail, Brigham moved to take over the church. Joseph Smith had decreed the leadership of the church would pass to his heirs. Brigham collected all the letters, to use as he saw fit over the years. Because I was blind and he knew I didn't believe in his folderol, he'd read them to me, to see what I thought. He called me his little Gentile. But he grew careless, and though I can't see, my hearing is very, very good. So I found them and hid them away. He despised me in my blindness, and it took him a long time to mark off those who might have, and then he just had me."

She didn't need to tell me what happened next. One close breath around Elder McMullin and she'd know what she was in for.

So Mountain Jim and Palmyra wanted a little peace and quiet and the only way that they'd ever get it was having a club to hold over Brigham big enough to make him flinch. If they didn't have that, their heads would be on his desk, come now, come later.

"When I get 'em," I says, "where can I find you?"

"We'll find you," said Mountain Jim. "You might get caught."

"They wouldn't have to torture me," I says. "I'd nobly tell them whatever they wanted to know flat out and save them the work."

I do try to be right honest about my best qualities, which is cowardice, chicanery, avarice, lechery, gluttony, sloth, blasphemy, mortal untruth, and, yes, I knowed even then what a good lawyer I would have made but life worked out better and I didn't even slip and get elected to Congress.

So Kelly loaded up and went back up the trail to Salt Lake, figuring that the news of the Elder's expiration would most certainly cause large red carpets to unroll and give me a clear shot at that goddamn Prophet.

The desert country rolled red and yellow before me and I made good time, coming up one dusk to a stage station and I thought I'd have a home-cooked meal and then bed down a few miles away so I wouldn't have to feed the bedbugs.

The stage station didn't have a coach in it, but there was a line of hay wains piled high with fodder. I rode past them and saw how the forage contractor had cut a lot of willows into the hay to bulk it up. That much woody stuff would damn near founder the horses unlucky enough to get it.

The contractor was a fat, rumpled, piggy redgait of an Irishman who had the leavings of a hundred dinners down his waistcoat. His teamsters was a rough-looking crew, all armed with pistols and knives. The station agent was a small bookish feller with garters on his sleeves and a popgun in his right-rear pants pocket.

I watered my horse and tied him to the hitching post and then I went in the low building, which was spotlessly clean. The three gents who belonged to the other horses were just inside the door, looking out at the contractor and the agent. Two of them was ordinary-looking youngsters. The third was an impossibly clean gent in a white shirt and black pants and boots and black silk coachman's gloves. He had a black spade beard and eyes that flicked here and there constantly. He had his right hand on the ivory grip of a Colt and a sawed-off shotgun in his left hand.

"Evenin'," I said.

"Are *all* our friends out there through unloading?" said the dandy. His voice was whispery; I thought it would be what a snake would sound like if he talked.

"Not yet," I said. "But they'll be done in five minutes if they don't smell whiskey."

The dandy laughed, a soft whispering sound.

"Pay up, Gilson!" the Irisher bellered. "Pay up, Goddamn you!"

"Let us now," said the dandy, and he walked toward the door on the balls of his feet, which were tiny for a man his size.

They went on out and I stood in the doorway, so I could see and be handy to cover behind the thick logs the place was built out of. I wondered idly how many folks was going to die in the next two minutes.

The dandy walked up to the fat contractor and said, very mild, "I believe that the KC stage line is unhappy with the quality of your hay."

The Irisher said something unpleasant, which he et next breath, because he was looking into a sawed-off double-bore. I've done that. Them bores look big as train tunnels.

The contractor's knees started to shake. The station agent took his popgun over to the teamsters, and them boys unloaded all their artillery right there. The dandy's friends hadn't even pulled their pieces out.

"Chain this bastard to that log," said the dandy. His sidekicks slapped the contractor face down on a pine log and chained him good and tight to it. They padlocked the ends of the chain and stood back.

"I'm Jules La Farge," said the dandy, "and the KC line

employs me to inspect purchased goods." He lifted a five-gallon can of coal oil and he poured it over the haystack, very slowly. He struck a patent match and touched it to the oil, which caught and burned smokily. Pretty soon the stack was well ablaze.

"When the fire gets hot enough throw the log in," says La Farge to his sidekicks.

Then he walked back toward the station door.

"Buy you a drink?" I says.

"Not during business hours," says La Farge. "But I think the office will close shortly."

The contractor was screaming his lungs out by now. He was sure he'd roast soon, and he was swearing that he'd bring in real hay and never even think of padding it out with brush again and he'll give the hay to KC for years and he will wash and currycomb this hay he brings in and he sounds awful enthusiastic and not 'tall like the surly feller he was such a short time ago.

La Farge and I listened for a while, me laughing and La Farge smiling, and when he went back out I followed along. I always have admired folks who are good at what they do.

"My good man," he said, "a word." He knelt and looked almost sorrowfully at the red-faced, sweating feller. "If you should forget our conversation here I will have to return. I do not like this godforsaken wasteland. I will kill you. I'm not to leave here for a couple of days. I'll also kill you if the hay the line wants is not here by sundown tomorrow. So I will have my associates unchain you. I think that then you should go and cut hay, yes?"

The Irisher allowed as how he would be cutting hay by lamplight and arranging it stem by stem any old way La Farge wanted it.

"Just good hay will do nicely," said La Farge, standing up. "Oh, I believe your contract has another . . . . . eighteen months to run?"

All the Irisher could do by now was nod and gasp.

There is men who sell buttons and patent medicines and there is men who sell fear, and La Farge, soft-spoken and foppish, was about the most frightening feller I was ever to see. Most gunfighters potted folks in the back (like me) but some liked a contest.

One of the teamsters suddenly plunged a hand in the footwell of his wagon, and La Farge shot him in the head before the man laid a hand on the shotgun there. The sound of the shot died away and the teamster flopped out of the wagon and lit with a thump in the dust, blood running out of his mouth.

"You know," said La Farge, thrusting the gun back in his hip holster, "I never could hit a damn thing aiming one of these. If I don't think about it, I never miss. Strange, don't you think?"

I shook my head. "No, same for me."

"Business is closed for the day, and I will join you in that drink, if any can be found here that is made of vegetable matter."

The station agent brought us a bottle of bonded whiskey and waved away our money. We invited him to join us but he said it was against Company rules, and he set to fixing dinner in pots that had been washed in living memory.

La Farge out of the office was a garrulous sort, and he told me a lot of funny stories about his days as a railroad agent, how he shot or hung them as wanted to rob the trains, and his days as a Union officer, hanging spies and saboteurs in New Orleans. The man was soaked in death, and I couldn't tell whether he had chose it or it found him. (It was to get him in a little over two years, a double charge of buckshot in the back. His killer was never found.) But La Farge that night was gay, and his assistants, too, Luke and Billy, learning the killer's trade.

Since the station was so spotless I bunked there that night, and I had no sooner put my head on my saddle than the door come banging open and two of them tall hats I hate so much come in yelling for the station agent.

The agent come out of the back yawning and scratching his head.

"Have you seen either of these people?" the lead Mormon said, in a raspy voice sounded familiar.

The agent shook his head.

"How 'bout him?" said the Mormon, holding up another handbill.

La Farge was walking fully dressed except for the sawed-off shotgun, over to where the agent and the new folks stood.

"Interesting," said La Farge, "what do you want him for?"

"Luther Kelly for murder, and Palmyra Young and Jim Belding for theft."

"Ain't seen any of them," said the agent. La Farge nodded sympathetically.

There was a fair hullaballoo outside, many riders. I thought I'd just lie where I was and let someone else look. La Farge went outside, floating along on those tiny feet.

After maybe fifteen minutes the Mormons rode off. They was mighty hungry for the three of us, if they'd be risking their horses on a dark moonless night.

I just waited, for they might well have left one or two behind to watch. My mind was racing. I didn't know how exactly to warn Mountain Jim and Palmyra. One thing for sure, it wasn't no passel of ignorant, crazy McMullinses out there. There was some hard men there. I wasn't worried about them tracking Jim and Palmyra down, I was worried they'd split up and drive my friends the one into the other.

La Farge come back in and walked over toward me and he sat down at a table and looked off from me.

"Just stay there. Luke and Billy are looking to see who might have got lost and stayed behind. Now, no one here will betray you, but the stable hands are Mormon boys and they'll be here at dawn. What do you wish to do?"

I didn't know. Best would be to ambush all the mounted men who had just passed, but that would raise a bigger stink than we already had.

So I told La Farge the truth. He put his head down on his silk-gloved hand and listened, nodding every once in a while, and I was only about half done when Luke and Billy come back.

"Please start over," said La Farge.

I did. I told them about Palmyra, her blindness, Mountain Jim, the McMullinses, Ouray, and how that passel that had just flown into the night was bent on murdering them over the letters they didn't even have. Worse yet, Palmyra was standing up to her own father and somewhat taller, by my reckoning. I had to get those letters or my friends wouldn't ever be safe. I didn't know what to do.

"Only one thing I can see to do," said Billy, drawling. Luke nodded beside him.

"We'll do what we can to break that mob up," said La Farge. "And I think I know where I can take them, a good place, one that I once thought I would retire to, but I am afraid my life is not going to . . . . . allow me to do so."

We packed up and got ready to go our ways, me to "stick my head in the lion's arse" as La Farge gleefully put it, and Jules, Luke, and Billy to stand between two people they'd never even met and death.

"Do you have anything that would be recognized as coming from you?" said La Farge.

I thought hard, and then I remembered the quilled and beaded bag Ouray had given me for Elder McMullin's head. I dug it out, and added a note I scribbled on KC line paper with a stub of a pencil.

We split up then, and I never saw La Farge again, though I've run on to Luke and Billy time to time. Those three went after them Mormon cutthroats like real cutthroats, and they stalked and harassed them—there was *forty* blasted Sons of Dan when they passed the stage station. When they got out in the desert Jules, Luke, and Billy'd get a couple every other day. Ouray watched some and decided he'd like to meet such public-spirited folks, so Owl-Walks-West slipped into camp one evening—almost getting shot, it had been a rough day on Jules and Company.

The Sons of Dan was scared out of their hair by then, and Jules quit killing them and just killed their horses. Not a one of the Sons of Dan came back, not even a horse with an empty saddle.

Then Jules and Company took Palmyra and Jim to a hanging valley hidden in the Colorado Rockies. You could get up to it only by going up a narrow goat trail—had to blindfold the horses—and once you came through the cleft in the rock a huge valley opened out, one with a small river—and here's the most curious thing—this river came up within a quarter mile of the cleft, and then it dived into the earth and where it came out no one knew. Sharp hornlike mountains stood clear around it, and the grass was rich and deep.

There was no way into it except that narrow trail, and one armed man could defy an army, the cleft was so narrow. Sheep would make it up there easy.

The Lost Cloud Valley, is what it's called. (Palmyra and Jim are still there as I write this, there in some ways.)

Me, I had an even less restful time of it, I'll tell you.

I went riding on toward Salt Lake City. No one bothered me all the way there. So I canters up to the porte cochere and the hedges and bushes and windows suddenlike was all pointing guns at my vitals. A couple of oxlike fellers in them copious hats drug me off my horse and sort of bounced me in the door to Brigham's study where they practiced their knots and glares and grunts for some time before lifting the chair that was now an intimate item of my apparel and dropping it from three feet up in front of the Prophet's desk so I could have a good view of him.

Brigham scowled at me and I scowled right back. He then motioned to his lackeys and they all stomped off leaving me all alone with this bloodthirsty madman, although truth to tell I wasn't no slouch in that department anymore either.

"Did my slut of a daughter give you the letters?" he hissed. He seemed to swell, like a scared cat.

"No," I says. "There ain't no letters she knows of."

"Lies," Brigham screamed. "Damned, dirty, blasphemous lies! I will by God have those letters! I'll have them, you Gentile shit!"

"There ain't no goddamn letters and I shot that bastard McMullin for you. Now let me go, I don't much like it here."

Brigham was wound up pretty tight. He come round and I thought for a moment he was going to smash me in the face. He glared for a while and then he pushed a lever on his desk.

The two oxen who had brought me in here came and untied me and picked me up and hauled me away. They opened a thick door with a key and I smelled the musty smell of basements. Something else, too, I couldn't quite place.

They bounced me down the stairs and into a big cell. As they slammed the door I caught a whiff of unmistakable stink and heard the thunderous murmurations of bowels could belong to only one man in all the world.

It was dark as the inside of yer pocket there, but I knew the farting lump on the damp straw pallet had to be my old chum the sutler, God's Own Atmospheric Disaster, Klaas Vipsoek. I wondered what chance I had that they'd burned his banjo.

"Wal wal wal," says a thick Southern voice. "What in Hell's Balls took you so damn long?"

"Mulebreath?" I said.

"At yer service, yah Yankee turd," said Mulebreath.

Klaas let off a great ripple of wind.

Mulebreath belched.

Here I am, I thought, touring the Golden West and I'm home with my kind of folks.

17

Klaas, Mulebreath, and Luther was let set a couple of days. Someone came by with a water bucket and dipper and they took the slops pail and brung it back, but there warn't no food delivered. I figured Brigham wanted us weak before making us dead.

After the first four hours Klaas's farts had numbed my nose and I couldn't smell anything. It kept the cell right free of vermin and the guard as far away as he could get without actually deserting. Mulebreath sang stirring martial airs and when he warn't doing that he refought the battle of Pea Ridge, Arkansas, in which he had heroically charged a Yankee ambulance and made off with the medicinal brandy. Single-handed. When I asked him if he shared it round he looked at me like I was daft.

Klaas woke up and scratched himself and stood up. He still had them spectacles upside down on his nose.

"Mulebreath," I says, "how did you and this fat Dutch bastard end up in Brigham Young's basement?" I had business here.

"It's a long damn story," Mulebreath said. "I could use a drink." He fished around in his possibles sack and came up with a big bottle of stump blower.

Mulebreath swigged mightily and passed the bottle to me. I choked and gagged but I got some of it down. It was a lot like drinking hot worms. My eyeballs began to dance in their sockets.

Mulebreath wiped his beard and moustache. It seemed that he and Klaas had arrived in the City of the Saints and they went in as partners on a small house nearly to the edge of town. Klaas saw possibilities in selling things no pious Mormon would touch but they would certainly buy. Mulebreath had thought the drivers who plied the Parley Canyon route were not much good with a mule.

Mulebreath had slept off much of the day's drunk on the roof of their humble dwelling. Klaas was sitting on the stoop playing the banjo. Two missionaries approached.

Klaas did not wish to leave off playing the banjo, largely because if he didn't he couldn't hear the missionaries blather. So one of them foully grabbed Klaas's banjo and jerked it away. The other began to read from the Book of Mormon. Klaas rolled up his sleeve and knocked the banjo-grabber halfway to St. Louis. Then he thrust a fearsome uppercut at the one reading— painfully and slowly as they do—which put out his lights. The slumberers were parked out in the mud for the hogs to root at and Klaas went back to his banjo.

A flying wedge of missionaries burst in and demanded Klaas quit playing the banjo. Klaas's slow temper was gone by now and he defended banjo and hearth and then he unbuttoned his flies and pissed on such Books of Mormon as had fallen near.

"So I looks up the street and there's this mob all wavin' Books of Mormon and they come up and was working on Klaas pretty good so I hauled out the frightful hawg and pissed on all of them but good. Then there was a general sort of a riot and when we come to here we was. Sort of seems unfair. I mean, they had every chance to stay away and not bother us. Yankees. Shit."

Mulebreath had another snort and so did I. Klaas scratched and farted and rubbed his sore jaw. He held out his hand for the bottle. Mulebreath gave it to him.

"Man out here can't tell a lie good ain't got many friends,"

I said. "Now will you quit lyin' to me and tell me why Brigham tossed a sutler and a teamster into his dungeons?"

"Iss tha truth," said Klaas.

"Bullfeathers," I said. "They come down on you because you knew *me*."

But how? We headscratched for a while and came up with not one good reason for them to be down here. Pissing on a few of the pesky missionaries would hardly have Brigham in the rage he was in. He was scared, and it made him angrier and angrier.

"Ah think these here Mar-mans is mighty strange fer the love of their God," said Mulebreath. He had a Southern accent so thick catfish could swim in it.

"I tink lots unmarked graves," said Klaas. "Also these bastards break my banjo."

"First useful act a Mormon done," I snarled. "Call the newspapers."

The light was pretty bad in our rathole, but I thought if I could get a rock somewheres and sling it in my shirt I could club a guard and we might be able to escape. More I thought on it the worse the idea seemed. There was at least twenty armed men up there and us three and Klaas was stove up some.

All of the time I was thinking I was running my fingers along the back wall, absentmindedly, and I come on a stone that moved a little. I worried it out and worried my ideas down to a nub and sat down on the pallet with the rock in my hand. I was far gone mopeful.

Another rock fell out of the wall. I got up and rushed to the opening and I could smell fresh air. I grabbed at the rocks and pulled a hundred pounds of them out at once. They crashed on the floor, but the guard didn't seem to hear.

"Boys," I hissed, "I think we got a maybe here." They come right quick. I stuck my hand through and waved it round and found nothing. There was a considerable draft of cool fresh air coming now.

Mulebreath stuck his paw through the hole and waved it so damned long I finally asked him what was he doing?

"Reachin' for Maggie's Lost Drawers," says Mulebreath. His trade whiskey breath caused my whiskers to stagger and fall.

We tore down more rock, getting it wide enough to let Klaas through.

"We could just leave him here to slim down some," I said. "It'd do him a world of good."

Klaas made foul suggestions for things I might do in the way of entertainment, once I got out and was next to bats, goats, and stumps. He punctuated his speech with an enormous blast of wind.

"We got to git him to where we can kill him goddamn good and proper," Mulebreath gasped. I was leaning on the wall for support. It fell away in front of me, with a crash I'd thought could be heard in Wyoming. The guard didn't come. Mulebreath padded off and stuck his head through the bars and came right back.

"He seems to be passed out halfway up the stairs," said Mulebreath. "Prolly 'cause of Klaas's last explosion. Maybe I was hasty. Maybe we shouldn't kill him."

Klaas rubbed his eyes with his hands. "I vondter vat happen to my banjo," he said.

"We'll find out," I says, crawling through the hole. I went along cool, sandy earth on my hands and knees and when I'd look up I could see some cool, gray light far ahead. I struggled toward it and soon I was going along behind shelving filled with rows and rows of canning jars.

I could hear Klaas wheezing and Mulebreath cussing sort of steadylike, just keeping his tongue in shape.

Canning jars. The light such as could make it down this far came from a cobwebby window fairly high up. The window looked big enough for me and Mulebreath to get through and I am such a noble character I thought even Klaas could make it if he starved down for a couple months and we greased him up real good. The others were coming on. Well, goddamn it, I didn't stuff all them pickled pig's feet down him nor them barrels of beer and sides of bacon.

The three of us stood there blinking in the soft new light.

"If she be sunny our eyes won't work," said Mulebreath. "We be blind as moles for fifteen minutes."

I carefully moved about forty jars of canned stuffs out of the way and slithered out and stood up. My forehead was running blood so I scrabbled in a corner and got a handful of dusty cobwebs and plastered them on the cut, which quit bleeding just like that.

Klaas struggled through and lay like a beached dolphin on the dirt floor.

"Kick in the ribs help ya up?" I inquired, my voice concerned as an undertaker's.

Klaas struggled to his feet and Mulebreath came through in a moment. He stood up and dusted off his buckskins and painted his tonsils with more from his jug.

"How'd you get that in here?" I asked.

"Them plumless fellers got tard a me crackin' there heads together, I said I'd walk peaceablelike if they left me alone." Mulebreath had developed a powerful personality in his trade and it stood him good in all weathers.

The light brightened and we got a good look at each other for the first time. We was filthy, stomped, bloody, battered, and half dead. So we laughed at each other.

"If our mothers could see us now they'd say I told ya so," I said. We hooted and then remembered we was sneaking out and cut off quick.

"Wal?" says Mulebreath.

"I need a big crock of chokecherry preserves," I said.

"Klaas's farts simple ya?"

All I said about it was that Brigham would perish of the apoplexy if he knew what was in that there crock. So we found it quick enough, and sure the crock had been moved recent and there was fingerprints in the dust.

There was water running over in the corner and when I went to it I found a slate table and sink, for washing the jars before taking them upstairs. I dumped the preserves in the sink and fished out an oilskin packet and washed the stickiness off with a bar of soap I found on the floor. I put the packet in my shirt and thought how much fun I was going to have with that bastard Prophet shortly.

There was a shadow pass the window, and I started. It must have been a guard.

Suddenly a door opened upstairs and we heard a foot step down. There was several women chattering away. We all took to what dark we could find.

Four Mormon ladies come down the steps one by one, blind in the gloom, and we bound and gagged them quick, Klaas getting his hand bit pretty good by one who was determined to scream. They was all wearing them tentlike plain blue dresses they favor, and Mulebreath and I slipped one each over our heads and we pinned the other two front and back on Klaas. The bonnets fit perfect.

We went bold as you please up the steps and through a short hall and outside down a servant's staircase and out through a gate in the hedge.

Klaas didn't betray us, which I thought uncommon kind of him. He hung on to his wind till we was safe away and near a protective bunch of traced-up oxen.

What with our heavy boots I was worried we would be spotted, but inspecting other Mormon ladies we was right in style, except for the whiskers, at least in most cases.

In three hours we had snuck down to the southbound trail.

We was battered and starved and mad as hell, so when a pair of wagons loaded with rutabagas come along we come aboiling out of the brush and I leaped up on the first wagon and knocked the driver off. Klaas sat on the poor bastard and farted, fatal for the victim.

Mulebreath used the leaded butt of a blacksnake whip. We hid the bodies under the rutabagas and went on down the road, loudly forming the Great Salt Lake Rutabaga and Revenge Company.

Mulebreath got tired of us poking along and he passed us, jug to lips, and held ahead of us about two hundred yards.

"I no usually a vinchful man," says Klaas, "but I vill haff blut for my banjo."

There was a good place to water the teams, and while we hid the bodies in the brush the mules drank their fill. One mule got excited, and was dancing around bidding fair to foul all the rigging. Mulebreath sighed, put down his jug, and walked over to the mule, who was rolling his eyes by now. Mulebreath reached up and grabbed the mule's ear and twisted it hard and pulled the mule's head down and breathed in to the critter's nose.

The mule stood there quivering. Both ears flopped down like drooping leaves. Its knees quivered and sort of collapsed together. The mule didn't fall, but it looked like you could knock it over with a feather.

"Anny a tha rest a ya pissants makin' trouble?" said Mulebreath.

The other mules looked right smart at him and seemed eager not to make trouble.

"I never seen that before," I said, awed.

"Taint nothin'," said Mulebreath. "That mule'll be fine in ten minutes. Easier'n beatin' on em." He took a pull from his jug and handed it to me.

"Well, we're out," says Mulebreath. "Now where do we go?"

I hadn't thought on it much.

We was all about ready to clean out Zion with an axe.

The rest of the day we took the wagons south. We'd have been discovered to have gone missing by now, and the bodies in the bushes would not stay hidden long. So about evening we each took a rutabaga for dinner and turned the mules loose and took off for the high country, without much of a plan. Ouray was too far south of us to help.

Around a meager fire that evening we toasted slices of rutabaga—didn't help much—and it seemed that the only thing left was a life of crime, at least long enough to get a stake together. We needed all the gear the Mormons had took.

"Well," says Mulebreath, "back in 'sixty-three when we was . . ."

Klaas jammed an ashy slice of rutabaga in his mouth.

"We ought not rob no one but Mormons," I said.

"Only veepon ve got iss Mulebreath's breath," Klaas observed.

Well, it would be grand in close quarters but otherwise not much help.

We gathered squaw wood for the fire and sort of moped at it. We was so far broke we hadn't the stuff to *rob* anybody with. It was an annoying situation.

It was a damp and chilly night and we didn't sleep much. Klaas had a bad cough and even his farts was diminished in range and force. We was so *sorry* that we couldn't do much but laugh on our miseries. We slunk back down toward the road and stood around all day, but there warn't anything we could manage come by.

That night we didn't even have the rutabagas to complain about, which made it a gray evening.

18

We didn't wander overmuch the next morning on account of starvation and blood loss. I made snares from some of my fringe but the gophers just chewed through the leather in no time.

We was resigned to starving to death in a copse of cedars while looking for large clouds of Mormon dust. The dismals had us all covered over. We was so hungry and wore down even Klaas's farts had paled off into silence. Mulebreath was too unhappy to let us know how the Civil War come out.

I thought I saw some dust over to the west and I dropped flat on my belly and wriggled over to take a look-see. There warn't much in the way of entertainment in camp, so Mulebreath and Klaas wriggled up, too. We was laid out like trout on a mossbank.

Suddenlike I felt this monstrous clamp on my neck, and I was lifted up bodily, feebly kicking my legs. I could barely see Klaas, who had been picked up, too.

Mulebreath was looking at something behind us and he looked awed and terrified. I could see the shadows of me and Klaas out on the ends of huge arms, and a shadow of the gent holding us, and I choked and swore humans don't grow that big.

Klaas and me was slowly turned around, to face the biggest

man I ever seen in my life. And that was how I met Liver-Eatin'
Jack Johnson.

"WHICH ONE A YEW BOYS IS KELLY?" says Jack, in a
voice so deep it damn near shook the hobnails out of my boots.

"Meeeeeee," I whined. Jack dropped poor Klaas on to poor
Mulebreath, making them unconscious. Jack set me down
gently. I'm three inches over six feet and I was craning up a lot
just to see the top of the son of a bitch. Jack allowed to seven
feet but I think he was taller. He had thick, coarse black hair,
beard up to his cheekbones and half down his chest, and a pair
of pale green, sort of soapstone-colored eyes, flecked in black
and flat as death.

His clothing was heavy buckskins and moccasins, all over
beads and quills, and as greasy as bacon flitches. He had a Green
River knife no more'n three feet long in a gold-worked black
leather sheath, and a Hawken .60 with a curly maple stock and
gold and stones worked into the wood. Jack always wore a
sorrowful expression, like he'd been called and couldn't come,
but he didn't lack humor, most of which was designed to drive
his friends to the madhouse.

"BRIDGER SAID YOU UZ SORRY," said Jack. "JACK,
SAYS BRIDGER, HE'S SORRY AND WE GOT TO HELP.
MEANIN' JACK GOT TO HELP. NOW THAT I SEED YOU,
I WONDER WHAT THE USE IS IN ANY OF IT. 'NUFF TO
MAKE A FELLER WANT TA END IT ALL."

"Huh?" I said intelligently.

Jack lowered his voice to what amounted to a whisper, it
was just loud enough to shatter the larger rocks around.

"Even muh old pard Spotted Tail was holdin' back when he
told me you'd eat mouse turds for beans and yuh couldn't find yer
way up a woman if you was follerin' a salmon. Coulda made a
decent picket rope out a that boy's hide, says Spotted Tail, but
he's so pitiful I didn't, I don't know why. Goddamn the pair of
'em, leave it to Jack, let Jack take care of it, he's big and dumb."

"Wha?" I says.

"He's off tryin' to diddle the Mormons is what Big Throat

and the Tail tell me. They say, 'Jack, we're fond of that boy, we don't know why neither, and would you go see him all right before them Mormons got him married off to forty wives and fucked to a standstill?' They tell me ya got the morals of a goat had an accident with the locoweed. Rides like a turd hit with a club and if it wasn't for them as took care a this hopeless pilgrim, least they ain't guilty a lettin' ya die a starvation and pox.

"SO THEY GIVES ME A BUNCH A WHISKEY AND TELLS ME THAT I'D BEST THINK OF THE DUMBEST THING TO DO I WAS IN YER BOOTS AND FOLLER THAT SIGN TILL I SEES YA."

"Gunh?" I said, my usual smart reply.

"Ain't got enough sense to roll out from under a horse that's pissin' on him, they say, if ignorance was a dick he could stand in New York and piss in California."

"I love yer aria," I says, "but is there a point to all this?"

"POINT? POINT? POINT?" Jack roars. "YA SUCKED-UP LITTLE PISMIRE, YA FUCKING LITTLE PIECE A IRISH DOGSHIT YA DAMN NEAR GOT YERSELF KILT. OUT-TREACHERIZING BRIGHAM YOUNG? YOU THINK I LIKE HAVING TA SKIN TWELVE MORMONS OUT TO FIND YER SORRY, BLEEDING DUMB SHIT ASS? I DON'T LIKE IT!"

Well, all this criticism about knocked me over. I felt proud of what I'd done and here Jack was saying I shouldn't have been caught in the first place. It was a good point. It hurt. I felt a twinge of shame. It was the last time, but there it was.

"DON'T KNOW WHY TAIL AND BRIDGER THINK YER WORTH SAVIN'," Jack roared. "BUT I'LL DO MY GODDAMNED BEST. WHO'S THE FAT DUTCHY AND THE DRUNKEN SKINNER?"

Mulebreath and Klaas was toppled together and out cold.

"Them's my partners, Klaas Vipsoek and Mulebreath Mucklebreech. They are even less than they look at the moment but you know how it is with partners."

Jack picked them up, each by a foot, and carried them both

to a spring come out of the slickrock wall. There was a good deep pool there. Jack dunked them both and kept hold of one ankle on each of them. After a moment the water began to foam and dance, as Klaas and Mulebreath tried to come up for air. Finally Jack pulled them out and dropped them on the grass.

Klaas hacked and coughed and spat and then he started to cuss in High Dutch. I couldn't understand a word of it, but then there ain't a hair's difference what a man says at a time like this from Armenian to Zulu.

Jack looked at Klaas and Mulebreath and shook his head. Jack, I was to learn, always looked so sorrowful that the rumor was when he killed somebody he apologized for it.

Poor Klaas sat up, moaning and holding his head and rocking side to side. He'd been worse handled than us other two and his busted teeth was paining him something awful.

He made the mistake of complaining about it, so Jack, with a sorrowful expression, produced a small pair of pliers from his possibles sack and started in removing the offending roots. Mercifully Klaas passed out soon from the pain. For a few minutes Klaas had flopped bravely out on the end of Jack's arm, even kicking Jack a time or two in the belly, which Jack didn't notice. Finally he laid poor Klaas's tormented carcass back out on the grass.

"He'll be feelin' better now," says Jack. "Be turrible them teeth gone and got infected."

"I ain't never in need of dental work," I says. "Got teeth hard as agates. If my jaw swells up, I'm just storing nuts there for the winter."

"Sorry about yer friend there," said Jack. "But if I hadn't tooken them roots out he could die on us. Damn them Mormons anyway. What'd he do to them?"

"He pissed on their book."

"Good fer him," Jack says. He pulled a worn leatherbound book from one of the many pockets on him and commenced reading the poetry of Keats. Now, that's a *book*.

Then Mulebreath struggled up from his sleep and he looked at Jack a bit and then Mulebreath fished out his jug and had a few snorts. He looked again and Jack was still there so he shrugged and stood up.

Jack walked up a little hill and whistled hard and shrill, a note like a shrike's, and pretty soon a gigantic Shire horse with a saddle on him looked like them howdahs you see on elephants and further had ten mules in a train tied to his tail.

Now, draft horses ain't usually seen saddle-broke, but considering that Jack weighed nearly five hundred pounds I thought it clever of him to find a horse bigger than he could eat at a single sitting.

Jack's horse was also the biggest damn horse I have ever seen and weighed close on to a ton and a half. His hooves was the size of big dinner plates. He was black as coal save for a white mane and white stockings and tail and a blaze down his nose. I'm tall and I couldn't see over the back of him.

Mulebreath and me heaved Klaas up on a saddle mule—there was four of them, I wondered who else Jack was rescuing this time—and we got on the others and Jack pointed his mammoth horse east and we soon was climbing up to the pines. It was high summer now, and only the distant mountains had snow on their peaks.

Jack stopped at the first ridge and looked back the way we had come. There was a big cloud of yellow dust back there maybe ten miles.

"Ain't but a dozen or so of 'em," says Jack. "Appeteezers. But we's to run, not fight."

I was sudden hot. I wanted a lot of blood for my troubles. I was very young. I am fairly old now and I *still* want the same.

"Wull," says Jack finally, "I guess we'll set a surprise for 'em at Parker's Cut."

Parker's Cut proved to be a narrow passage through a blue and yellow mountain seventy miles long that rears up from a baked plain. We went on through and then up a nasty switchback trail and finally out on the rim of the cliff four hundred feet above.

Then Jack got off his monstrous horse and commenced in to tossing chunks down into the cut. Rocks no more'n half a ton were just casually kicked over. He rolled bigger ones. Klaas and Mulebreath struggled to help and I went over to a horn of stone and up it to look at our pursuers.

The water that had cut a path through the rock had wandered some on its way down, and we couldn't see how it piled up. After a good two hours of heaving stone over the side Jack pronounced himself satisfied. The last boulder he rolled into the chasm was the size of a bungalow.

"Thirt' mile to the next break in the mountain," says Jack. "They'll just turn back now. But that Brigham's a dangerous one. You'd best not go near Utah for a long time. And don't never trust strangers you ain't been properly introduced to, could be some of his damn Sons of Dan."

I already knew the Sons of Dan, their theological arguments was pretty cheap.

'Tis true I ain't the most moral feller you will ever meet, mind you, the sins I have committed are all of them but for molesting children and voting Republican. But these here Mormons was nothing more than a gang of crooks and such respectability as they got is boughten. Buy enough of it, I guess it works just about as well.

We turned south and went by back trails and a week later we come on a camp that had Ouray in it, and Ouray had the checkerboard out with a partly played game on it, which he told me was the same game we'd been playing till just before I left. Could we please get on to these more important matters? After death, murder, dungeons, and so forth I find myself back playing checkers with a crazy Injun. Of course, what he was really pointing out was that life was doomed to continue and whinin' about it would help absolutely nothing at all.

By and by as Ouray was whacking his kings over my prostrate reds Jack wandered by with a stooped, small, gray-haired feller moved slow on account of a stiff knee. I give them barely a glance and commenced into trying to salvage my checker fortunes—I was about half interested in winning the game—and didn't pay no nevermind and Ouray pounced any-way, clacking over the last of my pieces and saying, "comes back even dumber," and other cheerful and endearing things. I was often having thoughts of things other than killing Mormons and it was good of them to distract me. (Not a good idea if you're going out to do some serious slaughtering to be much set on the outcome, makes you still in your reactions.)

Jack walked over to me with the small, gray gent beside him.

"This yere sorry pup is that Kelly ejit," says Jack, pointing at me like I was a smear on a newly whitewashed wall. "The one ol' Spotted Tail and Big Throat say seems likely. I think they both gone simple from age, myself."

The small, slender old man offered his hand, it was long and slender with very long fingers.

"Kit Carson," he said, "and I'm pleased to meet you, Luther Kelly." His eyes was pale blue, with a lot of humor dancing in them. I stood gapemouthed, for I would have thought Kit Carson would be only slightly smaller than Jack. The man had the frame of a twelve-year-old boy.

Only reason I'm alive today is because men who knew things kept me from dying of stupidity. I was ready to ride back and charge that Lion House alone, and of course I'd have died before I got through the gate.

"Luther," says Carson, "time you left this country. Seems Gus Doane could use you. He's going down the Snake River, by boat."

"What the hell does he need me for?" I says. I was thinking on having the Prophet slow-roasting over a fire before long. "Rivers is generally wet and can be counted upon to flow downhill. Even a damned army officer ought to be able to figger that."

Smart-mouthed male children occasionally get what they most need. In my case, I got the back of Jack's hand across my flapping mouth. I have been kicked by mules and have it hurt less. I sort of went end over end about forty feet before fetching upside down against a wickiup, my feet in the brambles, bleeding out my nose and seeing shooting stars in whole batches. Jack come and picked me up by my belt and walked to the creek and held me under till I began to thrash. Then Jack pulled me out and carried me back to Carson. Kit reached in my shirt and took the packet of letters I wanted Brigham to know I owned.

Carson carefully opened the packet and took out the letters and he read them one by one and dropped them into the fire. I started to splutter but Jack picked me up by the scruff of my neck and waved his fist in front of my face, so I quit.

When the last bit of blackened ash collapsed into the coals Kit sighed and said that any truth in these matters was no longer of any value to anyone.

"Churches ain't about truth anyway," says Carson.

It took me years to figure it out, why Carson burnt them letters, but I finally did. We ain't even ten feet from the jungle and death is very close.

"When you finally know that revenge is best as a late, cold supper then you will be ready to take on the damned Mormons," says Kit. "But now you need to get shy of this country."

"Headwaters of the Snake is pretty close to Zion," I said.

Carson looked at me for a long time before sighing and shaking his head a couple of times, and then looking up at Jack. Jack took a swing at me and missed.

"You win," I said, holding my hands palm up.

"Plummer's gold," said Carson. "Now have a cup of this here coffee and pay attention. You are about to repay all this good kindness so many folks have given you."

Beaten, stomped, used for bait, messenger boy, horseholder to a monster'd rip off the Devil's balls, bushwhacker, scalp-taker, murderer, road agent—no pimping yet, but I had hopes—my heart overflowed with fine feelings for these bastards.

Mrs. Kelly's nice young son was learning a lot, but nothing he'd care to tell her about.

19

Henry Plummer, Kit explained, was one of them people who is charming, handsome, and has the morals of a tick. He'd have made a ripping good senator or a grand Revivalist preacher. He got himself elected as sheriff up in Bannack, Montana Territory, where he had run to after getting in trouble in the Idaho goldfields. Not one to pass up an opportunity, he also led a band of road agents.

Stout old X. Biedler and the Vigilantes hung Plummer. (I admire X. Biedler for a lot of good character he's got. Some fool woman asked him if he "felt anything" when he hung Plummer. "Feeling! Damn right! I felt fer his goddamned ear!")

While Plummer had been working the goldfields and them as mined it down to Idaho, he stole over a ton of gold. He hid it behind a waterfall on the Snake River.

"Let me guess," I says, "when Gus Doane and me are fallin' to a foamy death I'm supposed to look careful on the way down and holler IN HERE! with my dyin' breath." I told Liver-Eatin' Jack, Kit Carson the Rope Thrower, Klaas Vipsoek, and Mulebreath what I thought of this idea. I grew eloquent on amusements free for the taking right out there in the sand and sagebrush.

Jack backhanded me so hard that it damn near spalled my

face off of my head, and I did a few turns before coming to rest against a stump.

Jack picked me up like I weighed nothing and dropped me back in front of Carson.

"Wonderful idea and I'm grateful for the opportunity. Ain't every young feller gets an opportunity like this. I'll faithfully execute it, you'll see. I am lucky to have such fine friends. AND I HOPE YOU ROTTEN SONS OF BITCHES ARE ALL PECKED TA DEATH BY HUMMINGBIRDS!"

"I see you get our point," said Carson. "Brigham will worry over whether or not the letters are in the hands of an enemy. He'll worry all the time. And now he'll never know."

Carson then told me about how Brigham had been guided to the Great Salt Lake, for which the Mormons graciously burned Bridger out in '57. No good deed goes unpunished, as we Black Irish know. And they hounded Bridger every little chance they got.

"Now this is a whole lot of gold," said Carson, "and gold is a fine thing, ask any man here."

Ask me. I'd take the damn gold and hire Jules La Farge and be damned to Bridger, Cody, and . . . . . . I looked at Liver-Eatin' Jack and knew I'd need heavier artillery. Longer I thought about it, divvying that much up into shares made the most sense, since I'd have to spend all of it staying well guarded if I just up and ran. I am not a terribly honest man, but I sure am practical, and if you believe that you'll believe anything. I was a ripe old seventeen now, and I happened to be where I was and with who I was with, and I'd killed twenty-two men for certain and about that many probably.

Poor old busted-mouth Klaas come over, his jaw swole out like canteloupe halves either side. But them little eyes of his was twinkling—however bad things was he still was always happy with it. All the years I knew him I never heard him whine once.

"Viss I had me banjo," Klaas hissed, over his butchered mouth. Goddamned if that bastard Ouray didn't stalk over to his cache and come back with one.

I have no idea how Ouray come by all the things he

has—ransom from folks who don't want to die of old age looking across a checkerboard at that crazy Ute.

Klaas commenced into whanging on that damned infernal toy and the night air was sullied with hideous planks and plonks all crapped over by Klaas's singing. This blugerss Dutch music is so rough on the ear that I saw whole troops of ground squirrels heading for other lands. The pain would break them every few yards and they'd clap paws over their ears and writhe in agony. Blugerss singing is whiny and at its best slobbered out over a busted set of yeller Dutch teeth by a fartulent sutler. The inventor ought to have lampreys stuck in his ears.

Carson and I walked away where Klaas's, er, music wasn't so near on to us.

"Jack will be running the ridges keeping an eye on you," said Carson.

"Doane bein' an army officer don't give me a whole lot of confidence in his naval capacities," I said. "Also, Gus is fearless and stupid, which is a combination makes me shaky."

Kit and I looked out toward a faint band of red on the far western horizon. Nightjars fluttered overhead and some landed near to gravel up their craws. I heard a coyote and then another, and pretty soon they was having singing conversations across the rocky, sandy miles.

A gurgle behind us told me Mulebreath had paused to wet his whistle before joining us. He'd found two more jugs somewhere and had been happily pulling on one or the other all day long.

"Klaas and me outher go in the mornin'," says Mulebreath. "He's needin' new teeth. That means Denver, it do, and I'm feared of him traveling alone with his teeth so bad busted. Could get the mortifaction and die."

"Take four mules and such saddles and gear as you need," said Carson, "we're well fixed."

The banjo music had stopped. Klaas farted companionably just behind us.

"Such good music," said Klaas.

"Yer good music cleared everything that can walk out for

175

twelve miles about," I snarled, "and I saw a herd of cedars crestin' that hill there—" I pointed "—tap roots flappin'."

"We got to clear away, anyhow," says Kit. "We're a danger to Ouray and his people just bein' here."

When we went back to the camp a squaw come and took Klaas by the hand and led him off to the spring. We followed after, wondering on what she was up to.

She'd made some poultices and packings and she shoveled them into Klaas's mouth and I swear I could *see* the swellings go down in his jaw. He'd been in terrible pain for a long time and his body relaxed not having to hold tight against the agony.

We left before dawn the next morning, Mulebreath and Klaas to Denver, and me and Kit and Jack north to hook up with Gus Doane, who was going to try to kill me every day for the next several months. I had quit complaining because Jack turned up the charge behind his swats just a little bit each time and about one more notch and my head would go flying off.

Here I'd always thought insolence was a virtue.

Until we were plumb away from Zion, we traveled at night. Two riders crossed the trail in front of us and Jack followed them a ways and he was gone for three hours and when he come back he'd fresh blood on his right sleeve. All he did was nod. Sons of Dan, scouts, could well be a passel of them just out of sight most anywhere.

Mild-looking Kit went to a little town we passed by and come back with a reward poster for me, Mulebreath, and Klaas, for having stolen thousands of dollars from Brigham and having very nastily raped several of his wives. Five thousand dollars reward for each of us. I'd never felt so worthy in all my life. It warn't exactly a letter of credit but it was a hopeful sign for the future.

"Five thousand dollars!" I says, puffing up some.

"What you say that we bung this overpriced little shit into yonder jail and go home?" says Jack to Kit.

"A suggestion worth talking about," says Kit.

"May you have twin doses of clap," I says.

Jack and Kit knew where they were going and so I didn't

fret overmuch, just watched what they were doing to add to my bag of tricks. We moved mostly at night for the cover and the cool. Sometimes we were caught by sudden rainstorms that might be drenching one spot and not a quarter mile away the rain wouldn't damp the rock.

There's no topsoil in this country, so there's nothing for rain to soak into. It all ends up as flash floods in the watercourses and you have to be careful crossing them and you never, never camp in them, for the night may be cold and clear and bright and twenty miles away thousands of tons of water comes down in minutes and gathers and roars off.

The first one of these I saw impressed me no end. I dropped my hat when I was crossing a dry wash and got off to get it and as I picked it up I felt the sand and rock under me lurch. Not a hundred yards up the draw a solid mass of water carrying trees and rocks in it was coming down on me. My mule bolted for the far bank and he scrambled up safe and so did I, but another five seconds and I'd have been pulped by the flood.

It passed by and in an hour the sun had baked all the steam out and it looked all innocent and dry again.

Carson was up high keeping watch and he motioned toward the flood plain so I took the mule and went down the little dry wash and out into the flat pan now had an inch of water in it. There was a mangled horse with a wrecked saddle flung boneless out on the stones, and farther out what was left of the rider, his clothes just a few threads and his face wore off by the rocks the flood had banged him against. I looked through the saddlebags nearby him and found only some jerky and dried apples. I shook my head. We could have buried him but that would have left sign, so he waited on his face for the sun and the buzzards. It was a hard country then.

We cut east and went on up toward the Tetons, through high passes, Jack leading on his Shire and me tailing holding the leadrope to the four pack mules.

The Tetons is a lovely sight. I suppose someday rich folk will have summer homes all over them, but they were good when I seen 'em for the first time. We camped low down below them and Kit caught trout with a bent pin for a hook and horsehair for line. They were fine fat fish, about three pounds apiece. Jack showed me how to cover them with mud and bake them so they was moist still when cooked.

We was still pretty cautious about the Sons of Dan, one or another of us keeping watch from a dark place all night. We went out every morning and checked real good for sign, but there warn't none. As far as they knew, we'd left the rutabaga wagons and gone straight up in the air. I hoped that Klaas and Mulebreath had a safe journey, and that Palmyra and Mountain Jim were to home in the high hanging valley.

One morning I got up and pulled my boots on and went for a walk to stretch the stiffness out, and I saw the whole meadow had sprouted big red-capped mushrooms with white stems and flecks on the caps. I gathered up a bunch of them just for nothing else to do, and carried them back thinking on cooking them up for our breakfast.

Jack took one look at the mushrooms and he nudged Kit who said, "Oh fer Chrissakes," and they got up and ran me back out to the meadow and then they made me wash my hands good. Seems that they weren't poisonous to kill you, they just made you insane for a week or three.

"How much of these does it take?" I says. One bite, says Kit and Jack.

I dried slices of these mushrooms down and packed the oilskin pouch with them.

Kit looked at me long as I bent to this simple task.

"Could be you've the right idea at that," he said. "I never would have thought of it."

Doane was late in coming, and we waited a week, through the summer storms where the clouds boil round your shoulders and the lightning comes from under your feet, and we ate good of rockchucks and beaver. The deer and bighorn sheep was so lean from the winter still that they had no taste at all nor fat, which is what cuts hunger.

Jack showed me how to make all manner of snares for rabbits up to grizzlies and some tricks of tracking I'd never have found on my own. My Creedmore was in the House of Brigham, no doubt, but Jack had a serviceable .45–90 for me and the same plain Colts I was so used to.

A week past the time we was to rendezvous, Doane came on a litter strung between two horses. He'd broke his ankle, he said, in an accident on the trail, a green horse had shoved Doane's mount off a steep trail edge. His ankle was bound so tight that the skin was blue. Carson looked at it and muttered something under his breath and he cut the bandaging away with one swift flash of his knife.

Carson looked up in the sky at something, shading his eyes, and when Doane did, too, Carson grabbed Gus's ankle and gave it a quick hard twist. Doane screamed and then he trailed off into describing Carson's lady ancestors for the last fourteen generations, and finally he wheezed to a halt.

"Thanks, Kit," says Gus, holding out his hand. Carson shook it.

"I didn't really mean all them things I said 'bout your womenfolk, Kit," says Gus.

"Well, if'n you didn't, I'd best give it another crank, for I must not have done it hard enough," says Kit, smiling.

Gus turned pale and put his hands to his face.

Then he stood up and put some weight on the ankle.

"Warn't broke," says Kit, "wrap it tight now—don't strangle it—and you'll be fine as a new penny in a week."

The troopers pitched a couple of bell tents and they moved about efficiently setting up a camp. We was near a lake, a small one, and I saw a cow moose across it, stepping in up to her hips to feed. I took the .45–90 and went off, and killed her with a shot to the head at two hundred yards. When we butchered her out we found her good and fat. The troopers had been living on bacon and hardtack and watercress picked for to keep the scurvy away. Scurvy still killed more folks in the west than anything else, of the lack of green vegetables.

That evening, at supper, Gus talked about his expedition. Gus was a terrible toady and a good officer. If he saw something that warn't right he'd say something. Even to journalists. So his superiors had, no doubt, decided to send him down the Snake in hopes of his being drowned or killed by Injuns. My favorite Gus story was the report he telegraphed from Texas to the War Department: "Out 3 mos; 1 Indian killed; my casualties 114; at this rate war will last 500 yrs; cost 100 billion dollars; and they will win. Lt. G. C. Doane."

In the morning when we awoke Carson stood up suddenly and he went dead white and I barely caught him before he fell. I carried him to his blankets and let him set there for a while. He kept pounding his breast like there was something in there that hurt and could be drove away.

"My heart says it's time I settled my affairs," he said.

He and Jack left right away, Jack to take him as far as Laramie, where he could ride the stage down to New Mexico where he lived.

I never saw Carson again, for he died shortly after he got home. But I did meet him, and I'm grateful for that.

20

The United States Army wasn't long on backstocks of boats. They had been good enough to send along some canvas ones made up during the War of 1812, green cloth things with waxed basswood frames. The frames was in great shape but the cotton hulls had gone down ten million moth gullets long since. Gus, walking gingery on his sore ankle, looked down into the crates and sighed.

"Perfect," says Gus, "I can't remember when I been so happy 'cept when we was half shot dead at the Wilderness and the supply folks sent us eighty wagonloads of shoelaces. I think bullets being expensive we was to strangle the Rebs with 'em."

Them boats looked just fine to me, I was full of the satisfaction for 'em. The trip was off, to hell with Plummer's gold, and I'd just slide on north for a while, there was new strikes every day here and in Canada.

Bad luck has a way of cropping up no matter how you try to keep it away and this time it was a weedy corporal name of Bok who hailed from some Maine outport. No doubt a small child and a number of shotgun-carrying not-yet-relations waited upon him. His English was too damn good for a soldier. Anyway, the mouthy fool says he can build us fine boats in jig time, so we can foller orders.

Worse yet, it turned out that he *did* know how. My last best

181

hope was that he was lying and it went up the flume in short order.

We marched off to a stand of lodgepole pine where we was put to work stripping laps for the hulls. Bok went off and found a couple dead spruce for the frames.

Laps is long flexible strips of wood you take off lodgepole like you peel celery. After they was peeled off we weighted them down in the lake so they'd stay wet and flexible. I warn't wholly disgusted, actually. My life was surely going to be one of narrow escapes, and if I ever needed to flee an island (I did, several times) it would be handy to know how to build a boat.

Bok was a natural leader and he soon had some of the soldiers gathering pitch and others whittling out keelsons and thwarts and crossties.

In a week the twenty of us had made up five small, narrow boats with high prows and sterns, sort of dorylike. They was caulked with pitch and the shredded roots of willow. We launched one, Gus spitting on it as we pushed it into the water.

"I christen thee the USS *Festering*," says Gus. His ankle was still paining him some.

Bok had chopped oars out of spruce and he bound the necks with copper wire and pulled wet rawhide covers over the blades so they wouldn't split and break on the rocks. The boats were sound, they took on no water at all. Last thing, he drove heat-hardened fir tholepins into the gunwales.

Teamsters had been moving supplies up from Fort Shaw and we had barrels of hardtack and salt pork, navigational instruments, and the sundry stores of medicines and condiments and soaps and ammunition and cooking pots and tents and several folding chairs, fer Chrissakes.

Finally, one morning we loaded the boats, even taking the chairs, and pushed away from the banks and headed for the Columbia River. We hoped. This country is so big it's hard to tell what goes where. There were a lot of wild stories about deep canyons and whirlpools and huge manlike creatures who could carry a moose and stank of sulfur.

This country had a detailed map. It was in Jim Bridger's

head. The government wouldn't really feel that the land was theirs until some poor soldier bled to death all over it.

The Snake was about two feet deep and rocky where we took off, and Bok's design for our boats might have worked if we were headed to sea, but the bumping on the bottom opened up hundreds of leaks in the pitched bottoms and soon we all had a foot or more of water in the boats. We went over a smallish waterfall that couldn't be seen from upriver, down a long green tongue of water and then into foaming backwash. Gus Doane's armada went down like five dropped rocks. Us bold sailor men bobbed and hollered in the icy water. I had my guns and kit tied to a shot length of punky log, so I floated over to the shore and got up on it and tucked my thumbs in my pockets and watched the fun.

The seaworthy barrels of hardtack and salt pork and bacon disappeared downriver, and would get to where we wanted to go much sooner than we would.

I saw Bok's head go under and then come up again—he had seen Doane go down and the boy swam to shore with the commander near unconscious and all cramped up from the cold of the water, which tasted of snow when you drank it.

There must have been a hell of a spring under that pool, because at the far tail end of it there was a cut through solid rock and the river was roaring like a huge engine through it.

I saw four men struggling wildly and screaming for help get sucked into that horror, and several more barely escape it, catching a backwash and drifting over to where Doane and I were. Bok was out in the pool, diving for the instruments.

"Shit," says Gus. He was thinking of the next-of-kin letters he was about to write.

Gus remarked explosively on the last of the ration barrels as it shot into the grinder, and then allowed as how if God would like to step down here for a minute Gus Doane would punch the celestial spots offen him and anyone else he cared to bring. I grinned at him and remarked on the comforts of blasphemy.

Us sorry, wet survivors gathered and built a fire and dried off our clothes and we spent a hungry night slapping the mosquitoes that whined in clouds around us. I had gone out to see if I could bag a deer or moose, but the noise of our disaster had made all the game take a powder. I went out again in the early light, and shot a deer, an old buck who was tough as the soles of my boots, but it was food.

Bok had retrieved two boats when I got back—he was diving down to them with a line and the soldiers then pulled them in. Most of the gear had been tied down so we really lost very little other than four lives. All of this could have been avoided if there was just someone walking the banks ahead, a duty that I volunteered for as I was unlikely to drown walking on land.

The third day I rashly called Gus "Admiral" and he chased me about three miles waving his saber and hollering how I was going to feed the maggots. He'd forgot his bad ankle and when his bile ebbed it hurt so bad he let me walk him back to camp with his arm over my shoulder.

"I don't think I'd have killed you," he said, for his fit of temper over he was feeling ashamed.

"Hell, I knowed that," I said. "We just blow off a little stink now and then."

Gus was not going to turn back and the private soldiers said they would go on, even though their sergeant was one of the men drowned in the maw of the river cut. Too, Gus Doane was one of those rare officers who men would cheerfully foller right to hell. They actually gave Gus Three Cheers and Gus was so moved he had to walk away because otherwise his men would see him crying.

"To hell with the Quartermaster Corps!" Gus shouted, and that was to bring another round of cheering, since the soldiers had no fine feelings for the outfit that sent them pork full of maggots, biscuits full of weevils, and nary a drop of whiskey ever.

"No pissant trickle is going to stop us!" says Gus. Well, I thought that this pissant trickle had done a good job of that.

Hooray.

"On to the Columbia!"

Hooray!

"Why ain't you cheering?" says Gus.

"I ain't a soldier, I ain't a fool, and I know what this country is like. We'll be lucky if half of us is alive at the other end. I'll go, but I won't cheer. I ain't the sort to do it," I says, and Gus just nodded.

"Jesus," says Doane. I didn't know what that was for.

"Go shoot us some camp meat," he says.

"There's half a deer left," I says.

"That's an order."

So I directed Gus to go piss a long ways up a rope. We was starved for amusement, you see.

"All right, all right," I says, wishing I'd kept a horse.

I shrugged and took off toward a benchland I could see about a mile away that showed the purple of prairie grass. It wasn't much of a walk and I wasn't in much of a hurry. I come up a little rise one side of which was falling away and I saw what was about the most discouraged-looking buffalo I ever seen.

He was an old bull with three working legs, and he was still fat and heavy, so he must have busted his right front foot a short time back. The eye on the side I was looking at ran blood and had been gouged out in a fight or fall. One horn was busted off and his hide crawled with bugs and ticks. When I walked round to the other side, I saw that eye was clouded. His tail was broke. He had an advanced case of the limps and staggers and something wrong with his nose that made his breathing sound like a steam freight on a damp night.

This poor old boy was tottering and far gone, so I just walked right up to him and stuck my Colt in his ear and pulled the trigger, which gave off a small click and not one thing more.

The bull froze, tensed, and he sniffed, and he turned his head and he bellered and then he charged. I run like a stripe-ass ape for a scabby little juniper nearby and scrambled up it. The bull come lumbering along—nothing wrong with that right front hoof now—and he slammed into my tree and busted it off. I flew about fifteen feet and landed hard and the bull charged past me, one foot missing my head by a comfortable two, three inches, and mashing my hat about a foot down into the ground.

It took me a minute to get my breath back, and the bull had turned by then and was charging back. There was a little cave in a rock outcrop and I was about half wriggled into it when the whirring buzz of several rattlesnakes run me back outside again. I stood up and run to a rockpile and climbed up it and perched on one foot at the top, hoping that the bull would take me for a magpie.

He warn't having none of that. He come up, sniffed, and began to climb up toward me, hooking with his one horn. The footing wasn't good and I figured I'd run for the camp and so provide this monster with more targets, I was getting tired of being singled out.

I clambered down and run like hell smack into a thicket of chokecherry bushes, and damn near smack into a bear. It was a grizzly, and it stood up and said, "WWWWOOOOOO-OOOOFFF," utterly entranced by the sight of a man changing directions in midair. I turned at right angles and accelerated, humping my stumps along right smart and hearing hot pursuit behind me. I come to a downhill part of the trail and picked up speed. Bears can't run downhill very well, so my hopes rose, but not by much.

There was a mighty thudding crash behind me as the buffalo and the bear collided. A beller of rage from the bear, a beller of rage from the buffalo, and when I stopped to look back the sonsabitches had joined up and was after me again, partners in killing poor Luther.

No time for sniveling. I gained a few yards when my pursuers got jammed up squeezing through a passage between two boulders only big enough to let one through at a time. I was pouring on the steam. I rattled across some wind-sorted sand near the edge of the rim, looked down and saw Gus and the troops looking up, saw a nice soft red cedar maybe thirty feet down and since my pursuers were only twenty feet behind I hollered, "SHIT!" and jumped.

I lit in the brittle tree and busted off branch after branch with my face, ribs, knees, and various other parts and I come to rest in great pain on a sweet-smelling pile of busted-off cedar branches.

I took a couple of painracked breaths when there was this godawful crash and I turned my head and saw the buffalo with its head buried about two feet into the slickrock. It was all quivering in the hindquarters and obviously dead.

"Christ!" screamed Doane. "Here comes a damn bear!"

Grizzlies ain't awful good on the eyesight and the bear was descending clawing frantically for purchase on the desert air. It lit with a horrid thump on the now late Private O'Rourke and it rose up snorting and ran on to the river and jumped in and swam across and when it got to the far bank it went up the slope beyond, throwing gravel forty feet out into the river.

"Could I borrow one of you Colts?" says Gus, sitting down beside me. "To protect us from the meat you bring to camp?"

I told him of course and suggested where he might put it. Further, I resigned from this piss-brained expedition and I hoped they all drowned, a not unreasonable expectation.

I handed him the Colt I'd landed on. The barrel was bent over but I assured Gus that he could shoot around corners with it.

"Oh, bullshit," says Gus, tossing the gun into the river.

We was all starving and a couple of privates had quarried out a big lump of meat from the haunch of the bison and others was finding wood for a fire.

Various strange cuts of meat out of that poor buffalo were soon sizzling right on the coals on account of our cookware was under the river somewheres.

After an hour setting on the coals, the blackened lumps of meat was raked out and with a lot of grunting slabs of half-raw buffalo was cut off and handed round.

That meat was so damn tough I don't think I could have got a tooth in the gravy. I chewed some and gave up for it gave me charleyhorses in the jaws.

"We got to tenderize it," roars Doane, holding his jaw like it's sprained.

Our fearless, peerless, brainless leader put a big chunk of meat on one of the flat rocks around the firepit, picked up a long hefty log, raised it high over his head, and brought it down with all his strength on that there meat. That there meat shot thirty feet in the air, like it was India-rubber, while the club backed up the way it come and got Gus square in the middle of the forehead, making a sound like a melon dropped on slate.

Gus stood there for a moment with a cross-eyed look and a dumb smile on his face, and then he fell over backwards, giving himself another mighty blow when the club fell on him. He didn't feel a thing. (I been on a lot of expeditions. They all start out this way.—For that matter, they go on like that, too.)

A couple privates carried Doane down to the water and put cold cloths on the purple welt that used to be his forehead.

When Gus come to he asked for volunteers to go to Fort Shaw for supplies. The volunteers took off right brisk, looking sort of bashful, and I was sure they'd just keep right on going. (They did, but mailed in a supply list and where the expedition was. I couldn't blame them.)

We went back to building boats and about two weeks later the supplies come in, by mule train this time, since the desert was awful rough on wagons. We'd been living on anything that walked, crawled, or flew, and a few vegetables culled from the marshes.

We took off in calm water, rolling down the river, in a golden light past mountain sheep and deer.

For them, the Columbia; for me, Henry Plummer's gold.

21

Things went smooth for a few days, maybe even a week—hard to keep track when you're riding water toward the sea. Then one morning I spotted Liver-Eatin' Jack. He was standing on top of a cliff maybe a thousand foot high, pissing on a couple eagles below him. I waved and he give me an obscene Plains handspeak. Then the rock come in and the river bent a little and I lost sight of him.

We kept a look out for any of the four soldiers, but never seen any sign of them, I thought maybe there was a cavern under that horrible millrace where they had died, and they was stuck in it, forever.

The canyon walls was made of a soft, foamy lava that held water like a sponge. The rock was so soft that you couldn't climb up it—whole chunks of the cliff would pull away under the weight of a man. We stopped for fresh cold water at a spring on the south bank of the river and found all manner of fossil bones in a claybank near it. The bones was dark brown and all the lime had been changed to rock. Gus set the troopers to digging out the skeletons, including one of a big cat with two fangs that was each a foot long.

About the time that the river really calmed down we had got good at handling the boats, just when we didn't need it. Where the forks of the Snake come together we found a whole batch of Injuns on the banks, rooting around in some government issue ration barrels, for the last scraps of salt pork and hardtack.

"My, them Injuns look fat and happy," I says. "I wonder how they come by them good rations?"

"Kelly," Gus grated, "remember I know about you *before* you got here, and the army hangs deserters."

We hove to in an eddy and set off a fine old Injun ceremony, for they mostly all began to hop up and down and yell, "Pork and Tallow, Pork and Tallow," and I wondered who had read the ends of the barrels to them. (This was how Pocatello, Idaho, got its name—direct result of Gus's naval skills. I never tire of reminding him of it, though he does.)

We tried to camp there but the Injuns tried to steal everything, which I thought uncommon gall on their part— why, we'd only stolen their land, shot their families, cleaned out the game, and otherwise reduced them to beggary. It soon got to where someone was going to get killed so we up and loaded the boats and floated away in the dark. Not one among us had the viciousness to shoot these poor people.

Gus chanced the dark—we could see white water ahead near the shorelines but the water rolled on black and swift in the middle. The boat business made me nervous because it would be such an easy matter for someone to be up on a bluff with a buffalo rifle and we had no cover short of jumping overboard.

There was a big island we come to just at dawn that had so many blue heron nests in it that they were beyond counting. There was peregrine falcons and golden eagles on the walls of the canyon, some of the eagle nests were the size of haystacks they'd been in use so long.

Now, I know my true accounting of this expedition, this farcical voyage of exploration, will enrage our jingo historians, but I've been on a bunch of them and they are all alike. After all, Columbus was thinking he'd found China at first. Explorers is a simpleminded lot, with only the one virtue. They want to see things first, in the way a little kid will light up a stick of dynamite to see what happens. They *like* being froze, drowned, shot at, gnawed by strange critters, raddled by new diseases, and all them other things, and if you'd my experience you wouldn't lend them any more dignity than remarking these boys is combing the world for women who really *are* built sideways. (Teethadore Roosevelt was a prize example. I think he mashed his brain fooling with them Indian-club exercise things at Harvard.)

We come to another waterfall, a big one this time, and for a new twist Doane had a couple privates looking around down ahead. This was nice, as these falls was a hundred feet high and the pool below them was all jagged rocks. There was a couple hundred seagulls pecking away at whatever had gone over recently. The parts and chunks that was left.

Rainbows banded the mists the falls made and the muffled thunder of thousands of tons of water chewing slowly through the stones come right up through your bootsoles.

"Mild-mannered little thing," I says. "Why don't we just run it? Looks easy." I was hollering to make myself heard above the noise of the water. Gus scratched his ear.

"Go fuck a lame coyote," says Gus. "It's a nice day. Fuck two."

These noble speeches concluded I headed for the cliff by the falls and started down a goat path about as wide as this page, to look over the land and by the by peek behind the waterfall and see if Plummer's gold was all stacked up behind it waiting on Young Luther, the greedy little shit.

It would take a couple of days to portage around this big booming monster, so I had plenty of time to edge up close to the thundering cataract and see if there was an undercut. There was. There was also a greenish human foot sticking out of it. I tossed a loop of rope around the foot and hauled out the rest of him. I guessed him to be a prospector from his clothes. I fished around in his coat and found a packet of papers and the odds and ends of a smoker, but no money or wallet or nothing. I kicked the corpse over into the cataract. The river'd take him or he'd bob up and the troopers could dig him a quick grave.

The oilskin packet had a few daguerreotypes in it—a woman and small, towheaded children, an elderly couple, a pale-eyed gent in Union Blue—some letters, unreadable for the water that had soaked them. It's a lonely country and them as seeks their fortune here miss their families hard. And a map to the Lost Bullfrog Mine.

(After a few years of troubles that map caused me I got real hung on shooting bullfrogs with buffalo rifles. I'll tell you sometime.)

Since I was a humble civilian I tucked the packet in my shirt and said, "Yer secret's safe with me," to the corpse, wherever it may have fetched up. There was a good-sized cave behind that water, all full of spray and mist and very slick watery moss. I took a step and brought the other foot up. I felt a tiny stitch down under my bootsoles, and then my feet flew out from under me and I slid down a steep wet slick chute blind in the mist and darkness.

If the chute had gone out into the waterfall I'd have been pulverized food for the crawdads, but luck was with me and I only fetched up on the far side against a flat wall or rock that did not move overmuch. The wall was covered over by an inch of moss that evenly transferred the shock of my collision all over my body, leaving no joint still hinged.

"GODDAMNEDSONOFABASTARDINGBIT . . . . . ." I remember saying, just before thumping into the wall at a fast clip. I was sort of stuck there for a moment before slithering down like cowshit off a milking stall.

I rolled over to get my face out of the water on the floor of the cave, and fell off a ledge into deeper water. It woke me right up, as the pool was moving toward the white cascade of the falls. I swum like man never swum before. Didn't work.

I was so damn scared I even prayed some, in unorthodox wordings, as I was drawn into the thunder.

The falls took me down and plunged me deep, I wouldn't know how far. My ears hurt awful, and then I was popped right out over the fearsome curl at the front edge of where the falls hits the pool, and dogpaddling away from the mincer. There was a rock sticking up and I got a grip on it and dragged my sorry ass out on it and I lay there spewing water and wondering at still being alive.

I heard a whistle and looked over at the far north shore to see Liver-Eatin' Jack standing there. He give me the thumbs up sign and I nodded some, and then shook my head. It warn't *me* he was wondering about, it was Plummer's pocket change. Shit. Friends.

Jack grinned at me. I grinned back. The words I was saying behind my teeth were not nice words. At all. Jack scrabbled up a cliff two hundred feet high and was gone in less time than the telling of it takes.

Gus took the smallest of the boats and rowed out to where I was. I jumped in and sighed with relief. I still couldn't hear a damned thing, and I was bruised all over and pummeled about half to death. I was sure looking forward to dry clothes and trade whiskey.

I was slumped against the gunwale with my eyes half closed, and suddenly they flew open. There was an oar floating away. I sat up and looked at Gus, who was standing in the bows with his binoculars trained on the far bank. The other oar was out in an eddy, fifty feet away.

"What the fucking hell are you doing?" I screamed. Gus waved a hand back at me, to indicate he was busy and I should shut up.

There wasn't anybody on the shore. I hollered and yelled but it was futile, the falls covered my puny sounds like a rug.

I hollered for Jack, but he was nowhere to be seen. I was to be rescued. So why should he be worried.

The boat was moving. Not much, but it was. I turned and saw I couldn't reach the rock I'd been on. We were being drawn back toward the falls. Not quickly yet, but drawn nonetheless. I was too stunned and battered to get up and kill Doane. The one satisfaction I might have time for between now and dying and I'm too weak to take advantage of it.

Gus took the binoculars off his eyes and turned around, all radiant.

"A Harrington's Plover!" he said. "Not one has been seen in twenty years! What luck."

"Luck," I says, puking weakly over the side, "luck, you dumb bastard. WE'RE GONNA DIE NOW OF YOUR GOD-DAMNED HARRINGTON'S PLOVER. SHIT."

Gus looked confused for a few minutes and then he sat down hard in the bows.

"I see," he says. "It was just so exciting."

(Teethadore Roosevelt was a birdwatcher, too. I think they all ought to be hanged on account of how dangerous they all are. Or shot, or skinned alive, or dipped in tallow and set on fire. Something.)

The boat was picking up a little speed and the thundering maw of the waterfall was just a little closer each second. I saw a buffalo carcass come down, and it didn't come up. I'd lost my knife in the plunge and couldn't even attack Doane, who was sitting there looking embarrassed.

There was a whole tree, a cottonwood, that come over, one with the leaves mostly on it. It was crushed against the rocks and most of the small limbs snapped off. We was battered by twigs and chunks of wood. The trunk had wedged between a couple of big toothy slabs of lava.

I reached out to grab hold of the tree. I stretched as far as I could without going in. I couldn't get to anything. So I jumped out and swam to the trunk and got a deathgrip on a shattered stub of branch. Gus wasn't far behind me.

We shipwrecks clung and whined while the waterfall ate the boat.

"Harrington's Plover," I says, my teeth chattering. The water was damned cold. "Harrington's Plover. You stupid, accursed, moronic, goddamned idiot. I quit, if I get out of this alive I quit. . . ." I went on resigning for some time while Gus hung his head and nodded and apologized.

The soldiers had seen us in trouble and had a bigger boat, which four of them rowed out in and they stopped, sensiblelike, and threw out a line with a chunk of wood on it, not daring to get in to where the backwash was fast. I grappled with the rope and got a good grip on it and they hauled me back. I tried hard to talk them into leaving Doane clinging to the trunk of the cottonwood, but several of the soldiers allowed as how ol' Gus was all right with them, not too bright, maybe, but he meant well. They'd known lots of worse officers.

Doane got into the boat and we returned to shore without incident, and when I got my feet on dry land I fell face-forward and cussed into the sand. I was tired as hell and having just had death before my eyes and teasing I was maybe not so much in possession of my self as usual.

Gus still had his binoculars, and he was looking across the pool at the far shore.

"It's still there! The Harrington's Plover! See it?" he hollered, nothing daunted.

He handed the binoculars to me. I saw this not awfully impressing bird diddling on the sand. I gave back the binoculars.

Gus clapped them to his eyes and went on chortling.

The boom from the .45–90 sent Gus about twelve feet straight up and he lit looking wild-eyed around him. There I stood, the buffalo rifle on its bipod, arms folded on my chest. I could make out a few feathers still fluttering to earth over across the water.

Gus looked at me in horror. He clapped his binoculars back to his eyes.

"You murdering son of a bitch," he says.

Yup, I thought, that's me in a nutshell.

Not many folks get to render something extinct. I am happy to have been of service, and it is with pride I tell you a plover like that ain't never been seen since.

We packed up and went on down the river the next day, and now it was broad and purling. I saw a sturgeon in one pool that was at least fifteen feet long, and there were hundreds shorter than that. The river was gentle and fairly slow.

One late day we found a whole lot of dead folks on a ferry, so we got serious again.

22

We come on to the ghost ferry at last light, and the canyon made what little sun there was paler yet, with a yellow and unhealthy tint to it that made the green of the grass and the bushes rotten and putrid-looking. It was a place of death—there are such spots on earth—where crimes of such loathsomeness have been done that everything is touched by it, time, too. Some battlefields are like that, and the places where scaffolds stood and the innocent and the guilty was hung alike.

The ferry was deadheaded into the opposite bank, and we rowed over the placid water. Our heads in the boats were lower than the freeboards of the ferry. I gripped one and pulled myself up and blanched so quick Doane grabbed my britches to keep me from falling off. I turned and nodded and he heaved me over. First there were the five set against the little house for the tillerman. They had arrows in them and their throats had been cut clear back to the spine. The deck had thick mats of blood on it. There weren't any bloodstains around the arrows. The arrows had been shot into them after they were dead. And it took a lot more than five people to put this much blood on the decks.

"Injuns!" a soldier screamed behind me. He hung over a rail and puked his guts out before dissolving in tears.

Looks like Brigham Young's fair work, I thought, much like the Sons of Dan. But why? Most of the bodies must have been thrown overboard. I lifted a big tarpaulin in the stern and found them, stacked like cordwood. I wanted more than anything to see Salt Lake City again and be at the head of a conquering army when I did.

"Oh, my God," says Gus. He was as shaken as I was. We'd done our share of killing but hadn't gone on to butchery, at least not yet.

I tugged one of the arrows out of a corpse and held it close to my eye. The fletching was crude and the head was Injun, but it was flaked so finely it didn't look right with the shaft and the botched feathers. The feathers was pinions, all right, but they were swapped from the way the Injuns do it, the big part of the quill was forward.

We camped that night but didn't build a fire and all of us was watching the shadows. The air was so still above the water curtains of midges and gnats hung undisturbed, fish rose and ate them when they touched the water. There was a full moon and the light made ghosts, things moved. No one shot, but we all had our guns up one time or another, and our hearts in our throats.

Gus and the troopers dug a single grave in a small pocket of soft soil. We laid eleven bodies in it and covered them over and Gus read the Twenty-third Psalm. Whence cometh my help?

We piled the largest chunks of rock we could roll on top of the turned earth, to keep out the coyotes, skunks, and badgers.

We'd searched thoroughly for wallets, papers, letters, any name or date or address that would lead to the names of those under the cairn.

"They wasn't Injuns," I says to Gus, pointing to the crude shaft and fletching and the fine arrowhead. "For all we know, it could be robbers trying to have us think the Mormons done it."

Gus nodded. He finally sent three soldiers west to Fort Boise—the military was all the law outside of a few towns in Idaho—we had no horses and I had found some tracks headed off north, but it was useless to try going after them on foot.

Gus got to be unnatural silent for him, and he scanned the clifftops and wrinkled his forehead thinking. We abandoned a boat, leaving it on the opposite bank from the ferry, so that if folks needed to get across they could.

There had been enjoyable parts of the trip, deaths and murders aside. The birds was thick, other than that damned Harrington's Plover, and the canyons with the blacky-red lava walls held strange and beautiful light.

I hadn't seen Jack in a long time, which meant nothing. I supposed he was out there nearby. He was the size of a damn foothill, but he disappeared easy enough if he wanted to.

A couple days later—the river was pretty slow and we didn't make the kind of time we had upstream—we heard the rumble of a waterfall, and beached the boats and walked down to see how bad it was and if there was a good place to portage.

The falls was fairly shallow, only dropping maybe thirty feet, and the river had chewed hardest in the center, so the falls was shaped like a horseshoe.

I sauntered on ahead of Gus and managed to clamber down a narrow trail, and about halfway to the bottom shingle I swung my face to my left and saw a rattlesnake about the size of the Sons of Erin Fire Company's biggest hose, all rared back with his mouth open so far it looked like a porcelain dinner plate with fangs sticking out of it. I become one with the birds and even flapped my arms a bit before plunging into the cool green water below. I sunk down maybe ten feet before I come up, and the current was so gentle I could make way dogpaddling.

I clumb up on the rocks piled at the south end of the falls, and then I got to thinking that since Plummer would have come down from the North, like most folks, since there was no water south of the river, he'd likely have gone in here rather than on the heavy-traveled side. I swam up to the far south edge of the falls and put my hand through the curtain of water and there wasn't any water or force to speak of in it, it was only about an inch or so thick. I swam through the shimmering wall and there in front of me was a wide ledge, and on it was a batch of small crates, the size I expected the assay office in Idaho City used.

My heart was hammering. I hauled myself up and walked to the crates and pried off the rotted wood top of a crate with my fingers. I took out one of the bars and found a rock and hit it, and when I took it out to the light, it showed gray. Lead. I was full of the perplex.

On a hunch, I pulled off the top few layers of boxes and opened one in the middle of the pile, and when I picked up a bar, it was too heavy to be lead. I hit that one with the rock, it felt . . . . . . different. In the light coming through the thin curtain of water, I saw gold. Plummer's gold.

This presented me with a moral dilemma. Plummer had stolen this gold, killed for it, deprived women and children of its benefits, caused great hardships, and any decent, law-abiding citizen would inform the army, which would hold it until the courts of law returned the gold to the rightful owners.

So I put the bar of gold back, piled the lead on it, and picked up a lead pig and walked over to the curtain and stepped through it, barely managing to get a good foothold on a rock just the other side.

Gus was running up and down the shingle shouting and a couple soldiers was diving out in the pool.

"You see the body?" said Gus.

"Over here," I says. Gus looked over and gave a jump. I walked down to the shingle, and dripped my way to him, the lead pig in my hands. In the sun, I could see the hash mark of the Hudson's Bay Company on the bar.

"Whereinhell you been?!" Gus roared.

I told him I'd been near struck by a rattler and had found a cache of lead pigs behind the waterfall. (Hoping to Christ Gus had never heard of Plummer's gold.) Seemed to be left over from the fur trading days. I pointed to the hashmark and looked sincere.

Gus nodded and forbade any of the troopers to go into the backside of the waterfall. He'd already lost five and was not going to enjoy explaining how.

Good enough, I thinks, I can signal Jack to come on in and he can bag it up and pack it out after Kelly and the soldier boys is long gone.

I saw a sudden flash of white in a copse of red cedars a short quarter-mile away. Leaving Gus to go on with his lecture to his troops—he'd lost the thread and no telling when he'd be back on it again—I walked soft and casual toward the trees, casually carrying my pistol.

It didn't *seem* a likely spot for a bushwhacker, but I come on boulder to boulder for cover and I would have shot right pert if I'd seen another flash. Thank God I didn't.

When I was up to the sweet-smelling grove I heard a soft sobbing, breathless, tears spent. Just exhaustion, and waiting for something to come and kill the sobbing. Despair.

A little girl of maybe eight was slumped against a cedar trunk. She had one little hand on her hair, which was all matted and tangled, and she shook from fear and hunger.

I knelt down and looked closer for a minute. She sensed me there and turned her face to me and she screamed weakly and then she tried to stand up.

"I won't hurt you," I said, offering my hand. "And I won't let anyone else hurt you either." She looked about wildly for a way to escape, crying.

She scampered away, and ran to a wall of yellow rock maybe fifty feet high, and she tried to scrabble up it, tearing her fingernails and hands. I caught her and held her and she tried to scratch my eyes. She was too small and weak to do much, and she finally went limp, and I put her head on my shoulder and carried her out, saying over and over again that no one would hurt her. She relaxed, her whole body loosening, and then she clung tight to my neck.

I couldn't imagine how she had got here, unless someone had thrown her off the ferry and she grappled on to a log and came down the river, and the falls flung her up on the shore.

Her skin was near transparent, she was starving to boot. Children show that quicker than anyone.

The band of yelling loudmouthed men went silent and as soon as I come close to them they all stared and their foreheads puckered in pity.

We fed her bits of jerky and hardtack and plum preserves someone had hoarded up. She ate ravenous, and wanted more and right now, but I told her if she ate too much it would make her sick.

Any sudden movement or a shadow from a cloud would make her start and clutch tight to me. She had been terrified out of her wits and she was living on fear.

She ate a little more and I gave her sips of water, and then Gus mixed a little whiskey in water and gave it to her and she burrowed into my shoulder and went to sleep. We made up a bed for her, and when I would try to put her down on it she would wake up and cry and cling tighter.

So I sat through the night slumped up against a cedar, keeping her from nightmares, I guess. It was a clear night and a waning moon, it was peaceful by the river.

She woke in the morning looking much improved, children heal fast, too. One of the troopers had snared a groundhog and made up a rich, dark stew full of fat. The little girl tucked into it and when she finished a good-sized bowl she smiled and nodded at everyone.

"Do you have a name, child?" I asked.

She nodded her head and tried to speak, but her throat wouldn't work and no sounds came out. We bothered her with a couple of questions, but her voice was back with the bloody horror on the ferry and it would be a time before she could talk at all.

One of the soldiers pulled out a harmonica and played some lullabies and other sweet airs on it. The whole camp now turned completely around the little girl. There were near on to fistfights over who was going to feed her her soup, which was stupid, because she only allowed me to do that.

The rank black injustice of what had happened to this poor child set Gus in the only blazing fury I was ever to see him in. He was madder at Brigham Young than he had been at the Confederacy, and I do believe only his oath of duty kept him from heading for Salt Lake City in forty-foot bounds, there to tear Brigham in half with his bare hands, as so much more personal than a gun or rope.

The girl, who we had named Hazel Eyes, could likely nail

the gate on the Sons of Dan, but until she spoke there warn't any witnesses and I myself was trying to withhold judgment. It sure looked like them and the fact of the arrow, and the valuables just left—some jewelry and guns—and the throatcuttings all to the Prophet's specifications was a powerful argument. I suddenly quit wobbling. The Sons of Dan were bastards, they'd get death from me every chance, and it didn't matter a sparrow's fart if they was guilty of this crime. There were plenty of others.

It was time for me to go. There was a lot of river on to Fort Boise, and it went through country so parched and miserable a bird would have to pack a lunch to fly over it. There warn't any danger, that was upriver.

I explained this to Hazel Eyes, who looked at me gravely and nodded, and then she very practically adopted Gus for her new slave.

Doane thanked me civil and said he'd send a draft for my services if he had an address.

"Put it in the bank for her," I said.

I went up above the falls with four troopers and they rowed me across and we wished each other godspeed and I walked north. I thought the mountains looked about ten miles away, across a black lava plain dotted with sagebrush. Not the prettiest sight I'd ever seen but it didn't daunt me much 'cause I knew no better.

So I walked all the rest of that day, and I walked all night, and in the morning the mountains looked no closer. I hadn't much water, just a canteen, and I drained that and pressed on. I soon tossed away my clothes that was so hot, and in the afternoon I heard water rushing beneath my feet.

There was a mob of vultures circling above and the water was down below. I tore my hands bloody on the rocks. Gold and gray spots danced in front of my eyes.

I crawled under a ledge mostly out of my mind and I waited to die and I would have but for Jack, who come a couple hours later and he poured water down me and over me. My tongue was black and the size of a shoe.

Jack bundled me over a shoulder and about as casual as a

man hangs a bath towel at that, and he strode off for the far mountains, which got closer in a hurry as he loped in his moccasined feet. He stank of old grease and tobacco, and I stank of hopelessness.

In the middle of the night he stopped at a stream and we drank deep and I threw up. I felt some better.

In the morning we fed up good and Jack had packed a parcel of my clothes along—I hate admitting how stupid I was, even more I hate him knowing just exactly what I'd do.

My tongue had shrunk.

"I found Old Plummer's gold," I says.

Jack nodded.

"A cours' ya did," he says.

23

lummer's gold is still there, if you've a mind to go looking for it.

After I had recovered and we'd gone to Idaho City to get me a saddle and guns and such, we bought eight pack mules, to carry the gold off with. We had rawhide shoes for these pack mules made up, so they wouldn't cut their dainty feet on them black lava rocks, and stout panniers with pouches for the bars so the weight wouldn't slop around. We were in the gold moving business in a big way.

The night before we got to the falls we was all sound asleep under the stars when there was this sound like the biggest freight train in all the world went by ten feet away. The ground shook a little and we went back to sleep.

On we went in the morning, and we come on to the edge of the canyon. Me with my heart in my throat, and ready to tot up just how many of them bars there was. My own whorehouse, my racing stables, my watered-silk vests, all them useless things so nice to think on.

Well, the waterfall was gone.

Matter of fact the cliffs was gone and where the short falls had been there was this jumble of rock, chunks the size of houses, and the water roaring white through them.

I run on as many cusswords and ripe phrases as I had to hand, but I run down soon.

Jack looked at it impassive.

"WAUGH WAUGH WAUGH WAUGH," he roared. "WE'S SAVED FROM REESPECTABILITY! THANK GOD AMIGHTY!" And he laughed loud enough to spall chunks off the canyon walls.

Well, it was funny as hell. I'd had my hands on a three-million-dollar hoard of gold just long enough to find it, and now it was so gone it might as well been on the floor of the Pacific Ocean.

"Goddamn," I said. "You know, I have always had this fear I'd end up owning a big house with tennis courts on it. Pretty ladies in linen shirtwaists on it. My worst nightmare. Cold-eyed beautiful women on a lawn of a summer's morning. Makes me quake, fears me."

So us and them mules that we no longer needed turned round and went back toward Idaho City, biggest town in the state, with ten thousand miners panning and dredging for the gold. We sold the mules and bought some grub and went over the mountains to the Pahsimeroi country, desert and mountains, and over to Bannack in the Montana goldfields, where they hung Henry Plummer in '64.

Bannack was played out pretty good—just the Chinese working the old dredge tailings and a few miners digging little lodes of paydirt.

Jack and I parted ways there—he was going over to the high Absarokee to look around, and I hadn't anyplace much I was thinkin' on. I supposed I could winter over with Washakie, but the memory of Eats-Men-Whole was too bitter and new.

When I wandered into Fort Owen in the middle of October the colonel there was waiting on me and had sent a couple of soldiers down the Bitterroot to make sure I would stop. There was a thick envelope there, for me personally, and the colonel made it plain he didn't want me to read it there. I found a roadhouse a few miles north and I opened the thick vellum and saw a commission in the United States Army unaccountably made out in my name and a letter from U. S. Grant, which said in a friendly way I could ride posthaste to Laramie for further orders, or hang as the skulking deserter I was. Grant was General of the Army and was to be the next President of the United States. I'd heard he was a man of few words who meant every damn one of them he chose to utter.

I thought it best to feed all of it to the flames. The lieutenant's commission was a nice touch, but I had my doubts that I'd be commanding regular troops. The recruiting depot at Albany was a long way and a couple lifetimes ago. Why, in just three months I'd be eighteen. A few more years and they'd let me vote.

I bought a couple good remounts at Missoula and went up the Hellgate Road and cut down across the Great Divide at Monida Pass, and with the spares I was traveling fast, better than a hundred miles some days.

Washakie greeted me beaming and laughed about me and Jack and Plummer's gold. The old man had gone off against his old enemies, the Crows and Blackfeet, and had come back with a few scalps. Without me to gibber and faint he cut back his slaughters.

He'd been tending Eats-Men-Whole's bier, and the rawhide was fresh wrapped around the poles. A few tatters of the yellow silk scarf whipped in the wind.

I went on to Laramie the next morning, taking four days to get there, and wondering what in the name of God's Own Drawers I was going to be ordered to do when I got there. I hadn't any doubt that U. S. Grant meant every word he said. Hell, he could just ship me back to Utah, without horses, guns, and a head start I'd not last long.

The second packet told me to find Red Shirt—he was a warrior every bit as feared as Washakie, but young, with only a few dozen dead enemies to show. Washakie's thousands were trumps, no doubt.

Red Shirt's lodges were supposed to be clear up on the Bighorn, and any day they'd pack and go off toward the winter grounds on the Tongue.

It took me two weeks to find him. I was to talk with him about the Black Hills. The government was trying to avoid a war, especially with Red Cloud, who had run the army right out three times so far. Things had been peaceable other than the Fetterman massacre, and there was something prodding Uncle Sam to try to sweet-talk the Sioux and Cheyennes out of the Black Hills. The Pa Sapa, sacred ground, the Cathedral of the Sioux.

Gold. There was gold up there in the Black Hills and that one word could be whispered in the dead of night with a bad wind and ten thousand prospectors thousands of miles away would hear it by morning. They'd pour in in their thousands and then they would demand protection.

"So the Sioux should lie down in their graves now," I said, riding toward the Bighorn. Well, they'd be there soon and no mistake about it.

Red Shirt was the handsomest man I ever laid eyes on. He was the color of bronze, with broad shoulders and a small waist. His face was chiseled, and he had more laugh lines than anyone I ever saw but Washakie. He was a Santee Sioux, and their war leader even though he was barely thirty.

Red Shirt didn't like any of what he could see coming, but he was a dog soldier and couldn't run, even though he must have known that his time was going to be damn short.

The lot of soldiers isn't pleasant. You get to freeze, roast, or starve, and bleed and die for nothing. It don't matter if you're Red Cloud or Marechal MacMahon of France, the job's damned difficult.

Red Cloud had closed the Thieves' Road, had run the United States Army right out, and now the army had to come back because two drunken prospectors had found gold just under the grass roots, gold everywhere. Them two stumblebums signed the Plains tribes' death warrants. They probably couldn't even read.

Now, flannelmouthing is a gift I got, but I felt plumb inadequate to this task, of talking Red Cloud and Red Shirt and Crazy Horse into living on reservations and developing a taste for canned goods and an ear for the lower sort of preachers.

I liked Red Shirt. We rode side by side as the lodges went

north to the Tongue, and all Red Shirt knew was the sky and the grass and the water and the seasons and the buffalo. He'd been at Big Piney Creek, where he killed three soldiers and a man in dungarees—a few civilians went along to pot Injuns, to brag to the folks back home over—and he told me that when the Injuns split up to go off to their lodges for the winter, very few were going to brag on the victory.

The world seemed strange, Red Shirt said, it had turned and was no longer the world they had known. If a tribe had been as badly defeated as the bluecoat soldiers, it would be generations before they tried again.

But the whites didn't think that way. They'd be back, more and more of them until the tribes were massacred. Crazy Horse knew that. It was just that Red Cloud and Red Shirt and Crazy Horse were five thousand years out of fashion. Or whenever it was men began to plant grain and eat too much and stay in one place and invent slavery, cannon, and money.

"I don't understand what you do with gold," he said to me. "You cannot eat it or cure sickness with it or make useful things, you can only carry it from place to place. You whitemen are all crazed and lost. Your foolish prospectors cannot see the land they walk, our young men kill them with rocks. The miners act drunk when they have not had firewater in months, they stumble through the Sacred Hills and fall off rocks and die, they eat poison plants and go mad, they drink bad water, their clothes are thick with dirt. They hide from one another and all for something that they cannot use."

Well, I ain't never understood money either, come to think of it.

I suppose that I hoped that Spotted Tail could talk some sense into the Sioux—he *tried*, but they just couldn't see it. Not that anybody would be happy to lie down and die, or find it a good idea.

We was moving slow, north, and there had been skiffs of snow and the steel gray snow clouds grabbed the mountains close—it was deep winter up there already.

Good thing this particular chore had come to me, as it was to turn out. A couple of young braves come riding fast back down the trail and they said there was two wagons up ahead and whites in them. Just a driver for each was all they could see. Now if Red Shirt would just give the word, they'd go wipe them out.

"Making horrible noises, one in front," said the brave, "it hurts the ears."

A dim light come on somewheres in my mind.

"What kinda noises?" I says.

The driver was screeching and the thing he was beating on twanged like a bowstring, only higher and painful.

"Shit," I says, knowing just who was up a stump out there.

Moral dilemmas is horrible things. I wondered if I could live with having Klaas's tongue cut out and one or both of his hands cut off.

"These whites die," said Red Shirt. "They must know that is the fate of whites on this trail."

Klaas was a good friend and I thought maybe if I pleaded with Red Shirt I could get him and Mulebreath spared—I knew he was up ahead because of the fresh-broken whiskey bottle I had just passed. Jaysus Kay-rist.

Red Shirt shook his head. The braves went off and I thought that it meant they'd kill them two lunatics.

They didn't. Reason was an older man, called Water Prophet. He had rode up close and seen the mules clopping down the trail, Klaas bellering and plunking and Mulebreath in full Confederate uniform waving a saber and hollering at men who weren't there.

Folks we call primitive everywhere spare those obviously insane, so Klaas and Mulebreath was let be, protected even.

I cantered up ahead, passing a few naked birds likely knocked out of the sky by Vipsoek's blugerss, and I passed Mulebreath's wagon first. Mulebreath was leading Pickett's Charge again, I thought.

"Mulebreath!" I hollered. He looked at me bleared up.

"Kelly?" he says.

"Yes," I says.

"Well, goddamn," he says, falling off the far side of the wagon.

The screeching and twanging and pickled egg farts was a foul trail behind Klaas. My horse snorted and shied and shook his head. I come up on Klaas's blind side and after a moment I couldn't stand it no more so I reached over near him and fired my Colt about an inch from his right ear.

Klaas jumped about twenty feet straight up and lit yelling Dutchy curses. I watched happily as the iron-rimmed wheels of the wagon crushed the banjo. I even rode over and shot it so I could be sure that it's dead.

Klaas hauled back on the reins and stopped the mules. He was hopping mad, but the first thing he done is go back and see what was left of his deceased twangbox. He picked it up and waggled a finger through the hole I'd shot in the skin top.

"Shelly," Klaas snarled foamily. "You haff terrible idea of joke."

"Follow Me!" Mulebreath bellered, as his mules stopped and he fell hard on the wagon tongue.

We was distracted for a few moments pulling Mulebreath out from under some of his mules, who were trying hard not to step on him, but would pretty quick. We heaved him up into the wagon bed and I checked his pulse, which was slow, four or five a minute, but still there.

"Is it the catfish these Southern boys eat so much of does this to their minds?" I says, pointing with a shrug at the slumbering General Mulebreath in the wagon.

First I noticed a sign on the side of the wagon.

VIPSOEK & MUCKLEBREECH

PURVEYORS

OF

FINE

MUSICAL

INSTRUMENTS

Red Shirt had come up, and he was setting easy on his horse watching life unfold before him. I walked over to him and stood with my back to the wagons and Klaas.

"Kill them," I says. "Please."

"Can't," says Red Shirt. "Is that what you whites call singing?"

"No," I says.

I helped Klaas move Mulebreath's wagon off the trail and out of the way. And then Klaas's. They planned to go north and trade among the Injuns, said Klaas, which they could do with impunity now.

Red Shirt and I rode on. We talked of the coming council. Spotted Tail wanted full citizenship for his people and money for the land.

"What will we do with money?" says Red Shirt.

"Pay lawyers. That's what money is for," I says, and not joking.

"My people will vanish like grass before a fire," says Red Shirt. "I have nothing left to give them but hope."

He would fight.

I kept quiet, and wished I was somewheres else.

24

The Sioux on the Tongue was scattered up and down maybe fifteen miles of river. They'd made meat on the plains, and the drying racks were full and the caches packed and the last few berries gathered. There was plenty of saltweed for their horses, and cottonwoods to strip the bark from if the horses ran short of grass. The high hills cut that fierce north wind that could chill you to death in an hour if it was sixty below and the sun carried suns on its shoulders. Time of the sundogs, time of bitter cold. Hard country up there in Montana, hard country.

Spotted Tail stood beaming out in front of his lodge, all decked out in quilled white deerskins and beaded moccasins and eagle feathers and the only Royal Purple Hudson's Bay blanket I ever saw in all my life. He was a dude, that's for sure, looked good in his savage finery here and he'd look good in a stovepipe hat and tails years on when he wore them. (When he got into the tails he also discovered whorehouses and burlesque shows. He was the sort of charming scoundrel who made money only to spend it all on beautiful women. No fool he.)

(He was to die of ice cream, and that story is another time, but suffice it to say if he hadn't had a mouthful of fresh peach ice cream, and he hadn't been thinkin' so hard on the charms of Sally Parmenter, who was like a whole lot of fresh peach ice cream, he'd have minded things like the flash of a rifle shot from a nearby ridge. The second shot got him, and I'm sure he couldn't be bothered hearing the first, and, well, boys, there you have it, and us all.)

He nodded to Red Shirt, and he made a short welcoming speech, much of it praise for the child of his heart, Stands-in-the-Fire-and-Argues. He remarked on how I fucked turtles, I ate things a coyote would run from, I had amazing talents for treachery and cowardice and ingratitude, and so forth and so on and I will have to admit that no one who knows me well could find much fault with Spotted Tail's speech.

It is customary for the recipient of such an honor to respond gratefully, so I remarked upon how white his brains had bleached his deerskins, how swift he was to fly from enemies, how quick to toady up to anyone who could shoot, and how the scalps on his warpole was sent to him a dozen at a time from a wig factory in Cleveland.

I thanked him for having given me such a good seat at the Big Piney massacre, and though I saw many there I hadn't seen him. I finished off with a fond description of his little habits with ducks and groundhogs and all the civilized greetings out of the way we both turned to Red Shirt, who had been stifling his laughter with the back of both hands.

"Why don't you two get married?" says Shirt, taking the prize for most vicious undercut.

We went into Spotted Tail's lodge and et dog stew and cattails. He asked after Washakie and I said he was fine, for an old fart, but he needed more Blackfeet hearts to eat and a couple young men to torment with his infernal bloodlust.

Red Shirt told Spotted Tail of the two spirit-touched whites coming along, and he gave a pretty good imitation of Klaas singing blugerss, and plunking sounds.

"I know him," says Spotted Tail. "Is that really how the whites *sing*?"

"He was an opery star fore he fell on hard times," I says. "His partner was a hero in the Civil War. He was shot through the head six times at Kennesaw Mountain but the holes healed up and he's here now." I had just reduced everything south of the Mason-Dixon line, but not by much.

"My scouts say that the fat one's farts are simply awesome," says Spotted Tail.

"Nothing to them," I says. "When he's serious all the skunks sue for peace."

I was dead tired for some reason and half loopy and Spotted Tail, ever the gracious host, offered me a pile of robes in his lodge and only offered threats of mutilation and death as a hostly entreaty to stay a while.

The lodge was warm and I slipped my boots off and slept hard.

Spotted Tail woke me after a while, and he sat crosslegged and tucked his chin into his hand.

"What do we do?" he says. "The Teton, the Brulé, the Santee, the Hidatsa, the Oglala? The Cheyenne and Kiowa?"

I could tell him if he'd listen, for Spotted Tail, though no saint, had a broader mind than any other Sioux.

"You got to do it quick. There's rumors of gold in the Black Hills. You and Red Cloud and Red Shirt and Crazy Horse need to make peace and demand full citizenship and much of the gold. And do it now. Do it tomorrow."

"I know all of this, Kelly," he says. "Try and explain that to my people, who have no written language and who obey the words of their fathers. Our land is alive, our mother, when we walk upon her we do so gently for we can feel her skin and breath. Your white laws change with the winds. Name me a tribe that has prospered under white rule. The Cherokees? The Iroquois? Is there a mention anywhere of even the name of the tribe that greeted Columbus?"

"Then nearly all of you will be killed."

"Better than starving to death on a broken land and listening to sermons."

Well, he had a point. The young men wanted war. They always do. Go to Arlington, look at the tombstones. Eighteen, most of 'em.

In the morning quite early I got up and went to the Tongue to wash. The water's sweet and the grass is thicker there than other places. Soon the lodges would be bermed with snow and the gambling and the stick games—storytelling games, really—would go all winter. The little children would wrestle in the lodges and the old men would tell stories and brag some and the old women would tell stories on the old men and it warn't a bad sort of life, one that wouldn't last much longer.

I walked to windward of the camp and blenched at a faint sauerkraut-and-rotten-egg stench on the wind. That could only mean that Klaas and Mulebreath were drawing nigh. It would be so like Klaas to search among the savages for converts to his twanging and screeching.

There was a hooting mob of young braves riding around the two wagons, and behind them were four fellers trussed up and hung over their horses. Klaas and Mulebreath were safe—if they just did as they were accustomed to they would excite only pity for their insanity among the savages.

"Four missionaries," says Spotted Tail at my elbow. "Mormons. So I give you a gift. You figure out a torment for them and if it is good we will not treat them as we usually do."

He meant skinned alive and slow-roasted.

Red Cloud come along behind the young braves. At a hand signal from Red Cloud the four were jerked off their horses and then hung from the limbs of a nearby cottonwood.

"Council time," says Spotted Tail. "Leave them hang for now."

There were so many there that the council had to be held outside, no lodge was big enough to hold them all. And it went fast for an Indian council, the chilly wind helped it along.

Red Cloud was the most imposing figure I have ever seen. If he walked into a roomful of drunks they'd be sober in three minutes. He stood with his sons behind him all in red blankets. He got his name because when his warriors rode behind him, they looked like a red cloud.

There was Touch-the-Clouds, a seven-foot Teton Sioux—that's seven feet before the eagle-feather headdress, mind you—and Little Big Man—who weighed a hundred pounds without his collection of scalps, two hundred with. Crow Killer, Magpie, Many Snows, Crazy Horse, Gall, Rain-in-the-Face, and many dog soldiers, who would not retreat. They fought tethered to a stake, and they could not leave off fighting until another dog soldier had pulled the stake up.

There was about four hours of flowery speeches and a ruck of chest-beating and brave boasts. Spotted Tail spoke for an hour, telling them to take the whiteman's road and sell the land for money, not for blood.

If that damned idiot Fetterman had known his business and done his job they wouldn't have had so much hope. Wiping out eighty stupidly led troopers and casuals was a mite different from fighting Little Phil Sheridan, who killed everyone, because he liked problems solved up good and no relapsing.

Klaas had come up and we stood well away from the circle, and when Little Big Man spoke he thought all whites should be killed, beginning with the seven in camp. It was a nice, easy, conservative policy but I still didn't like it.

He was downwind of Klaas and it may have made him tetchy, I allowed to Klaas, who grinned at me with his pale blue store-bought teeth.

A warrior I didn't know was reciting his genealogy, and so I turned to Klaas and answered a few of his questions about the council and what was to become of the missionaries. I explained I had to come up with something original or they'd be skinned.

"Mormons," said Klaas, lisping a little. "Vy not sent letter to Brigham Young?"

"A letter?"

"Sureness," said Klaas. "I am yalso tattoo artist."

Klaas was always good in a pinch, I'll say that for him.

Mulebreath announced that he had woke up by giving off a loud rebel yell and poking the saber through the canvas top of the wagon.

"Ze south risess," said Klaas. "I hope he won't start shooting at our hosts, here."

We run like deer to the wagon and pounced on Mule-breath, who had got down with a buffalo rifle he'd managed to fit a bayonet on.

Mulebreath fought us off pretty good till he lunged at me with the bayonet and managed to get it buried in a water barrel that hung on the side of the wagon. Unarmed for a moment, the Great Confederate Hope was treacherously beset by his friends, one of whom cracked him on the head with a Colt, and the other sat on him. Mulebreath's speech got fainter and fainter, on account of he couldn't breathe.

We trussed him up good and put him in the wagon, not forgetting to gag him good, too. Fine he wanted to insult the damn Yankees, not fine if he should wake up knowing exactly where he was. Spotted Tail, for one, could savvy English.

"You got your tattoo implements here?" I says. "Not much of a market, is there?"

"Alvayss carry my tattoo things," says Klaas. "Can't leave them to happy home. Wife hates that I even *retired* tattoo artust."

"Why was she stupid enough to marry you?" I says.

"Good qvestunn," says Klaas. "Potherss me lot."

Red Cloud had called for me, and I explained that these here missionaries was no worse than a mild case of ringworm. If they was properly treated, they'd go back to their hive and bother the Sioux no more.

Red Cloud nodded.

The warriors pegged the missionaries out, face down on the prairie, and I had Klaas tattoo Scripture, a mite altered, and what I remembered of my theological discussion with Elder McMullin. The very best things I thought of gave Klaas the laughing fits and caused the wobbling of his tattoo arm.

When their back parts was all covered we turned them over and Klaas scribbled all over their fronts.

Then we tied them on their horses facing backwards, and sent them south.

I wouldn't dream of telling you what I had Klaas write, as

my family already blames that Luther for encouraging poor behavior in my nephews and nieces and all. I'm fifteen hundred miles away, I didn't know that my voiced carried that far.

As they was leaving—two young warriors was to dump them at the closest trading station—the ungrateful bastards said horrible things to me, not one word of thanks, after I saved their lives. Just human nature, I suppose. (Had to do the same to some Baptists, which left the Sioux to the Catholics and Episcopalians, but at least they wash.)

A party of twenty Teton Sioux showed up, with two dozen fresh scalps. They were killing every prospector that they could find.

The exercise might have been good for them, but the matter of keeping the whites out wouldn't be that easy. The Injuns I knew then hadn't numbers big enough to count the whites, and they couldn't see what was coming. How were they to know? They'd won a cheap, easy victory over Fetterman. So that is how it was supposed to be.

They were my friends, and I was to help hunt them down and stick them on the reservations, and if you'd seen what I was to see later, you'd have done so, too.

Klaas and Mulebreath and me wandered down to the Canadian River country. There we saw hundreds of thousands of buffalo carcases left to rot, and at one rail siding we saw piles of hides stacked to thirty feet, and the pile was a mile long.

I had come out here not long since, and I knew that the time for this land to be what it was hadn't much sand left to run. It was going quick as the blood of the buffalo.

I wanted to see as much of it as was left before the land was all over red and the flies was breeding.

25

I like hunting, mind you, but this slaughter was a bit rich even for someone as bloodthirsty as I am. Oh, you hear these days about the slaughter of the buffalo was done to open up the plains to the plow. That may be, but it was also to starve the Injuns out and force them to the reservations. And it warn't just the buffalo. There was government money for deer and elk ears, and furs, and a buffalo hunter, after he'd shot all his skinners could manage, would shoot any other walking food.

The government paid inflated prices for furs—the Hudson's Bay Company was eager to trade guns and ammunition straight over for furs, long as the guns wasn't used on Canadian Territory.

The buffalo was shot in the winter, for the best fur on their robes. A hunter would set up on a high place and lung-shoot the animals. They just bled to death inside and they'd wander around for an hour or two before quietly lying down. After the hunter had killed as many as he could, the skinners would come in and jerk the hides off, using teamed horses. They'd cut out the tongues and pickle them.

After a number of articles in homemaker's magazines, the fine old American custom of a buffalo roast at Christmas was started. It was also a fine old American tradition at Easter, New Year's, and Aunt Grizelda's wake.

The hunters started first off down in the Canadian River

country, now the Indian Territory, and they worked north from there. There was three great herds—Canadian River, Central, and Yellowstone.

There was a fourth herd up in Canada that the Canadians was killing off even faster than us, to make Canada unattractive to Red Cloud, Crazy Horse, Gall, Rain-in-the-Face, or any other war leaders.

We wagoned past stands where hunters had set and shot up to three hundred buffalo from a single place. We were in Kansas now.

I'd seen Buffalo Bill Cody once before, when he was with that idiot Custer, who had shot his wife's mare while chasing buffalo. But we didn't have words. I thought Bill had been embarrassed by the company he was keeping.

This time it was in a little Kansas town name of Larned. Bill was hoot-owl drunk and riding a stump that some kind soul had put a saddle on. The stump was unlikely to throw him or step on him.

A good barkeep does that, and the barkeep at the Mint Saloon was a princely good barkeep. If a drunk got to clacking his knees together or he dropped his eyeballs in the dice cup, the barkeep would walk him out back to a good-sized shed and tie one of the drunk's feet up to an eyebolt three feet up from the floor. This kept the drunk safe until he come out from under enough to reach up and untie the knot. The shed's floor was covered in sawdust, which soaked up the puke. Damn classy place, you ask me.

I inquired of the barkeep as to who the drunk in the quilled and beaded, bright blue fringed leather coat was. Why, the barkeep says, that's Buffalo Bill Cody, and I think he's about ready for the shed.

Bill had come up in the world, largely due to the efforts of a sawed-off teetotaling scribbler name of Ned Buntline. Oh, Cody was brave as hell—he literally had no fear bones—and Cody was trustworthy, brave, honorable, and a crack shot and horseman. (If you're planning to have a war, Indian or otherwise, you need a treacherous, greedy, conniving, unprincipled swine like . . . . . . uh . . . . . . Luther Kelly, war is a serious business. In theater, Bill shone, and he was to make many people wealthy. Bill hated money; he could go through it like crap through a goose.)

Klaas and Mulebreath about beat each other to pieces getting through the doorway and they was soon drinking redeye by the quart and grazing on the free lunch. Klaas had put a hundred dollars in gold on the bartop, and he and Mulebreath was determined to spend it all right here.

It weren't long 'fore Klaas had powerfully defeated his thirst. He tried to clamber on to a poker table to deliver a speech and the table done collapsed into matchsticks. I helped the barkeep haze the Dutch rummy out to the shed, and soon Klaas was snoring peacefully, one fat Dutch foot hitched up to a ringbolt. And pissing in them green-and-white-checked pants that he likely stripped off a dead drummer.

Mulebreath had drunk enough so he decided to fight the War all over again, and the barkeep stood fast in front of Mulebreath's charge, and cracked him a good one with a leaded pool cue.

I took this heaven-sent opportunity to rifle the wagons and ship the banjos East to a music store in Cleveland. (After all these years, I sort of wonder where they ended up.)

A pair of teamsters took my gold and the banjos and I never saw any of 'em again. I was planning on tying a good one on and I was afraid that if I was suffering lots and hangover'd half to death I'd commit murder if Klaas started in on his infernal blugerss.

All this accomplished, I attacked the Sinner's Cider with glee, and sometime the next day, or the one after that, I was escorted to the Hitchfoot Hotel. Klaas, moaning and snuffling, had at last managed to untie his foot. He crawled off in search of healing potions, at leastways that's what I think happened, and I awoke in ten or twelve hours feeling that I had been dancing with a train, and that I had dined in the sewers of hell.

My right big toe was swollen and throbbing—my boots had gone missing—and here I had my first full-fledged attack of gout.

(Perhaps this was the cause of my further misfortunes with Ned Buntline, who I hated on sight.)

Buntline had run on to Buffalo Bill some months before and he was busily churning out reams of abominable tripe just as fast as his pencil could scritch.

Bill and I met whilst puking into the sawdust in the Hitchfoot Hotel and never you mind the legends. It ain't as Buntline has it. Listen and I'll tell you how it was.

Buntline would scribble something like "Buffalo Bill pulled his steely gaze away from his rifle sights and pondered the dark gentleman [me?!] to his left who had just killed fifty-three Sioux with seventeen shots and was presently reading Keats to his horse. 'Pardner,' said Bill, offering his hand, 'you must be the famous Yellowstone Kelly. No one else I hear of reads Keats to his horse.' BLAM. Another forty-three savages fall whilst Bill is composing a sonnet to his lady."

This is how it really was when we first met, formal-like:

"Uuuuuuuuuuuuuuuugggeeeeeeeeeeeeglurb glurg Oooo," says Bill, through the foamy stream of bile he was a-pukin' into the sawdust, and some on a couple fellers who was out cold yet.

We moaned and puked and struggled with the knots so we could get back to the saloon. Every hair on my head hurt, and so did my teeth, all of which seemed to be growing pelts.

"Pass me the bucket," says Bill. "I think I'll have an attack of the thundering drizzlies now." Which he did.

"I can't remember when I've had such fun," I says. "Musta been the church apple-bob."

"Godfuckingdammit my guts is on fire," says Bill, which is a long way from Keats. "I believe I shall bob for such of my innards as came up in the last toss," he says, contemplating the puddle in front of him. "Why, I do believe there is a kidney rising up and sinking down there. Look!"

"Lord, hell of a stomach I got—I don't think anybody has thrown anything that far, ever. Maybe I can get a job in the circus. Moan."

We went on in this cheery vein for a while, for what can

you do but laugh. Brains combined, we had no trouble getting each other untied. We leaned against each other and sort of tacked and yawed back to the saloon. We tilted one against another like a couple of hairy deadfalls and after waving one or another appendage Sam the barkeep come cheerily down, looking at us like we sashayed in stuck to someone's shoe.

"We have returned," says Bill. "Looking and feeling our very best."

Sam nodded and served us each a big glass full of fresh oysters, hot sauce, gin, and three or four more soothing ingredients.

"Congratulations fer gettin' the knots undone," says Sam. "Now get these down and we'll see about a real drink.

"If ya got to puke, do it in them spittoons," he went on. "I gets annoyed ya puke on my bar. I hang ya all the way in the air overnight if ya do that."

Sam run a no-nonsense joint and that was that. We gurgled and swallered and the sweat run in rivulets off us from the hot sauce and we gripped the bar hard as we could to keep the room from dancing around.

A sawed-off weasel with a pad and pencil slithered up, and he made an infernal racket with his scribbling. Scritch scritch and so forth. I had grabbed an empty whiskey bottle by the neck and I was praying for the strength to brain him with it, but it looked to be a bust cause.

"Ned Buntline," he says, offering a paw.

I reeled off a string of curses would have paled Calamity Jane, and Calamity could outcuss Sherman.

Critch scritch scritch critch.

There was a mighty farting and belching and stench and the liquid sound of Dutchy moanings crawling over store-bought teeth. Klaas had arrived again.

"Kelly," he said, "you no-good sonbitch, vott you do mit banjos?"

"Nothing," I says. "I've been in the Hitchfoot Hotel there."

Klaas looked at me blearily for a while, then he signaled to

Sam, who brought him a fiery oyster special. Klaas drank it down and seemed to glow with health all of a sudden.

"I buy drinks!" he said.

"Could you please kill him," I says, pointing a feeble finger at Buntline.

Buntline went on scribbing.

"The two scouts, recognizing each other as noble Christian gentlemen, paused in their slaughter of the howling savages . . ." Buntline read from his pad.

"KILL HIM!" screams Cody and me.

Klaas picked up the malevolent little dwarf and carried him to a window over the slops pit. We heard a wail and a splash.

By and by, as we recovered, we thought we might cut our losses and so we took the wagons—Mulebreath was damn near dead in the back of one—and we left town to heal up at a quiet spring. Bill and I had only a fair hangover and Mulebreath could walk to town if he'd a mind to. I soothed my gouty toe in the spring. We had the blind staggers. My brain felt like it was crawling with fleas, and Bill held long conversations with something green and scaly and had purple teeth and was after him for money.

My toe hurt too bad to bother much with whiskey visions.

The third day we was there a godawful stink of decay come up the wind and a line of skinner's wagons come into view, all piled high with hides. The skinners was coated and crusted with blood, everything dark brown and stinking, everything, clothes and hair and beards. They lived in clouds of flies, though it was late enough to trim them down some.

The horses pulling the wagons shied and fought, wild from the stink of blood.

There must have been a hundred wagons, and the skinners was drinking from stoneware jugs, which they mostly did all of the time. Being drunk, they could mostly stand the life. The skinners was men with poor eyesight. The hunters, who had good eyesight, made the money, and the skinners died of skin infections for three dollars a day and bacon and beans.

A few skinners a little cleaner than the others was riding

out to the sides to look for Injuns. I saw one high up on a ridge, just setting on his horse, against a lowering mackerel sky. I wondered if the Injun knew that what he was seeing before him was the death of his people, in those stacks of hides and gouts of blood from the mouths of lungshot buffalo. Like the tale of the apprentice sorcerer spills the potion on the grass, which turns black and curling, dies, and the stain spreads faster and faster, and it was too late with the first drop to stop it.

26

oys will be boys and Bill was a boy all of his life, as open and honest as the morning sun, and plain damned dumb about all of the crooks that would hang off him like ticks all his life. Buntline made Bill famous, and Buntline got rich off Bill, and Bill spent his money on beautiful women, whiskey, cards, and his friends. Not a bad life, now is it?

Bill was making good money, a few hundred a day when he was working, which consisted of carrying a sixteen-pound .45–120 and a bipod to a hilltop and shredding buffalo lungs with it. He left the hard work to his skinners, but he was a most generous employer, giving them whiskey in addition to bacon and beans. He even bought them coffee.

Buntline was pretty indestructible, his hungry sense of how much he could make off of Bill holding him close, even though Bill and I played an endless succession of practical jokes on him, jokes designed to maim or to kill. (I cannot forgive him for marking me as "Yellowstone" Kelly. It's annoying to get a nickname that sticks like paint on you.)

I tried the buffalo hunting trade but didn't take to it much, as I didn't need the money that bad and the Injuns was tumbling to what the buffalo hunters were doing to their way of life, and what they did to buffalo hunters they captured would make your hair stand on end.

I shot buffalo till March of '69 and then I sold my traps and recommended my skinners highly to the next set of clumsy butchers who wanted to get rich killing critters that wouldn't even run. I ain't making a case for how fine a feller I am, I'd have gone on if I needed the gold.

Klaas had gone off to St. Louis with a hot notion of setting up a medicine show, which he did mostly, I think, to have an excuse to play his damned banjo.

He thought a life peddling Chief Mushbutt Stump Water, a fine formula he had come by in a poker game, was the finest sort of life. I told him I hoped that the stump water would cure the rolling fits caused by his infernal blugerss music. I further hoped that his flatulence would be much reduced.

"You havff poor tastes," says Klaas, shaking his head as though he'd just gotten a fatal diagnosis.

"I like 'em and I think I'll keep 'em," I says.

April come and the grass greened up, so I said tall grass and deep watering holes to Bill and such friends as I'd made. At the Hitchfoot Hotel and better establishments. I purchased at great expense several ounces of fleas and bedbugs and I sprinkled them around Buntline's room. I had hoped he'd be bit so bad and itch so much his scratchings would bleed him to death. All them fellow bloodsucking parasites went off to chew on everybody else, leaving Buntline alone as a professional courtesy.

I'd had it worse than usual with the gout and such from the farewell party Bill throwed me—it lasted three days and resulted in two deaths, one accidental and the other more or less. The dead fellers had gone up on the roofs to sing, and one was drunk and clumsy and fell off the rooftree headfirst onto a pile of dressed stone, and the other was some mistook for a lovesick tomcat and blowed near in half by a feller nursing the whips and the staggers.

I headed north, queasy at the movement of my horse and near worried to a frazzle about catching the clap or the syph from the whores—you know how it is when you're drunk and reckless—and my throbbing big toe kept me from thinking of anything else, mostly. By the time I had crossed the Niobara and the Platte some days later I was eating good and hardly shaking and twitching at all and there was no untoward burnings down there when I drained my tanks.

What was on my mind was the Big Dry, the country to the east of the Judith Basin, up in Montana Territory, between the Yellowstone and the Missouri. I'd heard from Bridger that even the trappers hadn't gone there—too dry—and the mountain ranges were like islands, unconnected bunches of mountains, not all stuck together like the Rockies. Out east was the Badlands, the Mal Pais, and the Black Hills the Plains tribes were going to die for. The badlands was shaped by the wind, not by water, and ghosts sang and danced in the night.

There might be an abandoned city or castle, no one knew. So I aimed to go through and find what there was there.

I made for Billings, one of the major ports of trade, where the shallow-draft steamboats transferred their cargo to bigger steamers for the run down to St. Louis. From Billings I thought I'd head down the north bank of the Yellowstone till I come to a good place to cut upcountry. I figured it would be quiet there and I could damn sure lose myself there, and I needed quiet and a place to get lost in.

The tale I will now tell you is true, as incredible as it seems, and will perhaps point out why I am not overfond of governments. Or them as runs them.

I bought four mules in Billings, big matched cream-colored bastards out of Thoroughbred mares and the tack for them and two mule-loads of canned delicacies, and in mid-May I paid off a ferryman to haul me and my gear across the Yellowstone. I packed up and led the four-mule string north and east, to what I did not know.

My God, what a country, where rising plains stretched for sixty miles any way you cared to look and the coulees and cutbanks was pale yellow, red, and chocolate and the sage fairly made soup of the air. I feasted on antelope ribs and such canned goods as suited me. I found sweet water by looking for Injun plum trees, easy to see because their leaves was two-toned and lightly hung and they flashed and shimmered like nothing else and could be seen at ten miles. The air was so clear that I swear I saw colors for the first time, all the usual tints, shades, and tones, but more so. No sign of another human being. I should have stayed there.

One night I come to a good place to camp particularly late, and I unrolled my blankets hard by a short cliff no more than fifty feet high. It had a little spring of water coming out on one side and the smell of wild strawberries all round it. The cliff looked a little odd even in the pale starlight, and I was tired and slept soon after a cold supper. A coyote opera went on just long enough to send me to sleep. I am fond of the coyotes, you see, they share many character traits with me, and though I can't sing a note I wish I could every time I hear them.

The morning sun come up on me and I squinted out and went back to sleep and dreamed of monsters charging out of a cliff wall and it woke me up and by God, they were there. There was two heads sticking out of the cliff face, huge horrible things all gone to minerals, but they had once walked the earth.

They were about six feet across, these heads, with a bony flaring helmet in back and three good-sized horns a foot thick at the base. They had horny, lizard-looking mouths and their jaws was set open, and supported by limestone columns that had been protected by the fossils above.

For a moment I wondered if these damn things was still around, before deciding that if they were they'd have run everything else out long since and pretty well own the damn continent. A quick figuring told me a buffalo with a head that big would be fifteen feet high at the shoulder and a couple of dozen feet long. My .45–120 would mean no more to this beast than a gnat's bite to a man.

The countryside was full of such marvels. I found a shoulder blade off something that was nine feet by five—a man's is the size of his hand, and also a lot of shark's teeth, perfect triangles about a foot on each side.

Strange country, it was. Quiet during the early part of the day, nothing but the dust, the hoof sounds, the jingle and creak of tack, wind in the afternoon, thundershowers before sunset, and then at night the tortured hills and cliffs gave off weird music, moans and cries and shrieks that made the mules jittery and me pretty spooked, too. I didn't believe in ghosts, but out there it pretty much stood to reason.

By and by I came over a divide so scant I didn't even notice it and the streams, such as they were, began to head north. I went up the easiest route, toward the breaks of the Missouri. The big river pooled some here and I could see where it had wandered over the land. What pushed the river is a mystery to me—there weren't any mountains hemming it in.

From a clifftop maybe two hundred feet above the brown water I watched many steamboats going up and going down. Upstream they was hauling miners and supplies. Downstream they hauled those who had gone broke or struck it rich or the coffins of those who had enough money in their pockets to be pickled and sent back to where they'd come from. Damn lonely country here to be buried in, if you believe all that Christer claptrap about Judgment Day and the resurrection of the dead, you'd suspect this country was forgotten even by God. No one would recall to blow the trumpet here.

There was Injuns to the south, east, and north, and I had had a bellyful of the wars. I hoped for nothing more than maybe finding an island range and maybe wintering over in it, far away from the army and Injuns, living simply and peaceably in a range of mountains no one much wanted.

These pleasant reveries was all sort of stumbling through my mind and the steamboats was whistling jolly tunes below, and all of a sudden the mules gave off bellers and run right off the cliff. I looked back and thought for about half a second, and I went over, too.

A huge pale river-bottom grizzly was coming at a dead run. I had a glimpse of an arrow buried in his hindquarter. I scrambled down the cliff, which was a soft sandy thing, more like earth than rock, and I grabbed a handy cedar about three feet long and hung on.

The bear was stymied—my horse and the mules was dead a couple hundred feet below. The bear kept taking swipes at me and damn near did knock me off with showers of small rocks he dislodged time to time.

I clambered up to sit on the cedar, which obligingly started making cracking noises, and it bent down just enough to scare me good and then quit. I could see below me and it was sheer, right down to the sausage meat that used to be my horse and mules. I couldn't recall when I'd last been so happy.

My remarks on this subject scorched and blackened all about me for fifteen feet. The bear joined in the chorus.

Someone was loudly bellering from a steamboat below. When the bear went off for a moment I could hear, faint and far off below me, the stentorian pipes of Lt. Gustavus Cheney Doane, USA.

I thought I'd best jump.

"We'll save you," hollers Gus.

Certain death, I thinks, so why jump?

Seems that Gus had been buying them fancy books with the engravings of insane Swiss climbing up rock faces with tent pegs and rope and had talked someone in the government into outfitting him with all sorts of expensive mountain-climbing gear, so Gus could do what Gus does best, busting the various parts of Doane but nothing fatal, goddamn it.

In jig time a boat was lowered—all of a foot and a half, these steamboats didn't run to freeboard much—and Gus and three stout lads rowed over to the cliff face and they scrambled up to maybe fifty feet below me, where the cliff turned sheer.

Gus commenced hammering tent pegs into cracks and come up maybe halfway to me when the slab he'd loosened with his hammering fell off and damn near killed his troopers before landing square on the boat, which went to matchwood instantly.

The river belched and gurgled appreciatively, and soon all the foam was gone, too.

"How can I ever thank you enough?" I says to Gus.

"I was looking for you as a matter of fact," says Gus. "I have a major's commission for you."

"A WHAT?"

"You have your choice," says Gus, "either accept the

commission or I hang you for desertion. U. S. Grant himself ordered me to find you and present you with your choice. He has a task someone like you can do."

I began to beller out patriotic hymns somewhat altered for the occasion, and then I commenced on Grant's family tree.

"Now if you'll excuse me," I says, "I'm going to go and commit suicide."

"You can't commit suicide," says Gus. "It's a violation of regulations."

"Oh, I think I'll just jump," I says. "Save us both a lot of trouble and inconvenience. But before I die why would good old Unconditional Surrender make me a major while cruelly leaving you a mere lieutenant?"

"It's a long story," says Gus.

So far I thought the whole business was funny.

The steamboat captain come backing and pulling his boat near on to the cliff, and a couple of deckhands leaped out and made the boat fast. There was no current to speak of here and the boat come so close to the cliff it must be sheer below the waterline, too.

Gus and I sat up there chattering for two or three hours until some soldiers appeared on the cliff above me and they tossed down a line and hauled me up. Gus was still high and dry and if I still had my horse I would have made my escape and to hell with U. S. Grant. Finally the steamboat captain pieced together a ladder (over my heated protests) and Gus clambered down to safety, too damn spry for my comfort.

Gus took me to what passed as his stateroom, which stank of sprouted grain and old salt pork, and he handed me my commission and my death warrant before allowing me to burn both of them in the brazier.

Seemed that the Sioux was raising hell and Grant wanted some of them to come to Washington and parley. Kelly, who was well known for surviving encounters with the Sioux in most improbably curious circumstances, was to carry the message. The last three messengers had been skinned, no doubt alive, and the hides returned with rude messages on them in Sioux pictograms and English and French. The hides all more or less told Grant to put them where the sun don't shine.

"Red Cloud is up toward Canada," says Gus.

"Why the major's commission?" I asked, not thinking I'd get an answer.

"I have never really understood the army," says Gus, "but here it is with all pay and rank long as you don't mention them."

"No one would believe me," I says.

"There's something else," says Gus, "and it is so strange you may think that I am joking. I'm not. This order simply cannot be written. We have found where John Wilkes Booth is hiding, up in Canada. You are to go there and kill him."

"Ah, Gus," I says, "I am truly sorry that such a fine officer as yourself has taken up smoking opium in large quantities. Why don't you have some more and we'll say no more about it."

"Kelly," says Gus, whipping out his Colt and tapping me on the temple with it, "I am authorized to shoot you if you won't do as Grant requests. And I will."

Damn, that was a persuasive argument.

"John Wilkes Booth is as good as dead," I says. I had got the notion that it would be one or the other of us, and that kind of arithmetic.

"So where the hell is John Wilkes Booth," I says.

"In Canada, working as a storekeep on the Belly River."

"Do the Canadians know this?"

"Of course," says Gus.

"I see," I says.

"No, I don't think that you do," says Gus. "But Grant does and the Canadians do, and we very much need Booth removed."

"What possible use can the damned Canadians have for John Wilkes Booth?" I snarled. I was confused and that always makes me angry.

"Guano," says Gus. "Bird shit to you."

"Of course," says I. "I knew we were headed for guano all along, knew it deep in my soul."

"If you kill Booth, we can tell you the rest of the story," says Gus.

"I don't want to know the rest of the story," I says.

"Good," says Gustavus Cheney Doane, Lieutenant, United States Army.

27

Any lingering suspicions I had about being in a madhouse flew off during the next three days. I thought at least one telegram of inquiry was in order. Maybe Gus had been grazing overmuch in the locoweed, maybe he was an opium addict. So I sent a telegram to U. S. Grant.

Telegram: ARE YOU OUT OF YOUR MIND?   LUTHER KELLY

Telegram: YES.   UTAH.   BEST USG

Telegram: HOW DO I KNOW ITS YOU?   LUTHER KELLY

Telegram: TRUST ME.   USG

I had always wanted to see Canada and I just enjoyed the hell out of being the national shuttlecock and being hung in Utah is considered a better fate than having to live there. There was something awesome in the casual way the President had gone and set ol' Luther up. I had no doubts about him being quite ready and able to have me hung.

It sounded like him. Grant never gave back an inch of territory once he had it. I believed him, yes I did.

My view was reinforced by the sudden arrival of William

Tecumseh Sherman, who stepped off a steam packet, marched up to the saloon where I was oiling my tonsils, and kicked my arse into the street and down to his stateroom to check on his soldier and to look me up and down like a prize hog before bracing me good and having me recite my orders.

"I will hang you," says Sherman, "with great pleasure. Do not fail us. If you bugger this up, your best bet is to head north and live out your days with the Eskimos."

Then he frog-marched me out and kicked me down the gangplank. There was a grizzled old sodden loafer who looked at this little drama and said, "It were the General Sherman."

"I know," I says, picking myself up out of the mud.

I tracked down Gus Doane and whined at him for a while and he offered the peculiar comfort that perhaps it was all for the best; no one could quite figure out whether to shoot me or hang me and this venture seemed to be a guarantee of one or both.

Full of the sorrows and a lot of old Tanglefoot I commenced into riding north, with no clear idea where I would be going. I was soon out of range of the army patrols watching the trails, up in the last great hunting ground pretty much untouched by the whites. There was deer thick in the coulees and buffalo and antelope on the plains, flights of ducks and geese numbering in the thousands. I could collect all the sage hens I could eat for a month with an hour's work with a throwing stick, and the plovers covered the ground in packs. Them plovers was wonderful eating, they are all gone now, not one survived. The sandhill cranes was a treat, stuffed with the wild rice that grows along the little streams.

John Wilkes Booth or whoever seemed an easier task than the Sioux or Cheyenne nations, so I elected to swing up north toward the little crossroads where Booth was thought to be storekeeping at.

I had some real qualms about just going up and shooting a citizen of Canada. It was a lot tougher job up there as the Mounted Police was a dedicated lot and they never give up. Down here in America the law usually gave up half a day's ride from the closest saloon.

(Americans don't hold grudges like them damned Canucks. They still holler for my head on a quarterly basis.)

There ain't no markers on the border between Canada and the United States, and just when I crossed over I'll never know, but the rolling plains of Alberta was just like northern Montana. The grass waved like a sea and brushed my horse's shoulders, there was the same wandering buffalo trails—cut through the grass on a zigzag, hundred yards to the left, hundred yards to the right.

I made camp and got to bed early and woke up at a noise and I grabbed for my rifle and had it trained on Liver-Eatin' Jack's heart. He had snuck up on me and dropped a large fishbowl on the rock nearest my head.

"Mornin'," says Jack. "You ain't no better at stayin' alive; try as I did to make you learn you just won't do it."

I put down the rifle and propped myself up on one elbow and commenced dusting the shards out of my hair. I invited Jack to go breakfast on himself. I put my head in my hands and moaned. Not only was I on this murderous fool's errand, I was going to be watched every inch of the way. I couldn't run nor hide nor fight fair.

"Washakie sends his best and wanted me to tell you that both his wives is pregnant," says Jack.

"He got any idea who the father is?" I snarled.

"Washakie don't care," says Jack. "After all, the children is the point. Hell, he even likes *you!*"

I sighed. Well, what the hell.

"This Booth feller," says Jack, "he ain't going to be like you think."

"I don't got to think on him," I says. "I just got to kill him quietlike. I don't understand any of this."

I wondered suddenly why Jack knew any of this. He read the question in my face.

He just shook his head and looked toward the far horizon.

"Time I think it'll quiet down along comes somethin' worse'n ever."

It occurred to me that I didn't even know who Jack was, or

what he'd been before the mountains got him. It also occurred to me that the reason Jack wasn't to kill Booth was if something went wrong it would be hard to sweep a seven-foot-two five-hundred-pound carcase under the rug. There wouldn't be too many could fit Jack's description. There were a lot of folks who could easy fit mine. Well, boys, there you have it.

I packed up and we moved north. After a little sleep we went on in darkness. The Cree could read our sign, and the Chippewa, too, but with Jack's draft horse and my two geldings, we could easy be one of the Metis going back to a homestead. (The Metis was half Injun, half French and they used carts to haul in. They was all Catholic, sort of.)

We backed and filled for a day near the trading post Booth was supposed to be working at. I went on in that evening, and the gent behind the counter matched the picture I'd been given, and he limped on the broken ankle he'd got jumping from Lincoln's theater box to the stage.

What happened next? Well, by God, Booth was syphilitic. The syph had got to the stage where it was eating his brain and he twitched and staggered and hopped and drooled. He had a couple of retired soldiers to watch him. Her Majesty's government was keeping its hands clean by letting the syph kill him, whereupon he would be dissected and pickled along with the sixteen pages of Stanton's diary. All placed along with other such relics of empire in a special room at Westminster.

I tucked my possibles in a saddlebag and rode back to where Jack was keeping himself.

"Why in the hell didn't they just send you?" I says.

"I'm mortal tired of this kind of work, Luther," says Jack, "I won't do it anymore, so I had to find a replacement. That's you."

"Do I have to kill the guards, too?" I asked, knowing the answer.

Jack nodded.

"What if I don't? What if I just say no. Ride south," I snarled. "Refuse to be dragooned into this."

In a second Jack's Green River knife was at my throat.

"All you had to do was ask," I says, more cheery than I felt.

"I'm askin'," says Jack. "You got a real talent for this work. I seen it, and so did Washakie. A real talent."

"Can't be no favor," says Jack. "Yore pecker is in Ulysses's pocket and no two ways about it. Sentiment is noble but hangin' is sure."

"How'd you get into this?" I asked.

"Volunteered," says Jack.

"Volunteered like me?"

Jack looked even more mournful. "No," he says finally, "I ain't as smart as you, Luther. I offered. You'll be better at it than me. You say you don't believe in nothin', but you do. Don't matter anyway, boy, you been chose."

So that night I did in the guards, easy work, the trading post was well out of the way and over the months they'd got slack and careless. Washakie had taught me how to slip a knife into a man's neck so silent you wondered if it happened at all. So I had been in school all of this time, so to speak. I wondered what they could have seen in me, or perhaps it was something in myself I didn't want to look at at all.

Booth screamed when I padded up to his bedside—he had to be tied in at night, his twitches was so bad. I smothered him, so I'm a hero sure enough.

Booth's emaciated body being such a big prize Jack chopped it up and smashed the teeth in. We tossed the contents of the store outside, and found Booth's diary—made interesting reading later—and we hauled the two corpses of the guards inside and set fire to the place. We headed south that night, and the store burned like a beacon we could see from every rise all that night, and part of me was burning in it, too. I felt the less after Booth, and I was not to get it back easily.

About fifty miles north of the border I heard an unmistakable sound—plank plonk dreedle plong twang—and there was a whiff of sauerkraut and sewage on the breeze. A high, desperate female trillings and a dog coughing itself near to death.

Yup.

Up the trail come Klaas Vipsoek, M.D. these days, in a fancy Conestoga followed by two Democrat freighters and a buggy behind with the female assistants and a cage for the geek.

The sideboards of the Conestoga proclaimed Chief Moo-tay-tun-tun's Stump Water, which cured malaria, yaws, tuberculosis, cancer, gangrene, blood poisoning, gunshots, dandruff, and psoriasis. It also was a sovereign remedy for warts, tree stumps, and crop blight.

"SHIT!" says Jack and me simultaneous. Here we'd been off on the lonely Road of Empire and here come Klaas right behind like a stubborn case of clap.

"Skelly! Shack! How glad!" says Klaas. He still had on them checked pants, though what color they was eluded me, and a fine watered-silk waistcoat and a creamy big hat mostly pale save where Klaas had fingered it after greasing his wagon axles.

"SHIT!" says me and Jack again, shocked plumb out of inventiveness.

"I play blugerss," says Klaas, taking a mighty whang at the banjo on his fat knee. "You coming to medicine show tonight?"

"SHIT, NO!" we says.

"Oh," says Klaas, looking hurt. "You want to say hello to Mulebreath? He's in the geek cage."

"Well goddamn," I says, "finally found a job for the old boy that's fitten."

There was an explosion of feathers coming off the surrey. I could hear Mulebreath pronouncing maledictions upon foul Yankee poultry.

Jack and me was both fond of Klaas; the atmosphere aside, he was the soul of kindness and the father of ill winds, and we couldn't no more stick to our first resolve than we ever did. Klaas and Mulebreath had a way of becoming catastrophes, never having the slightest intention of doing so.

By and by we wanders into a Metis town, Saint Something or other. The Metis had been the mainstay of the Gentlemen Adventurers of Hudson's Bay, both as trappers and as voyageurs. They still lived with many Injun ways.

The town was three crude stores and a clabber of huts around them and a muddy street full of dogs and pigs and mud.

There was a nice little clapboard mackerelsnapper church with a grim gent in a black cassock peering out, alert for signs of approaching sin. The medicine show had been some advertised, for a nice crowd awaited Klaas and Company, and trestle tables had been set up with food and drink for the asking. Nice women in white aprons starched enough to turn arrows handed out sandwiches.

Klaas and his assistants set up the folding stage and then the assistants went around back to dig a pit for Mulebreath, and as soon as that worthy was installed and an iron grille placed over his pit Klaas commenced into selling his stump water. His claims was as utterly preposterous as any other doctor's and since they was delivered in that cheese-thick Dutchy accent no one had the faintest notion what he was saying anyway. No one much cared as there was two dancing girls wearing not much doing snakey wiggles and the men was all panting like old dogs in August. Their wives was glaring beadily at them, and watching for any sign the menfolk might slip away.

There was an occasional cloud of feathers reaching well over the top of the stage.

The assistants passed among the crowd with trays of little cups had a sample of the stump water in them.

It was terrible what commenced happening then. The formula for the stump water was secret, but a whiff of it had me thinking it had opium, red pepper, spirits of hartshorn, wormwood, and bulk Oriental spices of the, uh, rejuvenating sort. All who had partook of the stump water got this beady glaze in their eyes and began to paw the earth and scratch some here and there.

"Make fer the high ground!" yelps Jack, spotting a particularly strapping wench headed his way and hitching up her skirts.

We dashed for our horses, Jack's new lady love eating up the ground in twenty-foot leaps, and I made it up into the saddle and sunk in my spurs and the horse dashed away about twelve feet before the rope sprang taut to the stump I'd hitched the skittish son of a bitch to.

I took such velocity as I had as the horse went ass over ears and I hit the ground running and never mind the breathy cries behind, and Jack's pitiful wail, "Luther, I cain't hit no woman! Luther! Help, Luther!"

I did not look back.

Fortunately, there was a canoe left untended, and I leaped into it and commenced paddling right smart, about twice the speed of the *Delta Queen* trying to make New Orleans before the whorehouses all closed.

I cannot describe the scene, like so many other massacres I have escaped words fail me. Also I *never* look back, because it might slow me down.

I could hear, however, an atmosphere rent with lustful cries, tearing cloth, Dutchy bellers of pleasure, assorted squeals and snorts, Jack's gratifyingly terrified yelps, all these sounds of catastrophe receding as I paddled like hell.

Once again sheer speed had saved me. I gathered nuts and berries for my supper and laughed in the ripening dusk.

28

Saint-Something-or-Other looked a lot like one great bridal suite after a shivaree. I had snuck up close at dawn to find that the celebrations was still going on, though greatly reduced in velocity. I poured the last of the stump water down a privy. Folks could get hurt with that stuff.

I noticed something swinging from the church steeple—it turned out to be the priest, his cassock somewhat torn and tattered. Whether he'd done himself in at the thought of some of the confessions he was going to hear or he had simply been lynched for making ill-mannered protests at the general debauchery I couldn't say, by dawn's early light. The sight of a priest swinging in the breeze is near as pleasing to me as a lawyer in the same fix.

There was a few setting hens in a coop that Mulebreath hadn't been given, so I had eggs fresh and raw for breakfast and I rustled up some trade coffee and since the ground was littered with household goods must have shot out when the cabin roofs blew off it was a small matter to find utensils, a few of which warn't even sticky.

There were shreds of buckskin where Jack had gone down, and the ground was tore up something awful. Looked like a twenty-mule team had got stuck there.

I was sorting through the wreckage of Klaas's Conestoga in hopes of a seegar when a moan caught my attention. There was a feeble scrabbling under a big chokecherry bush and a flash of human flesh never much out in the sun. I walked over to see if I could possibly be of assistance.

Klaas was shoved back in there sort of like a fish took a wrong turn at the waterfall and landed in a thicket. He was all over bruises and contusions and looked, uh, spawned out. He was moaning and pointing to my right boot. There was his blue china teeth still bravely buried in the whalebone of a bustle. I couldn't recall any bustles on the Metis women but then I was only there a minute.

I handed Klaas his teeth and he gratefully took them and scraped off the few stays still stuck in them and popped them into his swollen lips.

"Skelly," says Klaas, "less go back to Utah, the Mormons iss less dancherous."

"Maybe for you," I says. "All you did was piss on that book. I shot a lot of them. Also recall the rude messages you tattooed on the missionaries."

"Yess," says Klaas, "between us there is difference."

"This sort of thing ever happen before?" I says, looking at what was left of a peaceful and thriving community of simple farmers and trappers.

"First time I sell this stoomp vasser," says Klaas. "Would they prosecuite for stoomp vasser?"

"Good thinking," I says. "You could have tried it out on a dog or Mulebreath or something."

"Did zat," says Klaas, his teeth slopping around his gums. "Terrible old hound, near death, goes after wife of mayor of St. Joseph. Big scandal. She leaves husband, buys the dog blue velvet coat with brass buttons."

"Oh, horse shit," I says, amused.

"Mayor shoot dog, she shoot mayor," says Klaas.

After this touching rendition of careless love, which, fer Chrissakes, turned out to be true, Klaas picked himself up to his full and ponderous height and he began picking through the rubble for a bit of clothing.

I got my horse and left, figuring that Jack wouldn't be able to straddle anything for a few days.

Heading south, I covered as much ground as I could, eating only a little jerky and drinking sparingly when I did. I was looking for Red Cloud, because Grant was calling him in with a simple message. Come in now, or we will hunt you down, and leave not one in ten alive.

Grant made that kind of war. He would send whatever Sherman felt he needed in the way of troops, and then they would take the field and not come back till the last Injun was dead or shipped to a reservation.

The first day I thought I might be close enough to Red Cloud to see a scout or two, I got captured by a little river as I watered my horse.

That had been my plan all along, but not to be captured by Little Big Man, who loudly told me he still thought all whites should be exterminated. One brave, feisty little bastard, was Little Big Man, though a bit single-minded about certain things, at least for my tastes. For one thing, he proposed that what I taste with be torn out at the roots, and the real unpleasantries would then commence.

We come on to Red Cloud's lodges soon enough. Little Big Man delivered me and then he threw an absolute blue boomer over having had to do this at all.

Red Cloud got his hair up and reminded Little Big Man that the Sioux was pretty much in Canada and he, Red Cloud, had promised to keep the peace.

(The Canadians are Brits, of course, and unlike us once they run the Union Jack up the pole, everybody around best abide by the laws, or they'll hang you right smart.) There was a good militia and some troops and the Mounties here and there.

Red Cloud went on yelling at Little Big Man for a while, and Little Big Man finally told him to go piss up a bear's ass, and then Red Cloud yelled at Spotted Tail, who just grinned and gave him a pipe of tobacco.

Red Cloud headed off to find a dog with a callused butt to

work off a little steam on, and I set down next to Spotted Tail just outside his lodge and et dog stew and plums and root salad.

"Politics, politics," says Spotted Tail.

"Politics is no fun at all," I says.

Little Big Man had made me more than a mite nervous, and Spotted Tail fetched me a bottle of whiskey, which I drank slowly to damp down the whips and jangles.

"Little Big Man consumes himself and others with his hate," says Spotted Tail. "He does the whiteman's work for him. A warrior consumed by hatred will make many mistakes, and just when many depend upon him."

I couldn't blame Little Big Man, really. Half of his band had died of smallpox and his father had been shot down like a gopher as the blind old man walked to a spring for some water—just a passing hunter trying out the sights on his rifle. Oh, you read about the savagery of the Injuns, it warn't nothing to ours. Very thorough we were, not even sparing the day-old babies.

So I sat there with Spotted Tail and we sort of kept track of him and his progress around the camp by the yelps of startled dogs surprised from sleep by a mighty kick from Red Cloud's War Toe.

He come back, still fizzing like a heavy charge of soda water, rage running out his ears and his fingers beating rapid time on his leggin's.

"We go back to the Tongue tomorrow," says Spotted Tail.

"You ought to go, like Grant asks, to Washington," I says. "Might save your people. If you see how many whites there are and watch guns and bullets being made . . ."

"The young men would never believe us. They could call us fish-hearted. The young men are young; they think bravery solves all."

We was interrupted by someone falling into the campfire. Spotted Tail dragged him out and I looked at his contorted face—he was having some sort of epileptic seizure—and the feller foamed and twitched for a few minutes and then he sat up

246

and he commenced to sing of buffalo and great battles and the death of the Sioux Nation.

And so I met Sitting Bull, He Who Sees Long, and folks will tell you he was a war chief. He warn't, he was a prophet. Sides, he'd not have lived long making war, for he would get these attacks fairly frequent, the more so when there was excitement around. (He was always right in his predictions, sort of, because you couldn't really make out what he meant till it had happened. It would be clear as a bell then. For instance, he saw many bluecoat soldiers falling head first into Sioux camps just before the Little Big Horn. He also saw many white hands pulling the buffalo beneath the earth. So Custer got his and they danced for joy and was starved into submission a short time later.)

Spotted Tail propped Sitting Bull up against a willow backrest and he just laid there breathing shallow and exhausted. A thin strand of saliva ran from his mouth to his eagle-thigh-bone breastplate, glinting gold in the firelight.

Out in the soft dark a dog yelped off Red Cloud's foot. It must have been a big dog, and a warrior, too, because Red Cloud yelped and commenced into cussing in that bass viol voice of his.

Sitting Bull opened his eyes and smiled, a weak and gentle smile. His eyes was soft and gentle and glazed and rolled up a bit in his head.

"Long road, no grass, no buffalo, many graves, many Sioux in one grave, dark where they fall down, fall down, fall down," Sitting Bull said, his voice like the rasp of grass in the wind. He went back to sleep.

"How much would the Black Hills be worth?" Spotted Tail says suddenly.

I had to think about it.

"I'd demand twenty million dollars, and twenty percent of the metals," I says. "And I'd be damned careful about who was keeping the score."

"And what will we do with the money?" Spotted Tail

asked. "Buy a thousand blankets apiece? A thousand rifles apiece? And the horses to carry them all?"

Red Cloud limped in out of the dark. His hand was bloody, where the dog had bitten him.

"Shit," says Red Cloud. Diplomatic language, shorn of embellishment.

I liked it.

"We will go to Washington in early summer," says Red Cloud, "And Kelly will be our interpreter."

"Now just a goddamn minute . . ." I spluttered.

"Little Big Man is waiting," says Red Cloud.

"Honored at the appointment . . ." I mumbled.

"Oh, this will be *fun!*" says my good friend Spotted Tail, no doubt considering the comic possibilities.

Winter was late in coming. We moved south slowly, and I fell back into the easy rhythms of a winter Injun camp. They provided for me well. For the first time in years I held a young Indian woman in my arms, and I thought of Eats-Men-Whole and I wept. The girl looked at me with her dark eyes and she reached out her hand and touched my tears. It unmanned me completely. She dressed and slipped away. I never learned her name.

29

itting Bull and Crazy Horse. Strange, good men, half in another world. Doomed. They both shone with a mad light, a pale nimbus. In the firelight, their shadows were larger than other men's.

Crazy Horse was mostly off studying battlegrounds and trying to make his young men into soldiers, which they hadn't any good strong natural talent for. They were brave as hell, but tribal warriors rather than the cold professionals who had taken war over almost everyplace else.

Spotted Tail gave me a lodge and we spent pleasant days at chess. Alone of the Sioux, Spotted Tail knew that they could not win, and that the things they needed to win were as foreign to the business of being Sioux as the dust on the moon, and as far away in time as Elijah.

When an Injun fights, see, it is a good brave fight and everything is settled, the enemy is dead or beaten, the songs are made, the dances danced, the scalps hung on the warpole, and life goes back to hunting buffalo.

I warned Spotted Tail about the buffalo. Everything the Sioux ate or made depended on the buffalo. Little Billy Sherman would be after them like *they* was the enemy. I hadn't seen what he done to Georgia and Mississippi, but I'd heard after he got through with it a bird would have had to pack a lunch to fly over it.

249

When the wind was from the south, where the Republican River herd was down to a handful, it stank of rotten blood.

In February, during one of them warm lulls, I headed south with Red Shirt to see what was going on. He was the bravest man I'd known, and he never felt a need to brag on it. He never abandoned a battle till the air was about half lead and only after he had reflected on it considerable and had a pipe or two of tobacco and a nice nap, as he did not wish to be thought overhasty in his judgments.

The Sioux was all bored as hell and the more they sat around and pumped one another up the more they thought the Big Piney was the sort of battle they'd fight. Fetterman and his eighty men wasn't even loose change to the U.S. Army. So the worse the bragging got the dumber the boasts. God, the sorrow that come of that fool Fetterman.

But when Red Shirt spoke everybody shut up, because he reduced everything down to the most boiled-off and unpalatable of forms, and there it was, boys, and don't sing me the chorus again. The bragging was grating on him, and that's why we left.

Travel was pretty easy, our biggest problem was fording the rivers, because fords is shallow that's where the ice builds up, too. The williwaw or chinook wind would bust the ice out of the rapids and stack it in the fords—and it was too busted up to walk on. Each time we had to cross a river it took the rest of the day to dry out our traps. We crossed the Missouri by the government ferry and no one looked at us twice, figuring I was a scout and Red Shirt was a whiteman's dog, a paysoldier.

Red Shirt found the Union Pacific railroad line a great horror, and he saw immediately how fast troops and horses could be moved on it. The Plains tribes' best defense was their speed, but no horse could go sixty miles in an hour, and no horses could carry ton upon ton of supplies on their backs. The black plume of coal smoke writ on the winter air lingered for a long time, and made everything behind it dark and stinking.

The hunters was working north, starting where there was the fewest Injuns, after the Kiowas and Comanches were crushed, and so north. We passed buffalo hides tiered up waiting

on the freights, stacks a mile long and twenty feet high and forty feet deep. Big lobo wolves howled off in the distance, so fat they could barely walk. They wasn't a danger at all, there was more carrion than a million wolves could eat, and there never was many of them.

At one of our camps I went off to take a shit and over a little rise I come face-to-face with a big dog wolf, head on him three times the size of the biggest dog I ever seen, and feet the size of dinner plates. He looked at me with his yellow eyes and yawned. Them ivory choppers in his mouth seemed to go back in there all the way to his ass, which was plump. Noble animal, waddled when he walked.

The sight bothered me and I snapped at Red Shirt over nothing and he just looked at me sadly. A part of me was dying, but *all* that the Sioux had known was, I felt petty and mean and cheap.

However bad it was for me, I always had other places I could go, but Red Shirt was over soon, and he knew it. I got to wondering how he stayed sane.

He would be brave for his people, of course, and see what he could do for the living after their lives was gutted with a dull antler.

We run on to Bill Cody down in Kansas, he had gone in for lace at the throat of his cossack-type shirts, and real gold buttons and beaded gauntlets near up to his armpits, and high polished black boots clear up to his crotch, looked like they'd take three sweating assistants and a railroad crane to get on and off.

The loathsome Buntline was still in attendance on Bill, but he tried to fluff us up some—named Red Shirt Chief Red Eagle. Red Shirt just smiled, pitying him. We was in a saloon at the time and the barkeep give us crap about not serving Injuns. I offered to eat the barkeep's lungs and that shut him up some. Then he threw a drink at Red Shirt and I was over that bar like that and punching him silly, and Bill and Red Shirt hauled me off him and we went to another place. Buntline soothed the barkeep by giving him money.

I took Red Shirt out to watch the horse soldiers drill at

Leavenworth, there was two thousand of them, and I said this was kind of a small part of them as could be sent against the Sioux, on trains.

We headed back up north, past spur tracks laid down to hold the hide cars, watched buffalo hunters on their stands shooting. Bam bam bam bam. Every thirty seconds, like they was automatic.

We watched the teams of skinners jerking the hides off with horse teams and the wolves, coyotes, foxes, ravens, and crows feasting on the carcases.

Red Shirt had already guessed as much as I showed him, but at least now he could say he had seen this with his own eyes. He doubted it would do much good. Young men are always ready to die bravely.

I learned of the death of Brigham Young, gone home to himself as God, no doubt. A pure bastard, and therefore a hero to thousands. It would have been a pleasure to kill him, and I regretted it hadn't fallen to me to send him to hell—I don't believe any of that stuff, but I could have made an exception in Brigham's case. Old scores was being settled without my having to be around. The best way, I can see now.

We got to the Canadian camp of the Sioux in May. After Red Shirt had addressed the council the Sioux going to Washington to meet with Grant formed up and with me at the head, all of eighteen, off we went to see the mountain. I herded everybody onto a train in Minnesota, paying for their tickets and assuming that my beloved government would repay me. (Forty years later they still haven't. It used to annoy me, but now the less the government does, the better, far as I'm concerned.)

One thing these Sioux was long on was dignity—you could have set fire to them and they damn well would have set there unblinking, amused at yet another obnoxious whiteman custom. In all that followed I never saw one show fear or anger, though there was some pretty sharp rejoinders that I will get to in a minute. Red Cloud and Spotted Tail and Hump and Red Shirt and Sitting Bull and Low Dog were a substantial bunch of men.

(Low Dog, by the way, ain't a comment on his character. It meant the low to the ground stance of a stalking dog and Low Dog stalked a lot of bluecoats. He favored a sharp hatchet.)

I bought some box lunches on the train and handed them out. The ham was spoiled. So I herded up my Sioux and headed them toward the dining car. Several matrons and mothers with small children fainted dead away, after some fairly piercing shrieks, and the waiters in the dining car gave me some backchat. I told them to telegraph the White House and the reply must have been pretty sharp, because at the next station we pulled off to get a private railcar for the rest of the journey, and a gourmet car and kitchen behind that.

Everything was laid on a little too well, you ask me. The railroad furnished us with oysters and lobsters for supper. The Sioux, who lived fifteen hundred miles from salt water, thought the oysters was gobs of snot and the lobsters was lice of great size, but hardly fit food for warriors. I raised hell in the major-domo car and got us beefsteaks. Other than Low Dog getting a sneezing fit from his first glass of champagne, which he took as an attempt to poison him. He made straightaway for the steward, knife in hand but I leaped over two tables and brought him down before he could avenge himself. Things was only mildly eventful until we got to Chicago.

Christ on a stickhorse.

We had a bit of a layover and some officious ass of a provost marshal sent a brigade of troopers to guard us. They was armed right down to the bayonets, and Hump and Low Dog began to sing the deathsongs of their warrior societies. It took all of my considerable tact—my revolver in the provost's ear, the fool come to parley—and a blistering telegram from Washington to get everybody out of a fighting mood. I thought that a last stand by six half-drunk Injuns armed with lobster forks against the power and might of the American Nation would amuse historians no end.

After the troops had slunk off I took my chums out for ice cream, which I purely am glad I did, because they loved it and were to go on asking for it throughout the trip. (I broached the idea of free ice cream forever to President Grant. He thought it was a good idea.) Then we went on to a burlesque show.

This was a great hit with them, too, and Low Dog got into the whiskey at intermission and as soon as the show started again he leaped up on the stage and whipped out his pecker and caused a smallish riot. I led the other five in a death-or-glory charge and we swept up Low Dog and his tool and went out the stage door and through the shadows to the club car.

Several policemen showed up and suggested strongly that we stay in the club car until a puller come along to take us farther on our journey.

Off to see scruffy little U. S. Grant, who intimidated me because he had done a job or two in his time. Like on me, for instance.

We went past steel mills glowing with hot metal, and cranes and ships of giant size. The Injuns pressed their faces to the dirty windows and counted and thought. Such mechanical monsters weren't even in their dreams. Even with the stench and filth the plants were impressive, something out of hell.

My six friends counted men and factories.

Out west the rifles boomed and the buffalo dropped and as long as grass should grow and the waters flow the sacred Black Hills would belong to the Sioux.

And I am the goddamned King of Siam.

30

itting Bull began to have more seizures the closer we got to Washington. I think it was the poisonous air. He'd been quiet and sort of out of the prophecy business, but late one night he let out a beller and tumbled from his berth to the rocking floor, foaming at the mouth and drumming his heels on the floor.

He had had a vision of the Black Hills crawling with whites, a deep shaft in the heart of the mountain, down below the sea, allowing who knows what evil to escape. The sacred White Mountain was defaced by carvings of giant heads chiseled by a dark force that had a white face and a big moustache, and he saw the Sioux starving, massed rifles shooting them, the dead dumped in a common pit, laid out in rows, while the birds pecked at their eyes and the winter wind blew.

Sitting Bull seemed calmer. He never went to war, but he could see the future, and that is handicap and heartbreak enough for any man.

He was real weak and shaky after his fit and the others gathered round him and fed him and held cups of water to his lips. Whatever awe the tall buildings and giant machines may have caused the Sioux, they gave no sign.

When we finally chuffed down off the Piedmont into Washington we was tired and out of sorts. They was all sick from the unfamiliar food and the lack of sleep. After a lifetime of sleeping in buffalo robes they didn't find the Pullman bunks any too restful, and of course the sheer racket of modern cities compared to the silence of the plains kept them awake. We all regretted having come at all.

Spotted Tail reminded me once again that he'd just as soon no one knew that he spoke English considerably better than I did. He thought me, he said, a fine feller who would do a fine job of interpreting and how were my balls anyway?

When the train pulled in to the station there wasn't no brass band or red carpet and I wondered if the government here had plumb forgot or what. There was a tall, dark-complected feller in a clawhammer coat standing easy under his stovepipe hat and finishing the last of a thick seegar.

I come down off the club car and nodded to the gent.

"I am Commissioner Parker of the Indian Bureau," he said. I looked at him close, and he looked more like my friends in the car than he did me.

His eyes was twinkling. "General Grant who is now President Grant is a simple soldier," he said. "My Iroquois name is Donegahwa, the Keeper of the Western Door of the Long House of the Iroquois."

This was, since the Iroquois were my neighbors when I was growing up, like saying you were President of the Five Nations of the Iroquois.

Grant must be so far gone in whiskey he thinks appointing an Indian to the Indian Bureau is going to make him friends? How many Injuns *vote*, fer Chrissakes.

My puzzlement showed in my face, I guess.

"Have you been here before?" Donegahwa asked me. "Mr. . . . uh . . ."

"I'm terribly sorry," I says, "the name is Kelly. Luther Kelly."

"Not *Yellowstone* Kelly!?" says Donegahwa.

"Goddamn it," I roared, "I got to turn this train around and go skin that flannel-mouthing goddamn shithead scribbler. . . ."

"It's too late," says Donegahwa. "Far, far too late."

The six Sioux come down off the train, a little wobbly at

walking on something that don't move. I looked at Red Cloud, Spotted Tail, Red Shirt, Sitting Bull—all steady on his pins— and Hump and Low Dog. I thought it was too late. This Donegahwa feller seemed about too smooth by half.

"He's Indian," says Red Cloud, eyeing the clawhammer coat and the stovepipe hat and the polished box-toed boots.

"Yes," I says in Sioux.

"Well," says Red Cloud, smiling, "tell this mangy white-man's cur he is less than the fart of a toad and I would like to kill him and I will at the first opportunity!" All said cheerylike.

"This is Red Cloud and he's pleased to meet you," I says to Donegahwa.

"Excellent!" says Donegahwa.

"Lizard puke!" says Red Cloud.

"I hope I may be of help to you," says Donegahwa.

A translator's life can be a hard one, but I did my best. Donegahwa was genuinely trying to help, and Red Cloud heaped insult after insult upon him, faithfully mistranslated by Luther. I was a little annoyed with Red Cloud and furious with that damned Spotted Tail, grinning like a gargoyle throughout.

Donegahwa had horsecabs waiting for us, and we drove to a good hotel, where the bellboys smirked at the Indians and the doors had a number of round plugs in them, where someone had to get into the room to carry out the corpses of those who didn't understand these newfangled gaslamps.

We was descended upon by drummers and pimps, and the Injuns didn't understand a word, but as my anger rose they fell in behind me and the pimps left, shaking their fists. I had some high words with the walrus-moustached manager, and his house cop joined in, and we had a nice little Donnybrook going there until my Sioux friends showed up fingering their tomahawks and knives, and quite obviously ready for serious business. The walrus moustache and his cheap thug jumped into the elevator, which warn't there. They went through the roof of it a couple floors below, and the collision greatly reduced their health.

"Ah, Kelly," says Red Cloud, "how savage life is here! I almost wish that I could read and write."

I was mopping the blood off a cut lip when a spit-shined young captain come stomping up the stairs and asked to have a private word with me.

"None of these barbaric, bloodthirsty, savage, renegade piles of coyote shit speaks English," I says, watching Spotted Tail lick his chops, "so speak your piece."

"General Grant wants to see you alone, and right now."

I explained that I was off to see the Great White Father, and I'd appreciate it if they didn't molest nor kill nobody until I got back. I told Spotted Tail in Sioux if there was a problem to demand that they be taken to the White House.

There was a snappy hansom awaiting with a grim-looking sergeant in it and we took off at a fast pace for the White House, an ugly building where ugly things was thought up, usually.

President Ulysses Simpson Grant, a short rumpled feller you'd have thought a feed and grain merchant from some Illinois backwater had you met him on the street, was awaiting "Major" Kelly in a fine billiard room all hung with portraits of former Secretaries of State, where the real mendacity and chicanery is practiced, with seasoned players like England. Grant was smoking a seegar and sipping whiskey and he motioned me to a sideboard where the fixings lay. We was alone.

We talked of nothing much for a bit, until I was some settled, and then he asked me courteously about the Booth affair, and I told him it didn't amount to much.

"Don't suppose it would pay to go after the folks who were in on the assassination of Lincoln," I says, feeling some righteous and disgusted. Well, hell, I was young.

Grant just shook his head. "More government I see more damned unbelievable it gets," he says. "I'm President. I wish I could shoot about half of Washington tomorrow. Lincoln's dead, and all that would happen if we went after them as deserves it is that the South would be plundered for another twenty years. It will take the nation generations to heal anyway, I can see no point in adding to the trouble."

We blew smoke toward the ceiling.

"I've failed a few times in life," Grant said, meaning his

failed business efforts. "And I don't know if I can do this job but I have to try. I'm the only man enough voters think on to get elected. I have no more stomach for righteousness. So you did burn his diaries."

"Yes," I says. "I did everything I was ordered to do. Now, if you don't mind, a question. Why the false-front major's rank?"

"Oh, that," says Grant. "We always have need of a few rascals and rascals only understand threats of a dire kind. Your pay is accumulating. If you would like a few medals that's easy enough."

"Why me?"

"Bridger and some others said you were likely. Some I oughtn't to tell you about. And I won't."

Grant walked over by the window. "If the American people knew how badly they were served by their government they'd rise up and hang us all. And that would do no one any good. Hang a few guilty men and tens of thousands starve for years."

"Am I likely to be called again?" I says, about half angry.

"Nothing immediate," says Grant, twinkling. "But that could change in a matter of seconds."

We'd run out of those topics. Grant asked if Red Cloud and Company needed anything.

"Abolishing the whites," I says. "Short of that not much. It's terrible for me to watch these good people go down like grass before a mower. They were living just as their fathers had."

"Sherman will be after them and he'll contrive to bring them all in or kill them all. Bill is a kind man, and he'd leave no eye open to weep. If *he* had his way, though of course we'll torture the survivors with missionaries and poison them with government rations. Give them schools and such. It will never take the place of what they had."

Grant went on to explain that the treaty Red Cloud and the others had signed in 1868 did give them some lands as long as grass should grow and rivers flow, but the treaty that got signed wasn't the treaty that got read to them.

"Would it have mattered if it had been the one?" I asked.

"No, it wouldn't matter," said Grant. "They can come in

now or we can chase them down. One way or another they will have to come in. One way or another."

"The gold in the Black Hills will do it," I says.

Grant looked off toward the horizon, pain in his face. A soldier, he'd dealt out more blood and death than any other man on the planet, and now he was left with tending the wounded and small matters like the Germans in Mexico, the Russians in the Northwest, and the damned British, who was waiting for any old tidbit that might drop into their well-shaven jaws.

"What about this bird shit? I can assume that I can now be told about the bird shit?"

"The bird shit," said Grant. "They don't teach you about the effects of bird shit on the lives of nations. You have to come on it by accident and get elected President. I'd blow out my brains but I'm waiting for the bastards to top it."

Grant explained why I had to go to Canada and smother a syphilitic fugitive in the name of Manifest Destiny.

There were these islands off the coast of Peru, all covered with bird shit, millions of tons of it, and very valuable stuff it was, too. Bird shit was a large component of modern smokeless gunpowder. Smokeless powder was a boon to slaughter on the battlefield, because everybody could still *see* after the first volleys.

We own the bird shit concession now, but the British wanted it, to deny it to the Germans.

"Well," I says, "that makes about as much sense as fried ice."

"Indeed it do," says Grant.

I had another drink of whiskey and thought on what I'd just been told.

"You dragged me all the damn way here to tell me some fairy tale?" I says. I couldn't quite get comfortable with the why behind my murderous little foray up Canada way.

"Not much of a joke at all," said Grant. "But there you have it."

The world was a madhouse, sure enough.

"Your commission is based solely upon your liking for fairy

tales," said Grant. "You'd make a terrible officer. I was a good one, but since I got to be a general I'm spoiled. After a while the rotting corpses stink in your dreams."

My crazy uncle Angus, who used to read Thucydides to me, always said that nations conducted their affairs with the same sort of morality was exhibited at the Saratoga races by the whores. Actually, he said, musing, the whores win on points.

I liked Grant. He was a decent man in an impossible job, and probably thought that someone else could only do much worse.

"How come every time I turn round another of your fellers is up on charges?" I asked, bold in my disgust.

"Well," said Grant, "I can't actually tell the American people how rotten their government is, but I can drop a hint or two."

I laughed so hard I spilled whiskey on the carpet. Grant grinned. Well, he'd do to ride with, sure enough. There was a knock at the door and an aide scurried in and whispered something in Grant's ear, and then he scurried out again.

"The Frogs and the Krauts are fighting," said the President, "and that's too bad for the Frogs."

"Who recommended me to you?" I asked, thinking it was Gus Doane.

Grant shook his head. "Nope, not that name. Believe me, it's better that way."

I nodded. Well, it would come out in time.

"When I'm through here," said Grant, "I'm going to go back to Illinois and train horses and look after my grandchildren and I'll never tell them a damned thing. I hope none of them become soldiers, and if they do, I hope none of them are good at it."

I shook his hand and left. The cab ride to the hotel didn't take long. I stopped for one more drink before joining my chums.

The mirror behind the bar was distempered. I looked at myself and I seemed to be floating, drowned, in a dark green sea.

31

I n order to impress and scare hell out of Red Cloud and his
fellow Sioux, and show off what fine people us white folks
was, there was a lot of excursions to see this and that. For
openers, we went to some demented professor's laboratory
where the feller was working on a flying machine. Unlike
the clumsy gas balloons, the professor's thingismus would
prove that heavier than air flight was possible. It so far had
eluded folks, and the flights had been of short duration with few
if any survivors.

The Injuns and I stood around while the professor, who
hadn't washed in so long you'd of had to sand him good to get
a rope to stay on him, scribbled on a blackboard and hollered
"EUREKA" a lot. He was a mighty determined man, and the
day after we was there to his shop he wired down the safety valve
on the steam engine that was supposed to power the chamois-
skin-and-bamboo wings just right, and the engine split open and
poached him on the spot. At least he was fairly sanitary when
they hauled him to the undertaker.

"Big goddamn thing," says Red Cloud. "Our young men are
always jumping off buttes when they have chewed too much
jimson weed. If the Great God wanted man to fly he would have
given us wings and a place to go."

We got dragged to a Pennsylvania coal mine. The Indians
declined the offer of a ride down the shaft, so we just looked at

the surface works. When we walked through the sorting mill and saw dozens of ragged boys picking the slate from the washed coal the Indians looked sad and shook their heads. The boys had those pinched faces and bluish skins folks get when they never have had enough to eat.

A crowd of newspaper reporters followed us everywhere, always yelling for quotes, which I gave them, even pumping up the obscene ones given to me by the warriors.

The journalists was hard to discourage. They plagued us awful but finally come to do a service for us. What a job they got! Pry, pry, pry, and when they'd find something out the paper wouldn't print it.

The army put on a close-order cavalry drill demonstration somewhat marred by a dropped beat that caused two lines of troopers to crash into one another. In moments the field was littered with injured men and broken horses. The brigadier got so angry he had a fit of apoplexy and died on the reviewing stand.

"I'd hate to see the whites try to fuck," said Spotted Tail.

Every evening we went to a different burlesque house to watch the girls take off most everything, which entertainment us boys likes the world over. My charges was decorous and only made rude comments in Sioux. No one could understand them but me and all I really had to contend with was folks after me to explain, usually ministers slumming for Jesus.

We went to a display of oil products from Pennsylvania, and Spotted Tail said that the same stuff poured up from the ground on their lands.

We was taken to a symphony concert and enjoyed it hugely, the eighty or so instruments was fascinating to the Sioux. They loved the music, even though it was of a different tonal scale than Injun music.

One especially pestiferous journalist who had a nasty habit of showing up in your bathwater or under the bed got his but good one night. I HAD NOTHING WHATEVER TO DO WITH IT. Ahem. He was asked through an interpreter if he would like to become a member of the Turtlegooser's Society. Also the ceremony would make him blood brother to the Sioux Nation.

When he had stripped to the skin he was set upon by his fellow lodge members, who painted him red from head to toe and then tossed him into a huge hogshead out back of the hotel, which had a hundred-pound snapping turtle in it. The turtle's jaws had been wired shut, but how was he to know? He run off up the street in his paint, purchased for its resistance to every solvent known to man.

His newspaper expressed indignation, and, speaking for us, I expressed astonishment that such a cruel joke could have been perpetrated upon the poor man.

That backed the shoals of journalists off some, and then we was assaulted with wave after wave of lovelies, the sort who was game for anything as long as it caused eyebrows to rise.

The management of the hotel observed that they were not running a cathouse, and I said airily that I'd no idea whatever of what they could be talking about. I said this through a crack in the door, because a beautiful young woman of Prominent Family was lolling on the bed popping chocolates in her lovely mouth. Her husband was off yachting, the fool.

Occasional hasty conferences with my Sioux chums re-vealed that they didn't care if we never left the hotel again. I said this would pall, they said that they didn't think so. It did eventually for everyone but Hump, who had been seen clear by his spirit guide when he lay out in the wet for five days, neither eating nor drinking. Which, come to think on it, beats hell out of Yale.

Hump's prowess got grand reviews by word of mouth and he had ladies lined up taking numbers from Low Dog, who found the job of appointments secretary less taxing and he could sort of high grade the ore, so to speak.

Management was having fits by this time over our sporting life—some folks can't stand to watch others enjoying them-selves. They sent lawyers with writs, and I kept my head down, since there was no one else but Spotted Tail who could read English and he wasn't owning to it.

The day when all the Sioux and Kelly were to be formally received at the White House come and it was a most memorable day in all respects.

The day dawned with a screeching and caterwauling coming from Red Shirt's room, where one young lovely had crawled up the laundry chute and found him disporting happily with another young lovely. This brave who had counted over three hundred coup and scalped forty enemies and who was one of the bravest men I ever knew prudently took refuge under my bed, bidding me ring for room service and have them bring up tea and scones. He had taken a particular liking to both. Dulcet sounds of busting crockery and ripping skin soothed the rest of the Sioux awake. They came into my room following the heady scent of scones to find War Chief Red Shirt, the chickenshit son of a bitch, lolling on my bed drinking tea.

Also this paragon of a paladin was smoking one of my seegars.

The local haberdashers had give us all clawhammer coats and pinstriped trousers and boots and stovepipe hats. The Sioux wore everything but the pants. The pants bound some, they explained.

I thought a clawhammer coat and a breechclout looked mighty elegant, but it never did catch on.

First the presidential steam yacht *Columbia* was to take us up the Potomac, a filthy river full of oil and dead animals. We chuffed upstream, eating lobster salad and listening to the Marine Band play patriotic tunes. I had a chat with the concertmaster, during which money changed hands, and the band played music hall tunes that reminded us all of slim legs kicking high and feathers and pretty frocks and grand frolics. Soon the hidden jugs come out—they're always around somewhere, regulations or no, and we ended up smashing into the dock hard enough to cave in the bows. We stumbled furtively to the waiting hansoms.

We sort of poured ourselves through a side entrance and we was immediately met by stewards bearing strong coffee. We sobered up or something like it, and went on in to dinner. It was a men only affair, with Grant and his cabinet officers there and some male secretaries taking notes.

I was pretty damn drunk to interpret but figured since not one word could be depended on it didn't matter. I had to be wary of treating the Indian replies, with Spotted Tail standing smiling with that moon face over such long teeth.

After a lot of tommyrot and flowery phrases and an awful dinner of cold beef and vegetables we got down to the brass tacks. Grant said that the treaty they had signed about the Northern Plains and the Black Hills was not the one that had been read to them. Under the treaty that they had signed, the Black Hills was open for mineral exploration.

Then Grant said that soon the Sioux and Cheyenne would have to move to reservations and stay there, and that the government would supply all their needs, rations, blankets, farming implements.

Red Cloud said that he hoped the Kiowa were eating as well tonight as he was.

Donegahwa slammed his glass so hard it broke on the table. He said he had the rations in warehouses ready to ship but that Congress had failed to appropriate the money for transporting it. The Indian Ring (the usual thieves you find anywhere big money changes hands) was selling the Kiowa rotten and outright poisonous foodstuffs at ruinous prices.

Grant looked mighty uncomfortable. He'd tried to get an appropriation through Congress and he had failed due to the combined interest of the railroads, mining companies, and suppliers who didn't care whether the Sioux was starved to death or shot so long as they was out of the way.

Spotted Tail said that the Sioux wanted a big cash payment for the Black Hills. The others wanted to fight for them, but they had seen what white industry looked like. Spotted Tail cursed his fellow envoys and told them the Black Hills were gone, he just wanted to get something for them.

The dinner didn't last long, and we didn't linger.

Grant walked us out to the horsecabs, and he tried to make

small talk, asking Red Cloud what his best memory was of his trip to the East Coast.

"Little children working," said Red Cloud.

Grant looked ashamed and then he shrugged and walked back inside, a shabby little man in a warm coat with a lot on his shoulders.

As we was leaving the White House an earnest young man begged me to ask Red Cloud if he would come speak in New York, at the Cooper Institute. I told Red Cloud the only hope that he had was public outrage—the people could always pressure the Congress.

The six of them and one of me said yes, we'd go. I bought our tickets, and we left that evening. I am amazed at what happened there, and it was the only time I felt proud of my countrymen throughout the trip.

Red Cloud spoke at the Cooper Institute all right, with me interpreting, to a crowd of several thousand people who paid the greatest of tributes to him. They sat in stunned silence, and when he was through they applauded, not wildly, but with a heartfelt and solid thrumming that went on for fifteen minutes.

Red Cloud described the land of his people and the life that they had known, that they had not started any of this war or the others, that when the whites had killed defenseless old people gathering food, had raped women who were away from the band, and had wantonly killed the Sioux horses the warriors decided to teach them a lesson. He spoke of the treaty that was different from the one they had signed, how the Black Hills were the Sioux cathedral. And he spoke of the rations for the starving Kiowa that the Congress would not ship.

The outrage the speech summoned up caused a congressional inquiry, which discovered that Congress acted wisely with the good of all in mind.

We was gone west before any of that. Half of the buffalo were gone and the numbers of hunters was so swelled the rest seemed to wither to nothing in months.

"Why don't you whites skin us, too," Red Cloud said. "I could ride through the country that was mine as a saddle or boots on a whiteman's feet. The skin of our children is thin and fine, for they starve. It would make good glove leather. It could bind the books I cannot read."

More than anything the Sioux wanted schools for their children, all except Spotted Tail, who well knew that in the country of the blind the one-eyed man is king, and who could read very well, thank you.

We got to Minnesota, and our horses and gear was in fine shape. Grant had ordered some troopers to give us an escort, but we slipped away and were gone before they could saddle up.

"Come with us, Kelly," said Red Cloud. "We must take council and we do not understand white minds."

I nodded. I didn't know if I did either, but I'd do my best to help.